I0778406

*The Garden of Memories
and Other Stories*

Ruskin Bond is known for his signature simplistic and witty writing style. He is the author of several bestselling short stories, novellas, collections, essays and children's books; and has contributed a number of poems and articles to various magazines and anthologies. At the age of 23, he won the prestigious John Llewellyn Rhys Prize for his first novel, *The Room on the Roof.* He was also the recipient of the Padma Shri in 1999, Lifetime Achievement Award by the Delhi Government in 2012 and the Padma Bhushan in 2014.

Born in 1934, Ruskin Bond grew up in Jamnagar, Shimla, New Delhi and Dehradun. Apart from three years in the UK, he has spent all his life in India and now lives in Landour, Mussoorie, with his adopted family.

RUSKIN BOND

The Garden of Memories
and Other Stories

RUPA

Published by
Rupa Publications India Pvt. Ltd 2025
7/16, Ansari Road, Daryaganj
New Delhi 110002

Sales centres:
Bengaluru Chennai
Hyderabad Jaipur Kathmandu
Kolkata Mumbai Prayagraj

P-ISBN: 978-93-7003-468-6
E-ISBN: 978-93-7003-898-1

First impression 2025

10 9 8 7 6 5 4 3 2 1

The moral right of the author has been asserted.

Printed in India

Contents

Introduction

Memories can be a bit like plants, in that they require careful tending—regular revisits and loving attention—lest they fade away, forgotten. In my tenth decade of life, my garden of memories is no doubt as difficult to manage as it's ever been, but tending to it is a labour of love I am always willing to undertake. In it are the well-loved trees of childhood, the carefully preserved flowers of short-lived romances, and seeds that are still germinating, new ones added with every day that passes. I am fortunate that I am a writer—every time I put pen to paper, I am watering my garden, cheating time, and immortalizing it in the pages.

This special collection is an attempt to open that garden up to visitors, bringing together some of my most cherished memories. 'Of Childhood' contains stories about my family—my father, my mother, my grandparents, my uncle—both the joyful and the bittersweet. Stories like 'Boy Scouts Forever!' and 'Our Great Escape' are about childhood friends. It also has some of the fiction pieces I have written about childhood, such as 'The Night Train at Deoli' and 'The School among the Pines'.

'Of Adulthood' explores the later years, with stories about the people and the places I became acquainted with and grew to love as I too grew. 'A Love of Long Ago' is about fleeting romance, while 'Friends of My Youth' is about fleeting friendships; then there are stories like 'From Small Beginnings', 'And Now We Are Twelve' and 'Picnic at Fox Burn' that are about those connections that are for a lifetime.

Turning ninety-one may not have made me much wiser, but it has at least given me this lively, thriving garden, and the plants in it look happy. Life has been kind to me, and in tending to my memories and caring for those who love me, I wish to be kind to it in return. I hope this collection encourages you to tend to your own garden as well, for having memories of good times to look back on is one of the greatest joys of life.

Ruskin Bond

OF CHILDHOOD

The Photograph

I was ten years old. My grandmother sat on the string bed under the mango tree. It was late summer and there were sunflowers in the garden and a warm wind in the trees. My grandmother was knitting a woollen scarf for the winter months. She was very old, dressed in a plain white sari. Her eyes were not very strong now but her fingers moved quickly with the needles and the needles kept clicking all afternoon. Grandmother had white hair but there were very few wrinkles on her skin.

I had come home after playing cricket in the maidan. I had taken my meal and now I was rummaging through a box of old books and family heirlooms that had just that day been brought out of the attic by my mother. Nothing in the box interested me very much except for a book with colourful pictures of birds and butterflies. I was going through the book, looking at the pictures, when I found a small photograph between the pages. It was a faded picture, a little yellow and foggy. It was the picture of a girl standing against a wall and behind the wall there was nothing but sky. But from the other side a pair of hands reached up, as though someone was going to climb the wall. There were flowers growing near the girl but I couldn't tell what they were. There was a creeper too but it was just a creeper.

I ran out into the garden. 'Granny!' I shouted. 'Look at this picture! I found it in the box of old things. Whose picture is it?'

I jumped on the bed beside my grandmother and she walloped me on the bottom and said, 'Now I've lost count of my stitches and the next time you do that I'll make you finish the scarf yourself.'

Granny was always threatening to teach me how to knit, which

I thought was a disgraceful thing for a boy to do. It was a good deterrent for keeping me out of mischief. Once, I had torn the drawing-room curtains and Granny had put a needle and thread in my hand and made me stitch the curtain together, even though I made long, two-inch stitches, which had to be taken out by my mother and done again.

She took the photograph from my hand and we both stared at it for quite a long time. The girl had long, loose hair and she wore a long dress that nearly covered her ankles, and sleeves that reached her wrists, and there were a lot of bangles on her hands. But despite all this drapery, the girl appeared to be full of freedom and movement. She stood with her legs apart and her hands on her hips and had a wide, almost devilish smile on her face.

'Whose picture is it?' I asked.

'A little girl's, of course,' said Grandmother. 'Can't you tell?'

'Yes, but did you know the girl?'

'Yes, I knew her,' said Granny, 'but she was a very wicked girl and I shouldn't tell you about her. But I'll tell you about the photograph. It was taken in your grandfather's house about sixty years ago. And that's the garden wall and over the wall there was a road going to town.'

'Whose hands are they,' I asked, 'coming up from the other side?'

Grandmother squinted and looked closely at the picture, and shook her head. 'It's the first time I've noticed,' she said. 'They must have been the sweeper boy's. Or maybe they were your grandfather's.'

'They don't look like Grandfather's hands,' I said. 'His hands are all bony.'

'Yes, but this was sixty years ago.'

'Didn't he climb up the wall after the photo?'

'No, nobody climbed up. At least, I don't remember.'

'And you remember well, Granny.'

'Yes, I remember…I remember what is not in the photograph. It was a spring day and there was a cool breeze blowing, nothing like this. Those flowers at the girl's feet, they were marigolds, and the bougainvillea creeper, it was a mass of purple. You cannot see these colours in the photo and even if you could, as nowadays, you wouldn't be able to smell the flowers or feel the breeze.'

'And what about the girl?' I said. 'Tell me about the girl.'

'Well, she was a wicked girl,' said Granny. 'You don't know the trouble they had getting her into those fine clothes she's wearing.'

'I think they are terrible clothes,' I said.

'So did she. Most of the time, she hardly wore a thing. She used to go swimming in a muddy pool with a lot of ruffianly boys, and ride on the backs of buffaloes. No boy ever teased her, though, because she could kick and scratch and pull his hair out!'

'She looks like it too,' I said. 'You can tell by the way she's smiling. At any moment something's going to happen.'

'Something did happen,' said Granny. 'Her mother wouldn't let her take off the clothes afterwards, so she went swimming in them and lay for half an hour in the mud.'

I laughed heartily and Grandmother laughed too.

'Who was the girl?' I said. 'You must tell me who she was.'

'No, that wouldn't do,' said Grandmother, but I pretended I didn't know. I knew, because Grandmother still smiled in the same way, even though she didn't have as many teeth.

'Come on, Granny,' I said, 'tell me, tell me.'

But Grandmother shook her head and carried on with the knitting. And I held the photograph in my hand looking from it to my grandmother and back again, trying to find points in common between the old lady and the little pigtailed girl. A lemon-coloured butterfly settled on the end of Grandmother's knitting needle and stayed there while the needles clicked away. I made a grab at the butterfly and it flew off in a dipping flight and settled on a sunflower.

'I wonder whose hands they were,' whispered Grandmother to herself, with her head bowed, and her needles clicking away in the soft, warm silence of that summer afternoon.

The Old Gramophone

It was a large square mahogany box, well polished, and there was a handle you had to wind, and lids that opened top and front. You changed the steel needle every time you changed the record.

The records were kept flat in a cardboard box to prevent them from warping. If you didn't pack them flat, the heat and humidity turned them into strange shapes which would have made them eligible for an exhibition of modern sculpture.

The winding, the changing of records and needles, the selection of a record were boyhood tasks that I thoroughly enjoyed. I was very methodical in these matters. I hated records being scratched, or the turntable slowing down in the middle of a record, bringing the music of the song to a slow and mournful stop: this happened if the gramophone wasn't fully wound. I was especially careful with my favourites, such as Nelson Eddy singing 'The Mounties' and 'The Hills of Home', various numbers sung by the Ink Spots, and medley of marches.

All this musical activity (requiring much physical exertion on the part of the listener!) took place in a little-known port called Jamnagar, on the west coast of our country, where my father taught English to the young princes and princesses of the state. The gramophone had been installed to amuse me and my mother, but my mother couldn't be bothered with all the effort that went into playing it.

I loved every aspect of the gramophone, even the cleaning of the records with a special cloth. One of my first feats of writing was to catalogue all the records in our collection—only about fifty to begin with—and this cataloguing I did with great care and devotion. My father liked 'grand opera'—Caruso, Gigli and Galli-Curci—but I preferred the lighter ballads of Nelson Eddy, Deanna Durbin, Gracie Fields, Richard Tauber, and 'The Street Singer' (Arthur Tracy). It may seem incongruous, to have been living within sound of the Arabian Sea and listening to Nelson sing most beautifully of the mighty Missouri river, but it was perfectly natural to me. I grew up with that music, and I love it still.

I was a lonely boy, without friends of my own age, so that the gramophone and the record collection meant a lot to me. My catalogue went into new and longer editions, taking in the names of composers, lyricists and accompanists.

When we left Jamnagar, the gramophone accompanied us on the long train journey (three days and three nights, with several changes) to Dehradun. Here, in the spacious grounds of my grandparents' home at the foothills of the Himalayas, songs like 'The Hills of Home' and 'Shenandoah' did not seem out of place.

Grandfather had a smaller gramophone and a record collection of his own. His tastes were more 'modern' than mine. Dance music was his passion, and there were any number of foxtrots, tangos and beguines played by the leading dance bands of the 1940s. Granny preferred waltzes and taught me to waltz. I would waltz with her on the broad verandah, to the strains of 'The Blue Danube' and 'The Skater's Waltz', while a soft breeze rustled in the banana fronds. I became quite good at the waltz, but then I saw Gene Kelly tap-dancing in a brash, colourful MGM musical, and—base treachery!—forsook the waltz and began tap-dancing all over the house, much to Granny's dismay.

All this is pure nostalgia, of course, but why be ashamed of it? Nostalgia is simply an attempt to try and preserve that which was good in the past... The past has served us: why not serve the past in this way?

When I was sent to boarding school and was away from home for nine long months, I really missed the gramophone. How I looked forward to coming home for the winter holidays! There were, of course, some new records waiting for me. And Grandfather had taken to the Brazilian rumba, which was all the rage just then. Yes, Grandfather did the rumba with great aplomb.

I believe he moved on to the samba and then the calypso, but by then I'd left India and was away for five years. A great deal had changed in my absence. My grandparents had moved on, and my mother had sold the old gramophone and replaced it with a large radiogram. But this wasn't so much fun: I wanted something I could wind!

I keep hoping our old gramophone will turn up somewhere—maybe in an antique shop or in someone's attic or storeroom, or at a sale. Then I shall buy it back, whatever the cost, and install it in my study and have the time of my life winding it up and playing the old records. I now have tapes of some of them, but that won't stop me listening to the gramophone. I have even kept a box of needles in readiness for the great day.

In Grandfather's Garden

Though the house and grounds of our home in Dehra were Grandfather's domain—where he kept an odd assortment of pets—the magnificent old banyan tree was mine, chiefly because Grandfather, at the age of sixty-five, could no longer climb it. Grandmother used to tease him about this, and would speak of a certain Countess of Desmond, an Englishwoman who lived to the age of 117, and would have lived longer if she hadn't fallen while climbing an apple tree. The spreading branches of the banyan tree, which curved to the ground and took root again, forming a maze of arches, gave me endless pleasure. The tree was older than the house, older than Grandfather, as old as the town of Dehra, nestling in a valley at the foot of the Himalayas.

My first friend and familiar was a small grey squirrel. Arching his back and sniffing into the air, he seemed at first to resent my invasion of his privacy. But when he found that I did not arm myself with a catapult or air-gun, he became friendlier. And when I started leaving him pieces of cake and biscuit, he grew bolder, and finally became familiar enough to take food from my hands.

Before long he was delving into my pockets and helping himself to whatever he could find. He was a very young squirrel, and his friends and relatives probably thought him headstrong and foolish for trusting a human.

In the spring, when the banyan tree was full of small red figs, birds of all kinds would flock into its branches, the red-bottomed bulbul, cheerful and greedy, gossiping rosy pastors, and parrots and crows, squabbling with each other all the time. During the fig season, the banyan tree was the noisiest place on the road.

Halfway up the tree I had built a small platform on which I would often spend the afternoons when it wasn't too hot. I could read there, propping myself up against the bole of the tree with the cushions taken from the drawing room. *Treasure Island*, Huck Finn, the Mowgli stories, and detective novels made up my bag of very mixed reading.

When I didn't want to read, I could look down through the banyan leaves at the world below, at Grandmother hanging up or taking down the washing, at the cook quarrelling with a fruit vendor, or at Grandfather grumbling at the hardy Indian marigold, which insisted on springing up all over his very English garden. Usually nothing very exciting happened while I was in the banyan tree, but on one particular afternoon I had enough excitement to last me through the summer.

That was the time I saw a mongoose and a cobra fight to death in the garden, while I sat directly above them in the banyan tree.

It was an April afternoon. The warm breezes of approaching summer had sent everyone, including Grandfather, indoors. I was feeling drowsy myself and was wondering if I should go to the pond behind the house for a swim, when I saw a huge black cobra gliding out of a clump of cacti and making for some cooler part of the garden. At the same time a mongoose (whom I had often seen) emerged from the bushes and went straight for the cobra.

In a clearing beneath the tree, in bright sunshine, they came face to face.

The cobra knew only too well that the grey mongoose, three feet long, was a superb fighter, clever and aggressive. But the cobra was a skilful and experienced fighter, too. He could move swiftly and strike with the speed of light, and the sacs behind his long, sharp fangs were full of deadly venom.

It was to be a battle of champions.

Hissing defiance, his forked tongue darting in and out, the cobra raised three of his six feet off the ground, and spread his broad, spectacled hood. The mongoose bushed his tail. The long hair on his spine stood up (in the past, the very thickness of his hair had saved him from bites that would have been fatal to others).

Though the combatants were unaware of my presence in the banyan tree, they soon became aware of the arrival of two other spectators. One was a mynah, and the other a jungle crow (not the wily urban crow). They had seen these preparations for battle, and had settled on the cactus to watch the outcome. Had they been content only to watch, all would have been well with both of them.

The cobra stood on the defensive, swaying slowly from side to side, trying to mesmerize the mongoose into making a false move. The mongoose knew the power of his opponent's glassy, twinkling eyes, and refused to meet them. Instead, he fixed his gaze at a point just below the cobra's hood, and opened the attack.

Moving forward quickly until he was just within the cobra's reach, he made a feint to one side. Immediately the cobra struck. His great hood came down so swiftly that I thought nothing could save the mongoose. But the little fellow jumped neatly to one side, and darted in as swiftly as the cobra, biting the snake on the back and darting away again out of reach.

The moment the cobra struck, the crow and the mynah hurled themselves at him, only to collide heavily in mid-air. Shrieking at each other, they returned to the cactus plant.

A few drops of blood glistened on the cobra's back.

The cobra struck again and missed. Again the mongoose sprang aside, jumped in and bit. Again the birds dived at the snake, bumped into each other instead, and returned shrieking to the safety of the cactus.

The third round followed the same course as the first but with one dramatic difference. The crow and the mynah, still determined to take part in the proceedings, dived at the cobra, but this time they missed each other as well as their mark. The mynah flew on and reached its perch, but the crow tried to pull up in mid-air and turn back. In the second that it took him to do this, the cobra whipped his head back and struck with great force, his snout thudding against the crow's body.

I saw the bird flung nearly twenty feet across the garden, where, after fluttering about for a while, it lay still. The mynah remained on the cactus plant, and when the snake and the mongoose returned to the fray, it very wisely refrained from interfering again!

The cobra was weakening, and the mongoose, walking fearlessly up to it, raised himself on his short legs, and with a lightning snap had the big snake by the snout. The cobra writhed and lashed about in a frightening manner, and even coiled itself about the mongoose, but all to no avail. The little fellow hung grimly on, until the snake had ceased to struggle. He then smeared along its quivering length, gripping it round the hood, and dragging it into the bushes.

The mynah dropped cautiously to the ground, hopped about, peered into the bushes from a safe distance, and then, with a shrill cry of congratulation, flew away.

When I had also made a cautious descent from the tree and returned to the house, I told Grandfather of the fight I had seen. He was pleased that the mongoose had won. He had encouraged it to live in the garden, to keep away the snakes, and fed it regularly with scraps from the kitchen. He had never tried taming it, because a wild mongoose was more useful than a domesticated one.

From the banyan tree I often saw the mongoose patrolling the four corners of the garden, and once I saw him with an egg in his mouth and knew he had been in the poultry house; but he hadn't harmed the birds, and I knew Grandmother would forgive him for stealing as long as he kept the snakes away.

The banyan tree was also the setting for what we were to call the Strange Case of the Grey Squirrel and the White Rat.

The white rat was Grandfather's—he had bought it from the bazaar for four annas—but I would often take it with me into the banyan tree, where it soon struck up a friendship with one of the squirrels. They would go off together on little excursions among the roots and branches of the old tree.

Then the squirrel started building a nest. At first she tried building it in my pockets, and when I went indoors and changed my clothes I would find straw and grass falling out. Then one day Grandmother's knitting was missing. We hunted for it everywhere but without success.

Next day I saw something glinting in the hole in the banyan tree and, going up to investigate, saw that it was the end of Grandmother's steel knitting needle. On looking further, I discovered that the hole was crammed with knitting. And amongst the wool were three baby squirrels—all of them white!

Grandfather had never seen white squirrels before, and we gazed at them in wonder. We were puzzled for some time, but when I mentioned the white rat's frequent visits to the tree, Grandfather told me that the rat must be the father. Rats and squirrels were related to each other, he said, and so it was quite possible for them to have offspring—in this case, white squirrels!

My Father's Trees in Dehra

Our trees still grow in Dehra. This is one part of the world where trees are a match for man. An old peepul may be cut down to make way for a new building; two peepul trees will sprout from the walls of the building. In Dehra the air is moist, the soil hospitable to seeds and probing roots. The valley of Dehradun lies between the first range of the Himalayas and the smaller but older Siwalik range. Dehra is an old town, but it was not in the reign of Rajput princes or Mogul kings that it really grew and flourished; it acquired a certain size and importance with the coming of British and Anglo-Indian settlers. The English have an affinity with trees, and in the rolling hills of Dehra they discovered a retreat, which, in spite of snakes and mosquitoes, reminded them, just a little bit, of England's green and pleasant land.

The mountains to the north are austere and inhospitable; the plains to the south are flat, dry and dusty. But Dehra is green. I look out of the train window at daybreak to see the sal and shisham trees sweep by majestically, while trailing vines and great clumps of bamboo give the forest a darkness and density that add to its mystery. There are still a few tigers in these forests; only a few, and perhaps they will survive, to stalk the spotted deer and drink at forest pools.

I grew up in Dehra. My grandfather built a bungalow on the outskirts of the town at the turn of the century. The house was sold a few years after Independence. No one knows me now in Dehra, for it is over twenty years since I left the place, and my boyhood friends are scattered and lost. And although the India of Kim is no more, and the Grand Trunk Road is now a procession of trucks instead of a slow-moving caravan of horses and camels, India is still a country in which people are easily lost and quickly forgotten.

From the station I can take either a taxi or a snappy little scooter rickshaw (Dehra had neither before 1950), but, because I am on an unashamedly sentimental pilgrimage, I take a tonga, drawn by a lean, listless pony, and driven by a tubercular old Muslim in a shabby green waistcoat. Only two or three tongas stand outside the station. There were always twenty or thirty here in the 1940s when I came home from boarding school to be met at the station by my grandfather; but the days of the tonga are nearly over, and in many ways this is a good thing, because most tonga ponies are overworked and underfed. Its wheels squeaking from lack of oil and its seat slipping out from under me, the tonga drags me through the bazaars of Dehra. A couple of miles of this slow, funereal pace makes me impatient to use my own legs, and I dismiss the tonga when we get to the small Dilaram Bazaar.

It is a good place from which to start walking.

The Dilaram Bazaar has not changed very much. The shops are run by a new generation of bakers, barbers and banias, but professions have not changed. The cobblers belong to the lower castes, the bakers are Muslims, the tailors are Sikhs. Boys still fly kites from the flat rooftops, and women wash clothes on the canal steps. The canal comes down from Rajpur and goes underground here, to emerge about a mile away.

I have to walk only a furlong to reach my grandfather's house. The road is lined with eucalyptus, jacaranda and laburnum trees. In the compounds there are small groves of mangoes, litchis and papayas. The poinsettia thrusts its scarlet leaves over garden walls. Every verandah has its bougainvillea creeper, every garden its bed of marigolds. Potted palms, those symbols of Victorian snobbery, are popular with Indian housewives. There are a few houses, but most of the bungalows were built by 'old India hands' on their retirement from the army, the police or the railways. Most of the present owners are Indian businessmen or government officials.

I am standing outside my grandfather's house. The wall has been raised, and the wicket gate has disappeared; I cannot get a clear view of the house and garden. The nameplate identifies the owner as Major General Saigal; the house has had more than one owner since my grandparents sold it in 1949.

On the other side of the road there is an orchard of litchi trees. This is not the season for fruit, and there is no one looking after the garden. By taking a little path that goes through the orchard, I reach higher ground and gain a better view of our old house.

Grandfather built the house with granite rocks taken from the foothills. It shows no sign of age. The lawn has disappeared; but the big jackfruit tree, giving shade to the side verandah, is still there. In this tree I spent my afternoons, absorbed in my Magnets, Champions and Hotspurs, while sticky mango juice trickled down my chin. (One could not eat the jackfruit unless it was cooked into a vegetable curry.) There was a hole in the bole of the tree in which I kept my pocket knife, top, catapult and any badges or buttons that could be saved from my father's RAF tunics when he came home on leave. There was also an Iron Cross, a relic of the First World War, given to me by my grandfather. I have managed to keep the Iron Cross; but what did I do with my top and catapult? Memory fails me. Possibly they are still in the hole in the jackfruit tree; I must have forgotten to collect them when we went away after my father's death. I am seized by a whimsical urge to walk in at the gate, climb into the branches of the jackfruit tree and recover my lost possessions. What would the present owner, the major general (retired), have to say if I politely asked permission to look for a catapult left behind more than twenty years ago?

An old man is coming down the path through the litchi trees. He is not a major general but a poor street vendor. He carries a small tin trunk on his head, and walks very slowly. When he sees me, he stops and asks me if I will buy something. I can think of nothing I need, but the old man looks so tired, so very old, that

I am afraid he will collapse if he moves any further along the path without resting. So I ask him to show me his wares. He cannot get the box off his head by himself, but together we manage to set it down in the shade, and the old man insists on spreading its entire contents on the grass; bangles, combs, shoelaces, safety pins, cheap stationery, buttons, pomades, elastic and scores of other household necessities.

When I refuse buttons because there is no one to sew them on for me, he plies me with safety pins. I say no; but as he moves from one article to another, his querulous, persuasive voice slowly wears down my resistance, and I end up buying envelopes, a letter pad (pink roses on bright blue paper), a one-rupee fountain pen guaranteed to leak and several yards of elastic. I have no idea what I will do with the elastic, but the old man convinces me that I cannot live without it.

Exhausted by the effort of selling me a lot of things I obviously do not want, he closes his eyes and leans back against the trunk of a litchi tree. For a moment I feel rather nervous. Is he going to die sitting here beside me? He sinks to his haunches and puts his chin on his hands. He only wants to talk.

'I am very tired, *huzoor*,' he says. 'Please do not mind if I sit here for a while.'

'Rest for as long as you like,' I say. 'That's a heavy load you've been carrying.'

He comes to life at the chance of a conversation and says, 'When I was a young man, it was nothing. I could carry my box up from Rajpur to Mussoorie by the bridle path—seven steep miles! But now I find it difficult to cover the distance from the station to Dilaram Bazaar.'

'Naturally. You are quite old.'

'I am seventy, sahib.'

'You look very fit for your age.' I say this to please him; he looks frail and brittle. 'Isn't there someone to help you?' I ask.

'I had a servant boy last month, but he stole my earnings and ran off to Delhi. I wish my son was alive—he would not have permitted me to work like a mule for a living—but he was killed in the riots in 1947.'

'Have you no other relatives?'

'I have outlived them all. That is the curse of a healthy life. Your friends, your loved ones, all go before you, and in the end you are left alone. But I must go too, before long. The road to the bazaar seems to grow longer every day. The stones are harder. The sun is hotter in the summer, and the wind much colder in the winter. Even some of the trees that were there in my youth have grown old and have died. I have outlived the trees.'

He has outlived the trees. He is like an old tree himself, gnarled and twisted. I have the feeling that if he falls asleep in the orchard, he will strike root here, sending out crooked branches. I can imagine a small bent tree wearing a black waistcoat; a living scarecrow.

He closes his eyes again, but goes on talking.

'The English memsahibs would buy great quantities of elastic. Today it is ribbons and bangles for the girls, and combs for the boys. But I do not make much money. Not because I cannot walk very far. How many houses do I reach in a day? Ten, fifteen. But twenty years ago I could visit more than fifty houses. That makes a difference.'

'Have you always been here?'

'Most of my life, huzoor. I was here before they built the motor road to Mussoorie. I was here when the sahibs had their own carriages and ponies and the memsahibs their own rickshaws. I was here before there were any cinemas. I was here when the Prince of Wales came to Dehradun… Oh, I have been here a long time, huzoor. I was here when that house was built,' he says pointing with his chin towards my grandfather's house. 'Fifty, sixty years ago it must have been. I cannot remember exactly. What is ten years when you have lived seventy? But it was a tall, red-bearded sahib who built that house. He kept many creatures as pets. A *kachwa* (turtle) was one of them. And there was a python, which crawled into my box one day and gave me a terrible fright. The sahib used to keep it hanging from his shoulders, like a garland. His wife, the burra mem, always bought a lot from me—lots of elastic. And there were sons, one a teacher, another in the air force, and there were always children in the house. Beautiful children. But they went away many years ago. Everyone has gone away.'

I do not tell him that I am one of the 'beautiful children'. I doubt if he will believe me. His memories are of another age, another place, and for him there are no strong bridges into the present.

'But others have come,' I say.

'True, and that is as it should be. That is not my complaint. My complaint—should God be listening—is that I have been left behind.'

He gets slowly to his feet and stands over his shabby tin box, gazing down at it with a mix of disdain and affection. I help him to lift and balance it on the flattened cloth on his head. He does not have the energy to turn and make a salutation of any kind; but, setting his sights on the distant hills, he walks down the path with steps that are shaky and slow but still wonderfully straight.

I wonder how much longer he will live. Perhaps a year or two, perhaps a week, perhaps an hour. It will be an end of living, but it will not be death. He is too old for death; he can only sleep; he can only fall gently, like an old, crumpled brown leaf.

I leave the orchard. The bend in the road hides my grandfather's house. I reach the canal again. It emerges from under a small culvert, where ferns and maidenhair grow in the shade. The water, coming from a stream in the foothills, rushes along with a familiar sound; it does not lose its momentum until the canal has left the gently sloping streets of the town.

There are new buildings on this road, but the small police station is housed in the same old lime-washed bungalow. A couple of off-duty policemen, partly uniformed but with their pyjamas on, stroll about.

I cannot forget this little police station. Nothing very exciting ever happened in its vicinity until, in 1947, communal riots broke out in Dehra. Then, bodies were regularly fished out of the canal and dumped on a growing pile in the station compound. I was only a boy, but when I looked over the wall at that pile of corpses, there was no one who paid any attention to me. They were too busy to send me away. At the same time they knew that I was perfectly safe; while Hindus and Muslims were at each other's throats, a white boy could walk the streets in safety. No one was any longer interested in the Europeans.

The people of Dehra are not violent by nature, and the town has no history of communal discord. But when refugees from the partitioned Punjab poured into Dehra in thousands, the atmosphere became charged with tension. These refugees, many of them Sikhs, had lost their homes and livelihoods; many had seen their loved ones butchered. They were in a fierce and vengeful frame of mind. The calm, sleepy atmosphere of Dehra was shattered during two months of looting and murder. The Muslims who could get away, fled. The poorer members of the community remained in a refugee camp until the holocaust was over; then they returned to their former occupations, frightened and deeply mistrustful. The old boxman was one of them.

I cross the canal and take the road that will lead me to the riverbed. This was one of my father's favourite walks. He, too, was a walking man. Often, when he was home on leave, he would say, 'Ruskin, let's go for a walk,' and we would slip off together and walk down to the riverbed or into the sugar cane fields or across the railway lines and into the jungle.

On one of those walks (this was before Independence), I remember him saying, 'After the war is over, we'll be going to England. Would you like that?'

'I don't know,' I said. 'Can't we stay in India?'

'It won't be ours any more.'

'Has it always been ours?' I asked.

'For a long time,' he said, 'over two hundred years. But we have to give it back now.'

'Give it back to whom?' I asked. I was only nine.

'To the Indians,' said my father.

The only Indians I had known till then were my ayah and the cook and the gardener and their children, and I could not imagine them wanting to be rid of us. The only other Indian who came to the house was Dr Ghose, and it was frequently said of him that he was more English than the English. I could understand my father better when he said, 'After the war, there'll be a job for me in England. There'll be nothing for me here.'

The war had at first been a distant event; but somehow it kept coming closer. My aunt, who lived in London with her two children, was killed with them during an air raid; then my father's younger brother died of dysentery on the long walk out from Burma. Both these tragic events depressed my father. Never in good health (he had been prone to attacks of malaria), he looked more worn and wasted every time he came home. His personal life was far from being happy, as he and my mother had separated, she to marry again. I think he looked forward a great deal to the days he spent with me; far more than I could have realized at the time. I was someone to come back to; someone for whom things could be planned; someone who could learn from him.

Dehra suited him. He was always happy when he was among trees, and this happiness communicated itself to me. I felt like drawing close to him. I remember sitting beside him on the verandah steps when I noticed the tendril of a creeping vine that was trailing near my feet. As we sat there, doing nothing in particular—in the best gardens, time has no meaning—I found that the tendril was moving almost imperceptibly away from me and towards my father. Twenty minutes later it had crossed the verandah steps and was touching his feet. This, in India, is the sweetest of salutations.

There is probably a scientific explanation for the plant's behaviour—something to do with the light and warmth on the verandah steps—but I like to think that its movements were motivated simply by an affection for my father. Sometimes, when I sat alone beneath a tree, I felt a little lonely or lost. As soon as my father rejoined me, the atmosphere lightened; the tree itself became more friendly.

Most of the fruit trees round the house were planted by father; but he was not content with planting trees in the garden. On rainy days we would walk beyond the riverbed, armed with cuttings and saplings, and then we would amble through the jungle, planting flowering shrubs between the sal and shisham trees.

'But no one ever comes here,' I protested the first time. 'Who is going to see them?'

'Some day,' he said, 'someone may come this way… If people keep cutting trees instead of planting them, there'll soon be no forests left at all, and the world will be just one vast desert.' The prospect of a world without trees became a sort of nightmare for me (and one reason why I shall never want to live on the treeless moon), and I assisted my father in his tree planting with great enthusiasm.

'One day the trees will move again,' he said. 'They've been standing still for thousands of years. There was a time when they could walk about like people, but someone cast a spell on them and rooted them to one place. But they're always trying to move—see how they reach out with their arms!'

We found an island, a small rocky island in the middle of a dry riverbed. It was one of those riverbeds, so common in the foothills, that are completely dry in the summer but flooded during the monsoon rains. The rains had just begun, and the stream could still be crossed on foot, when we set out with a number of tamarind, laburnum and coral tree saplings and cuttings. We spent the day planting them on the island, then ate our lunch there, in the shelter of a wild plum.

My father went away soon after that tree planting. Three months later, in Calcutta, he died.

I was sent to boarding school. My grandparents sold the house and left Dehra. After school, I went to England. The years passed, my grandparents died, and when I returned to India, I was the only member of the family in the country.

And now I am in Dehra again, on the road to the riverbed. The houses with their trim gardens are soon behind me, and I am walking through fields of flowering mustard, which make a carpet of yellow blossom stretching away towards the jungle and the foothills.

The riverbed is dry at this time of the year. A herd of skinny cattle graze on the short brown grass at the edge of the jungle. The sal trees have been thinned out. Could our trees have survived? Will our island be there, or has some flash flood during a heavy monsoon washed it away completely?

As I look across the dry watercourse, my eye is caught by the spectacular red plumes of the coral blossom. In contrast with the dry, rocky riverbed, the little island is a green oasis. I walk across to the trees and notice that a number of parrots have come to live in them. A koel challenges me with a rising *who-are-you, who-are you.*

But the trees seem to know me. They whisper among themselves and beckon me nearer. And looking around, I find that other trees and wild plants and grasses have sprung up under the protection of the trees we planted.

They have multiplied. They are moving. In this small forgotten corner of the world, my father's dreams are coming true, and the trees are moving again.

Breakfast at Barog

It's well over seventy years that I actually breakfasted at Barog, that little railway station on the Kalka–Shimla line; but last night I dreamt of it—dreamt of the station, the dining room, the hillside, and the long, dark Barog tunnel—which meant that it had been present in my subconscious all these years and was now striving to come to the fore and revive a few poignant memories.

Should I go there again? The station is still there, and so is the tunnel. I'm told that the area has been built up over the years so that it is now almost a mini hill station. That wouldn't surprise me. Our villages have become towns, our towns have become cities, and in a few years' time our country will be one vast megacity with a few parks here and there to remind us that this was once a green planet.

I don't remember any dwellings around Barog, just that one little station and its one little restaurant with a cook and a waiter and its one little stationmaster. No, such a small station couldn't have had someone as important as a stationmaster. Someone quite junior must have been in charge.

Never mind. It was the breakfast that was important. And that I was with my father and on my way to Shimla and a boarding school. The boarding school was the least desirable part of the journey. It was almost two years since I had been in a school and I was perfectly happy to continue living in an ideal world where schools need not exist. The break-up of my parents' marriage had resulted in my being withdrawn from a convent school in Mussoorie and taken over by my father who was on active service with the RAF. It was 1942 and World War II was at its peak. Against all regulations he kept me with him, but to do this he had to rent a flat in New Delhi. Most of the day he was at work and I would have the flat to myself, surrounded by books, gramophone records, and stamp albums. Evenings I would help him with his stamp collection, for he was an avid collector. On weekends he would take me to see Delhi's historic monuments; there was no dearth of them. From the stamps I learned geography, from the monuments history, from the books literature. I learnt more in two years at home than I did in a year at school.

But finally he was transferred—first Colombo, then Karachi, then Calcutta—and it was no longer possible for me to share his quarters. I was admitted to Bishop Cotton's in Shimla.

We took the railcar from Kalka. It glided over the rails without any of the huffing and puffing of the steam engine that dragged the little narrow gauge train up the steep mountain. I would be travelling in that train in the years to come, but on this, my first to Shimla, I was given the luxury of the railcar.

It glided into the Barog station punctually at 10.00 a.m., in time for breakfast.

The Barog breakfast was already well known and I did full justice to it. I skipped the cornflakes and concentrated on the scrambled eggs and buttered toast. There was bacon, too, and honey and marmalade.

'Tuck in, Ruskin,' said my father, 'School breakfasts won't be half as good.'

He didn't eat much himself. There was a lot on his mind in those days, apart from his work. There was his estranged wife, my mother; my invalid sister, now with his mother in Calcutta; his frequent transfers; his own frequent attacks of malaria; and our future in India, once the war was over—for India's independence was just around the corner.

'When do we get to Shimla?' I asked, quite happy to remain in Barog forever.

'In a little over an hour. But first we go through the longest of all the tunnels on this line. It will take about five minutes. Time for you to make a wish.'

The railcar plunged into the tunnel and we were enveloped in the darkness of the mountain. I held my father's hand. A couple of soldiers sitting behind us broke into a song from an earlier war.

Pack up your troubles in your old kitbag,
And smile, smile, smile!

A glimmer of daylight appeared at the end of the tunnel and then we were out in the sunshine and the pine-scented air.

'Did you make your wish?' asked my father.

I nodded, 'I wished that my mother would come back.'

He was silent for a few moments. 'Do you miss her a lot?'

'I don't miss her,' I said firmly. 'I'm always happy with you. But you miss her all the time. I don't like to see you so sad.'

'I've often asked her to come back,' he said. 'But it's up to her. She wants a different kind of life.'

And that was true. She was still very young—in her late twenties—and she enjoyed parties and dances and a busy social life. My father was in his forties. He liked staying at home, listening to classical music. When he took a holiday, he went in search of rare butterflies. My mother was a butterfly too—pretty, merry, fluttering here and there—but most unwilling to be displayed in a butterfly museum.

I suppose for most of us, big or small, life is just a succession of making mistakes and we spend most of our time trying to rectify them. Marriage was a mistake for both my parents. And I was a product of that mistake!

In the time he had, my father did his best for me. And how proud I was of him when he accompanied me down to my new school! He was wearing his dark blue RAF uniform with its flying officer's stripes, and uniforms, especially officers' uniforms, made a great impression amongst schoolboys in those wartime days. I was received with respect and curiosity. Word went around that my father was a fighter pilot and that he'd shot down dozens of Japanese planes! He was another Biggles, that fictional aviator. Nothing could have been further from reality. My father did not fly at all. He worked for a unit called Codes and Cyphers, helping to create new codes or breaking down enemy codes. It was important work and secret work but there was no glamour about it.

Not that I was averse to the glamour of being Biggles Junior. In my previous school I'd been something of an outsider and the Irish nuns hadn't cared much for a quiet, sensitive boy. Here I was made to feel I belonged, and in no time at all I made a number of friends. It was already halfway through the school year but I had no difficulty in catching up with my classmates.

This was 'prep' school—junior school—and certainly more fun than senior school, still a couple of years away, would ever be... Still, I was always looking forward to the winter break, when I would be with my father again, for at least three months. And there he was, waiting at the Old Delhi railway station, as my train drew alongside the platform. He was still in New Delhi, at Air Headquarters, and I made the most of my time with him. Connaught Place was close by, and two or three evenings every week we would go to the cinema. There were four to choose from—the Regal, the Rivoli, the Odeon, and the Plaza, all very new and smart and showing the latest films from Hollywood. I became a regular film buff. The bookshops were there too, and the record shops, and Wenger's with its confectionery and the Milk Bar with its milkshakes, and Kwality with its ice creams. It was hard to believe that there was a world war going on in Europe and Asia and North Africa and the Pacific; or that the Quit India movement was at its height and that my father and I might have to leave the country in the near future. He spoke about it sometimes and of the possibility of my going to a school in England. We did not talk about my mother, but I noticed that he still kept a photograph of her in his desk drawer.

It was back to school in March, when the rhododendrons were in bloom. This time I went up with the school party, in the small train with its steam engine chugging slowly up the steep inclines. The journey took all day. We did stop briefly at Barog, but we were not allowed to get down from the train; one or two boys were certain to be left behind. I looked longingly at the little restaurant on the far side of the platform; but it was already teatime. Breakfast was for the railcar!

The school year rolled on. My father was transferred to Karachi and then to Calcutta. He had grown up in Calcutta and knew the city well. He wrote to me every week and in his last letter he told me what I could look forward to during the winter holidays—the New Market with its bookshops, the botanical gardens with an ancient banyan tree, the zoo, the riverfront, the great maidan where hundreds of people would be taking the evening air... I was hoping he would come up to see me during the autumn break, but instead I had news of another kind.

It must be difficult for a young schoolmaster, as yet untouched by tragedy, to tell a ten-year-old that he has just lost his father. Mr Murtough was given this onerous duty. And he did his best, mumbling something ridiculous about God needing my father more than I did and so on and so on...

My friends were more natural in expressing this sympathy—giving me their sweets or chocolates, offering to play games with me, talking to me in the middle of the night when they discovered I wasn't asleep... For the future did look bleak. I wasn't sure where I would be going next—my Calcutta granny or my Dehra granny, or my mother and stepfather... I did receive a letter from my mother, telling me that my father had died of the malaria that had plagued him for years; but it was an unemotional letter and it did little to bring me comfort.

But I did go to her when school closed for the winter and I was to spend the next few years in my stepfather's home. But that's another story.

I continued my school in Shimla, and every year in March, the small train would take me and my schoolmates up the mountain, through numerous tunnels and winding gradients, forests of pine and deodar, and we always stopped at Barog, before the biggest tunnel of all. But I never made another wish when passing through that tunnel.

That was over seventy years ago.

Is the railcar still running on that line? And do they still serve breakfast at Barog?

They say you should see Venice before you die. Or better still, Varanasi. But I'll settle for that little station among the pines. And if my father is standing on the platform, waiting for me, ready to take me by the hand, I'll be a small boy again and that railcar will take us to a different destination altogether.

Remember This Day

If you can get an entire year off from school when you are nine years old, and can have a memorable time with a great father, then that year has to be the best time of your life even if it is followed by sorrow and insecurity.

It was the result of my parents' separation at a time when my father was on active service in the RAF during World War II. He managed to keep me with him for a summer and winter, at various locations in New Delhi—Hailey Road, Atul Grove Lane, Scindia House—in apartments he had rented, as he was not permitted to keep a child in the quarters assigned to service personnel. This arrangement suited me perfectly, and I had a wonderful year in Delhi, going to the cinema, quaffing milkshakes, helping my father with his stamp collection; but this idyllic situation could not continue for ever, and when my father was transferred to Karachi he had no option but to put me in a boarding school.

This was the Bishop Cotton Preparatory School in Shimla—or rather, Chhota Shimla—where boys studied up to Class 4, after which they moved on to the senior school.

Although I was a shy boy, I had settled down quite well in the friendly atmosphere of this little school, but I did miss my fathers' companionship, and I was overjoyed when he came up to see me during the midsummer break. He had a couple of days' leave, and he could only take me out for a day, bringing me back to school in the evening.

I was so proud of him when he turned up in his dark blue R.A.F. uniform, a Flight Lieutenant's stripes very much in evidence as he had just been promoted. He was already forty, engaged in

Codes and Ciphers and not flying much. He was short and stocky, getting bald, but smart in his uniforrn. I gave him a salute—I loved giving salutes—and he returned the salutation and followed it up with a hug and a kiss on my forehead.

'And what would you like to do today, son?'

'Let's go to Davico's,' I said. Davico's was the best restaurant in town, famous for its meringues, marzipans, curry-puffs and pastries. So to Davico's we went, where of course I gorged myself on confectionery as only a small schoolboy can do. 'Lunch is still a long way off, so let's take a walk,' suggested my father.

And provisioning ourselves with more pastries, we left the Mall and trudged up to the Monkey Temple at the top of Jakko Hill. Here we were relieved of the pastries by the monkeys, who simply snatched them away from my unwilling hands, and we came downhill in a hurry before I could get hungry again. Small boys and monkeys have much in common.

My father suggested a rickshaw ride around Elysium Hill, and this we did in style, swept along by four sturdy young rickshaw-pullers. My father took the opportunity of relating the story of Kipling's *Phantom Rickshaw* (this was before I discovered it in print), and a couple of other ghost stories designed to build up my appetite for lunch.

We ate at Wenger's (or was it Clark's?) and then—'Enough of ghosts, Ruskin. Let's go to the pictures.'

I loved going to the pictures. I know the Delhi cinemas intimately, and it hadn't taken me long to discover the Shimla cinemas. There were three of them—the Regal, the Ritz, and the Rivoli.

We went to the Rivoli. It was down near the ice-skating ring and the old Blessington Hotel. The film was about an ice-skater and starred Sonja Henie, a pretty young Norwegian Olympic champion who appeared in a number of Hollywood musicals. All she had to do was skate and look pretty, and this she did to perfection. I decided to fall in love with her. But by the time I grew up and finished school she'd stopped skating and making films! Whatever happened to Sonja Henie?

After the picture it was time to return to school. We walked all the way to Chhota Shimla talking about what we'd do during the winter holidays, and where we would go when the War was over.

'I'll be in Calcutta now,' said my father. 'There are good bookshops there. And cinemas. And Chinese restaurants. And we'll buy more gramophone records, and add to the stamp collection.'

It was dusk when we walked slowly down the path to the school gate and playing-field. Two of my friends were waiting for me—Bimal and Riaz. My father spoke to them, asked about their homes. A bell started ringing. We said goodbye.

'Remember this day, Ruskin,' said my father.

He patted me gently on the head and walked away.

I never saw him again.

Three months later I heard that he had passed away in the military hospital in Calcutta.

I dream of him sometimes, and in my dream he is always the same, caring for me and leading me by the hand along old familiar roads.

And of course I remember that day. Over sixty-five years have passed, but it's as fresh as yesterday.

Life with Father

During my childhood and early boyhood with my father, we were never in one house or dwelling for very long. I think the 'Tennis Bungalow' in Jamnagar (in the grounds of the Ram Vilas Palace) housed us for a couple of years, and that was probably the longest period.

In Jamnagar itself we had at least three abodes—a rambling, leaking old colonial mansion called 'Cambridge House'; a wing of an old palace, the Lal Bagh I think it was called, which was also inhabited by bats and cobras; and the aforementioned 'Tennis Bungalow,' a converted sports pavilion which was really quite bright and airy.

I think my father rather enjoyed changing houses, setting up home in completely different surroundings. He loved rearranging rooms too, so that this month's sitting room became next month's bedroom, and so on; furniture would also be moved around quite frequently, somewhat to my mother's irritation, for she liked having things in their familiar places. She had grown up in one abode (her father's Dehra house) whereas my father hadn't remained anywhere for very long. Sometimes he spoke of making a home in Scotland, beside Loch Lomond, but it was only a distant dream.

The only real stability was represented by his stamp collection, and this he carried around in a large tin trunk, for it was an extensive and valuable collection—there was an album for each country he specialized in: Greece, Newfoundland, British possessions in the Pacific, Borneo, Zanzibar, Sierra Leone; these were some of the lands whose stamps he favoured most...

I did share some of his enthusiasm for stamps, and they gave me a strong foundation in geography and political history, for he went to the trouble of telling me something about the places and people depicted on them—that Pitcairn Island was inhabited largely by mutineers from *H.M.S. Bounty;* that the Solomon Islands were famous for their butterflies; that Britannia still ruled the waves (but only just); that Iraq had a handsome young boy king; that in Zanzibar the Sultan wore a fez; that zebras were exclusive to Kenya, Uganda and Tanganyika; that in America presidents were always changing; and that the handsome young hero on Greek stamps was a Greek god with a sore heel. All this and more, I remember from my stamp-sorting sessions with my father. However, it did not form a bond between him and my mother. She was bored with the whole thing.

My earliest memories don't come in any particular order, but most of them pertain to Jamnagar, where we lived until I was five or six years old.

There was the beach at Balachadi, and I remember picking up seashells and wanting to collect them much as my father collected stamps. When the tide was out I went paddling with some of the children from the palace.

My father set up a schoolroom for the palace children. It was on the ground floor of a rambling old palace, which had a tower and a room on the top. Sometimes I attended my father's classes more as an observer than a scholar. One day I set off on my own to explore the deserted palace, and ascended some wandering steps to the top, where I found myself in a little room full of tiny stained-glass windows. I took turns at each window pane, looking out at a green or red or yellow world. It was a magical room.

Many years later—almost forty years later, in fact—I wrote a story with this room as its setting. It was called 'The Room of Many

Colours'* and it had in it a mad princess, a gardener and a snake.

⌣

Not all memories are dream-like and idyllic. I witnessed my parents' quarrels from an early age, and later when they resulted in my mother taking off for unknown destinations (unknown to me). I would feel helpless and insecure. My father's hand was always there, and I held it firmly until it was wrenched away by the angel of death.

That early feeling of insecurity was never to leave me, and in adult life, when I witnessed quarrels between people who were close to me, I was always deeply disturbed—more for the children, whose lives were bound to be affected by such emotional discord. But can it be helped? People who marry young, even those who are in love in *Time Stops at Shamli and Other Stories*, do not really know each other. The body chemistry may be right but the harmony of two minds is what makes relationships endure.

Words of wisdom from a disappointed bachelor!

I don't suppose I would have written so much about childhood or even about other children if my own childhood had been all happiness and light. I find that those who have had contented, normal childhoods, seldom remember much about them; nor do they have much insight into the world of children. Some of us are born sensitive. And, if, on top of that, we are pulled about in different directions (both emotionally and physically), we might just end up becoming writers.

No, we don't become writers in schools of creative writing. We become writers before we learn to write. The rest is simply learning how to put it all together.

⌣

I learnt to read from my father but not in his classroom.

The children were older than me. Four of them were princesses,

---

*In *Time Stops at Shamli and Other Stories*.

very attractive, but always clad in buttoned-up jackets and trousers. This was a bit confusing for me, because I had at first taken them for boys. One of them used to pinch my cheeks and hug me.

While I thought she was a boy, I rather resented the familiarity. When I discovered she was a girl (I had to be told), I wanted more of it.

I was shy of these boyish princesses, and was to remain shy of girls until I was in my teens.

Between Tennis Bungalow and the palace were lawns and flower beds. One of my earliest memories is of picking my way through a forest of flowering cosmos; to a five-year-old they were almost trees, the flowers nodding down at me in friendly invitation.

Since then, the cosmos has been my favourite flower—fresh, open, uncomplicated—living up to its name, cosmos, the universe as an ordered whole. White, purple and rose, they are at their best in each other's company, growing almost anywhere, in the hills or on the plains, in Europe or tropical America. Waving gently in the softest of breezes, they are both sensuous and beyond sensuality. An early influence!

There were of course rose bushes in the palace grounds, kept tidy and trim and looking very like those in the illustrations in my first copy of *Alice in Wonderland*, a well-thumbed edition from which my father often read to me. (Not the Tenniel illustrations, something a little softer.) I think I have read Alice more often than any other book, with the possible exception of *The Diary of a Nobody*, which I turn to whenever I am feeling a little low. Both books help me to a better appreciation of the absurdities of life.

There were extensive lawns in front of the bungalow, where I could romp around or push my small sister around on a tricycle. She was a backward child, who had been affected by polio and some damage to the brain (having been born prematurely and delivered with the help of forceps), and she was the cross that had to be borne by my parents, together and separately. In spite of her infirmities, Ellen was going to outlive most of us.

Although we lived briefly in other houses, and even for a time in the neighbouring state of Pithadia, Tennis Bungalow was our home for most of the time we were in Jamnagar.

There were several Englishmen working for the Jam Saheb. The port authority was under Commander Bourne, a retired British naval officer. And a large farm (including a turkey farm) was run for the state by a Welsh couple, the Jenkins. I remember the verandah of the Jenkins home, because the side table was always stacked with copies of the humorous weekly, *Punch*, mailed regularly to them from England. I was too small to read *Punch*, but I liked looking at the drawings.

The Bournes had a son who was at school in England, but he had left his collection of comics behind, and these were passed on to me. Thus I made the acquaintance of Korky the Kat, Tiger Tim, Desperate Dan, Our Wullie and other comic-paper heroes of the late thirties.

There was one cinema somewhere in the city, and English-language films were occasionally shown. My first film was very disturbing for me, because the hero was run through with a sword. This was Noël Coward's operetta, *Bitter Sweet*, in which Nelson Eddy and Jennette MacDonald made love in duets. My next film was *Tarzan of the Apes*, in which Johny Weissmuller, the Olympic swimmer, gave Maureen O'Sullivan, pretty and petite, a considerable mauling in their treetop home. But it was to be a few years before I became a movie buff.

Looking up one of my tomes of Hollywood history, I note that *Bitter Sweet* was released in 1940, so that was probably our last year in Jamnagar. My father must have been over forty when he joined the RAF, to do his bit for King and country. He may have bluffed his age (he was born in 1896), but perhaps you could enlist in your mid-forties during the War. He was given the rank of pilot officer and assigned to the cipher section of Air Headquarters in New Delhi. So there was a Bond working in Intelligence long before the fictional James arrived on the scene.

The War wasn't going too well for England in 1941, and it wasn't going too well for me either, for I found myself interned in a convent school in the hill station of Mussoorie. I hated it from the beginning. The nuns were strict and unsympathetic; the food was awful (stringy meat boiled with pumpkins); the boys were for the most part dull and unfriendly, the girls too subdued; and the latrines were practically inaccessible. We had to bathe in our underwear, presumably so that the nuns would not be distracted by the sight of our undeveloped sex! I had to endure this place for over a year because my father was being moved around from Calcutta to Delhi to Karachi, and my mother was already engaged in her affair with my future stepfather. At times I thought of running away, but where was I to run?

Picture postcards from my father brought me some cheer. These postcards formed part of Lawson Wood's 'Granpop' series—'Granpop' being an ape of sorts, who indulged in various human activities, such as attending cocktail parties and dancing to Scottish bagpipes. 'Is this how you feel now that the rains are here?' my father had written under one illustration of 'Granpop' doing the rumba in a tropical downpour.

I enjoyed getting these postcards, with the messages from my father saying that books and toys and stamps were waiting for me when I came home. I preserved them for fifty years, and now they are being looked after by Dr Howard Gotlieb in my archives at Boston University's Mugar Memorial Library. My own letters can perish, but not those postcards!

I have no cherished memories of life at the convent school. It wasn't a cruel place but it lacked character of any kind; it was really a conduit for boys and girls going on to bigger schools in the hill station. I am told that today it has a beautiful well-stocked library, but that the children are not allowed to use the books lest they soil them; everything remains as tidy and spotless as the nuns' habits.

One day in mid-term my mother turned up unexpectedly and withdrew me from the school. I was overjoyed but also a little puzzled by this sudden departure. After all, no one had really taken me seriously when I'd said I hated the place.

Oddly enough, we did not stop in Dehra Dun at my grandmother's place. Instead my mother took me straight to the railway station and put me on the night train to Delhi. I don't remember if anyone accompanied me—I must have been too young to travel alone—but I remember being met at the Delhi station by my father in full uniform. It was early summer, and he was in khakis, but the blue RAF cap took my fancy. Come winter, he'd be wearing a dark blue uniform with a different kind of cap, and by then he'd be a flying officer and getting saluted by juniors. Being wartime, everyone was saluting madly, and I soon developed the habit, saluting everyone in sight.

An uncle on my mother's side, Fred Clark, was then the station superintendent at Delhi railway station, and he took us home for breakfast to his bungalow, not far from the station. From the conversation that took place during the meal I gathered that my parents had separated, that my mother was remaining in Dehra Dun, and that henceforth I would be in my father's custody. My sister Ellen was to stay with 'Calcutta Granny'—my father's seventy-year-old mother. The arrangement pleased me, I must admit.

The two years I spent with my father were probably the happiest of my childhood—although, for him, they must have been a period of trial and tribulation. Frequent bouts of malaria had undermined his constitution; the separation from my mother weighed heavily on him, and it could not be reversed; and at the age of eight I was self-willed and demanding.

He did his best for me, dear man. He gave me his time, his companionship, his complete attention.

A year was to pass before I was re-admitted to a boarding school, and I would have been quite happy never to have gone to school again. My year in the convent had been sufficient punishment for uncommitted sins. I felt that I had earned a year's holiday.

It was a glorious year, during which we changed our residence at least four times—from a tent on a flat treeless plain outside Delhi, to a hutment near Humayun's tomb: to a couple of rooms on Atul Grove Road; to a small flat on Hailey Road; and finally to an apartment in Scindia House, facing the Connaught Circus.

We were not very long in the tent and hutment—but long enough for me to remember the scorching winds of June, and the bhisti's hourly visit to douse the khas-khas matting with water. This turned a hot breeze into a refreshing, fragrant zephyr—for about half an hour. And then the dust and the prickly heat took over again. A small table fan was the only luxury.

Except for Sundays, I was alone during most of the day; my father's office in Air Headquarters was somewhere near India Gate. He'd return at about six, tired but happy to find me in good spirits. For although I had no friends during that period, I found plenty to keep me occupied—books, stamps, the old gramophone, hundreds of postcards which he'd collected during his years in England, a scrapbook, albums of photographs... And sometimes I'd explore the jungle behind the tents; but I did not go very far, because of the snakes that proliferated there.

I would have my lunch with a family living in a neighbouring tent, but at night my father and I would eat together. I forget who did the cooking. But he made the breakfast, getting up early to whip up some fresh butter (he loved doing this) and then laying the table with cornflakes or grapenuts, and eggs poached or fried.

The gramophone was a great companion when my father was away. He had kept all the records he had collected in Jamnagar, and these were added to from time to time. There were operatic arias and duets from La Bohéme and Madame Butterfly; ballads and traditional airs rendered by Paul Robeson, Peter Dawson, Richard Crooks, Webster Booth, Nelson Eddy and other tenors and baritones, and of course the great Russian bass, Chaliapin. And there were lighter, music-hall songs and comic relief provided by Gracie Fields (the 'Lancashire Lass'), George Formby with his ukelele, Arthur Askey ('big-hearted' Arthur—he was a tiny chap,) Flanagan and Allen, and a host of other recording artistes. You couldn't just put on some music and lie back and enjoy it. That was the day of the wind-up gramophone, and it had to be wound up fairly vigorously before a 75 rmp record could be played. I enjoyed this chore. The needle, too, had to be changed after almost every record, if you wanted to keep them in decent condition. And the records had to be packed flat, otherwise, in the heat and humidity they were inclined to assume weird shapes and become unplayable.

It was always a delight to accompany my father to one of the record shops in Connaught Place, and come home with a new record by one of our favourite singers.

After a few torrid months in the tent-house and then in a brick hutment, which was even hotter, my father was permitted to rent rooms of his own on Atul Grove Road, a tree-lined lane not far from Connaught Place, which was then the hub and business centre of New Delhi. Keeping me with him had been quite unofficial; his superiors were always wanting to know why my mother wasn't around to look after me. He was really hoping that the war would end soon, so that he could take me to England and put me in a good school there. He had been selling some of his more valuable stamps and had put quite a bit in the bank.

One evening he came home with a bottle of Scotch whisky. This was most unusual, because I had never seen him drinking—not even beer. Had he suddenly decided to hit the bottle?

The mystery was solved when an American officer dropped in to have dinner with us (having a guest for dinner was a very rare event), and our cook excelled himself by producing succulent pork chops, other viands and vegetables, and my favourite chocolate pudding. Before we sat down to dinner, our guest polished off several pegs of whisky (my father had a drink too), and after dinner they sat down to go through some of my father's stamp albums. The American collector bought several stamps, and we went to bed richer by a couple of thousand rupees.

That it was possible to make money out of one's hobby was something I was to remember when writing became my passion.

When my father had a bad bout of malaria and was admitted to the Military Hospital, I was on my own for about ten days. Our immediate neighbours, an elderly Anglo-Indian couple, kept an eye on me, only complaining that I went through a tin of guava jam in one sitting. This tendency to over-indulge has been with me all my life. Those stringy convent meals must have had something to do with it.

I made one friend during the Atul Grove days. He was a boy called Joseph—from South India, I think—who lived next door. In the evenings we would meet on a strip of grassland across the road and engage in wrestling bouts which were watched by an admiring group of servants' children from a nearby hostelry. We also had a great deal of fun in the trenches that had been dug along the road in case of possible Japanese air raids (there had been one on Calcutta). During the monsoon they filled with rainwater, much to the delight of the local children, who used them as miniature swimming pools. They were then quite impracticable as air raid shelters.

Of course, the real war was being fought in Burma and the Far East, but Delhi was full of men in uniform. When winter came, my father's khakis were changed for dark blue RAF caps and uniforms, which suited him nicely. He was a good-looking man, always neatly dressed; on the short side but quite sturdy. He was over forty when he had joined up—hence the office job, deciphering (or helping to create) codes and ciphers. He was quite secretive about it all (as indeed he was supposed to be), and as he confided in me on almost every subject but his work, he was obviously a reliable Intelligence officer.

He did not have many friends in Delhi. There was the occasional visit to Uncle Fred near the railway station, and sometimes he'd spend a half-hour with Mr Rankin, who owned a large drapery shop at Connaught Circus, where officers' uniforms were tailored. Mr Rankin was another enthusiastic stamp collector, and the two of them would get together in Mr Rankin's back office and exchange stamps or discuss new issues. I think the drapery establishment closed down after the War. Mr Rankin was always extremely well dressed, as though he had stepped straight out of Saville Row and on to the steamy streets of Delhi.

My father and I explored old tombs and monuments, but going to the pictures was what we did most, if he was back from work fairly early.

Connaught Place was well served with cinemas—the Regal, Rivoli, Odeon and Plaza, all very new and shiny—and they exhibited the latest Hollywood and British productions. It was in these cinemas that I discovered the beautiful Sonja Henie, making love on skates and even getting married on ice; Nelson and Jeanette making love in duets; Errol Flynn making love on the high seas; and Gary Cooper and Claudette Colbert making love in the bedroom (*Bluebeard's Eighth Wife*). I made careful listings of all the films I saw, including their casts, and to this day I can give you the main performers in almost any film made in the 1940s. And I still think it was cinema's greatest decade, with the stress on good story, clever and economical direction (films seldom exceeded 120-minutes running time), superb black and white photography, and actors and actresses who were also personalities in their own right. The era of sadistic thrills, gore, and psychopathic killers was still far away. The accent was on entertainment—naturally enough, when the worst war in history had spread across Europe, Asia and the Pacific.

When my father broached the subject of sending me to a boarding school, I used every argument I could think of to dissuade him. The convent school was still fresh in my memory and I had no wish to return to any institution remotely resembling it—certainly not after almost a year of untrammelled freedom and my father's companionship.

'Why do you want to send me to school again?' I asked. 'I can learn more at home. I can read books, I can write letters, I can even do sums!'

'Not bad for a boy of nine,' said my father. 'But I can't teach you algebra, physics and chemistry.'

'I don't want to be a chemist.'

'Well, what would you like to be when you grow up?'

'A tap-dancer.'

'We've been seeing too many pictures. Everyone says I spoil you.'

I tried another argument. 'You'll have to live on your own again. You'll feel lonely.'

'That can't be helped, son. But I'll come to see you as often as I can. You see, they're posting me to Karachi for some time, and then I'll be moved again—they won't allow me to keep you with me at some of these places. Would you like to stay with your mother?'

I shook my head.

'With Calcutta Granny?'

'I don't know her.'

'When the War's over I'll take you with me to England. But for the next year or two we must stay here. I've found a nice school for you.'

'Another convent?'

'No, it's a prep school for boys in Shimla. And I may be able to get posted there during the summer.'

'I want to see it first,' I said.

'We'll go up to Shimla together. Not now—in April or May, before it gets too hot. It doesn't matter if you join school a bit later—I know you'll soon catch up with the others.'

There was a brief trip to Dehra Dun. I think my father felt that there was still a chance of a reconciliation with my mother. But her affair with the businessman was too far gone. His own wife had been practically abandoned and left to look after the photography shop she'd brought along with her dowry. She was a stout lady with high blood pressure, who once went in search of my mother and stepfather with an axe. Fortunately, they were not at home that day and she had to vent her fury on the furniture.

In later years, when I got to know her quite well, she told me that my father was a very decent man, who treated her with great courtesy and kindness on the one occasion they met.

I remember we stayed in a little hotel or boarding house just off the Eastern Canal Road.

Dehra was a green and leafy place. The houses were separated by hedges, not walls, and the residential areas were criss-crossed by little lanes bordered by hibiscus or oleander shrubs.

We were soon back in Delhi.

My parents' separation was final and it was to be almost two years before I saw my mother again.

The Last Letter

AA Bond 108485 (RAF)
c/o 231 Group RAF Post
Calcutta
20/8/44

My dear Ruskin,

Thank you very much for your letter received a few days ago. I was pleased to hear that you were quite well and learning hard. We are all quite OK here, but I am still not strong enough to go to work after the recent attack of malaria I had. I was in hospital for a long time and that is the reason why you did not get a letter from me for several weeks.

I have now to wear glasses for reading, but I do not use them for ordinary wear—but only when I read or do book work. Ellen does not wear glasses at all now.

Do you need any new warm clothes? Your warm suits must be getting too small. I am glad to hear the rains are practically over in the hills where you are. It will be nice to have sunny days in September when your holidays are on. Do the holidays begin from the 9th of Sept? What will you do? Is there to be a scouts camp at Taradevi? Or will you catch butterflies on sunny days on the school cricket ground? I am glad to hear you have lots of friends. Next year you will be in the top class of the prep school. You only have three and a half months more for the Xmas holidays to come round, when you will be glad to come home, I am sure, to do more stamp work and library study. The New Market is full of book shops here. Ellen loves the market.

I wanted to write before about your writing Ruskin, but forgot. Sometimes I get letters from you written in very small handwriting, as if you wanted to squeeze a lot of news into one sheet of letter paper. It is not good for you or for your eyes, to get into the habit of writing small: I know your handwriting is good and that you came first in class for handwriting, but try and form a larger style of writing and do not worry if you can't get all your news into one sheet of paper—but stick to big letters.

We have had a very wet month just passed. It is still cloudy, at night we have to use fans, but during the cold weather it is nice—not too cold like Delhi and not too warm either, but just moderate. Granny is quite well. She and Ellen send you their fond love. The last I heard a week ago, that William and all at Dehra were also well.

We have been without a cook for the past few days. I hope we find a good one before long. There are not many. I wish I could get our Delhi cook, the old man is now famous for his black puddings which Ellen hasn't seen since we arrived in Calcutta four months ago.

I have still got the records and gramophone and most of the best books, but as they are all getting old and some not suited to you which are only for children under eight years old—I will give some to William, and Ellen and you can buy some new ones when you come home for Xmas. I am re-arranging all the stamps that became loose and topsy-turvy after people came and went through the collections to buy stamps. A good many got sold, the rest got mixed up a bit and it is now taking up all my time putting the balance of the collection in order. But as I am at home all day, unable to go to work as yet, I have lots of time to finish the work of re-arranging the collection. Ellen loves drawing. I give her paper and a pencil and let her draw for herself without any help, to get her used to holding paper and pencil. She has got expert at using her pencil now and draws some wonderful animals like camels, elephants, dragons with many heads, cobras, rain clouds shedding buckets of water, tigers with long grass around them—horses with manes and wolves and foxes with bushy hair. Sometimes you can't see much of the animals because there is too much grass covering them or too much hair on the foxes and wolves and too much mane on the horses' necks—or too much rain from the clouds. All this decoration is made up by a sort of heavy scribbling of lines, but through it all one can see some very good shapes of animals, elephants and ostriches and other things. I will send you some.

Well, Ruskin, I hope this finds you well. With fond love from us all. Write again soon.

Ever your loving,
Daddy

It was about two weeks after receiving this letter that I was given the news of my father's death. Those frequent bouts of malaria had undermined his health, and a severe attack of jaundice did the rest. A kind but inept teacher, Mr Murtough, was given the unenviable task of breaking the news to me. He mumbled something about God needing my father more than I did, and of course I realized what had happened and broke down and had to be taken to the infirmary, where I remained for a couple of days. It never made any sense to me why God should have needed my father more than I did, unless of course He envied my father's stamp collection. If God was Love, why did He have to break up the only loving relationship I'd known so far? What would happen to me now, I wondered…would I live with Calcutta Granny or some other relative or be put away in an orphanage?

Mr Priestley saw me in his office and said I'd be going to my mother when school closed. He said he'd been told that I had kept my father's letters and that if I wished to put them in his safe keeping he'd see that they were not lost. I handed them over, all except the one I've reproduced here. The day before we broke up for the school holidays, I went to Mr Priestley and asked for my letters.

'What letters?' He looked bemused, irritated. He'd had a trying day. 'My father's letters,' I answered. 'You said you'd keep them for me.' 'Did I? Don't remember. Why should I want to keep your father's letters?' 'I don't know, sir. You put them in your drawer.' He opened the drawer, shut it. 'None of your letters here. I'm very busy now, Bond. If I find any of your letters, I'll give them to you.' I was dismissed from his presence.

I never saw those letters again. And I'm glad to say I did not see Mr Priestley again. All he'd given me was a lifelong aversion to violinists.

Our Great Escape

It had been a lonely winter for a fourteen-year-old. I had spent the first few weeks of the vacation with my mother and stepfather in Dehra. Then they left for Delhi, and I was pretty much on my own. Of course, the servants were there to take care of my needs, but there was no one to keep me company. I would wander off in the mornings, taking some path up the hills, come back home for lunch, read a bit, and then stroll off again till it was time for dinner. Sometimes I walked up to my grandparents' house, but it seemed so different now, with people I didn't know occupying the house.

The three-month winter break over, I was almost eager to return to my boarding school in Shimla.

It wasn't as though I had many friends at school. I needed a friend but it was not easy to find one among a horde of rowdy, pea-shooting eighth formers, who carved their names on desks and stuck chewing gum on the class teacher's chair. Had I grown up with other children, I might have developed a taste for schoolboy anarchy; but in sharing my father's loneliness after his separation from my mother, and in being bereft of any close family ties, I had turned into a premature adult.

After a month in the eighth form, I began to notice a new boy, Omar, and then only because he was a quiet, almost taciturn person who took no part in the form's feverish attempt to imitate the Marx Brothers at the circus. He showed no resentment at the prevailing anarchy, nor did he make a move to participate in it. Once he caught me looking at him, and he smiled ruefully, tolerantly. Did I sense another adult in the class? Someone who was a little older than his years?

Even before we began talking to each other, Omar and I developed an understanding of sorts, and we'd nod almost respectfully to each other when we met in the classroom corridors or the environs of the dining hall or the dormitory. We were not in the same house. The house system practised its own form of apartheid, whereby a member of one house was not expected to fraternize with someone belonging to another. Those public schools certainly knew how to clamp you into compartments. However, these barriers vanished when Omar and I found ourselves selected for the School Colts' hockey team, Omar as a full-back, I as the goalkeeper.

The taciturn Omar now spoke to me occasionally, and we combined well on the field of play. A good understanding is needed between a goalkeeper and a full-back. We were on the same wavelength. I anticipated his moves; he was familiar with mine. Years later, when I read Conrad's *The Secret Sharer*, I thought of Omar.

It wasn't until we were away from the confines of school, classroom and dining hall that our friendship flourished. The hockey team travelled to Sanawar on the next mountain range, where we were to play a couple of matches against our old rivals, the Lawrence Memorial Royal Military School. This had been my father's old school, so I was keen to explore its grounds and peep into its classrooms.

Omar and I were thrown together a good deal during the visit to Sanawar, and in our more leisurely moments, strolling undisturbed around a school where we were guests and not pupils, we exchanged life histories and other confidences. Omar, too, had lost his father—had I sensed that before?—shot in some tribal encounter on the Frontier, for he hailed from the lawless lands beyond Peshawar. A wealthy uncle was seeing to Omar's education.

We wandered into the school chapel, and there I found my father's name—A. A. Bond—on the school's roll of honour board: old boys who had lost their lives while serving during the two World Wars.

'What did his initials stand for?' asked Omar.

'Aubrey Alexander.'

'Unusual names, like yours. Why did your parents call you Rusty?'

'I am not sure.' I told him about the book I was writing. It was my first one and was called *Nine Months* (the length of the school term, not a pregnancy), and it described some of the happenings at school and lampooned a few of our teachers. I had filled three slim exercise books with this premature literary project, and I allowed Omar to go through them. He must have been my first reader and critic.

'They're very interesting,' he said, 'but you'll get into trouble if someone finds them, especially Mr Fisher.'

I have to admit it wasn't great literature. I was better at hockey and football. I made some spectacular saves, and we won our matches against Sanawar. When we returned to Shimla, we were school heroes for a couple of days and lost some of our reticence; we were even a little more forthcoming with other boys. And then Mr Fisher, my housemaster, discovered my literary opus, *Nine Months*, under my mattress, and took it away and read it (as he told me later) from cover to cover. Corporal punishment then being in vogue, I was given six of the best with a springy Malacca cane, and my manuscript was torn up and deposited in Mr Fisher's wastepaper basket. All I had to show for my efforts were some purple welts on my bottom. These were proudly displayed to all who were interested, and I was a hero for another two days.

'Will you go away too when the British leave India?' Omar asked me one day.

'I don't think so,' I said. 'I don't have anyone to go back to in England, and my guardian, Mr Harrison, too seems to have no intention of going back.'

'Everyone is saying that our leaders and the British are going to divide the country. Shimla will be in India, Peshawar in Pakistan!'

'Oh, it won't happen,' I said glibly. 'How can they cut up such a big country?' But even as we chatted about the possibility,

Nehru, Jinnah and Mountbatten, and all those who mattered, were preparing their instruments for major surgery.

Before their decision impinged on our lives and everyone else's, we found a little freedom of our own, in an underground tunnel that we discovered below the third flat.

It was really part of an old, disused drainage system, and when Omar and I began exploring it, we had no idea just how far it extended. After crawling along on our bellies for some twenty feet, we found ourselves in complete darkness. Omar had brought along a small pencil torch, and with its help we continued writhing forward (moving backwards would have been quite impossible) until we saw a glimmer of light at the end of the tunnel. Dusty, musty, very scruffy, we emerged at last onto a grassy knoll, a little way outside the school boundary.

It's always a great thrill to escape beyond the boundaries that adults have devised. Here we were in unknown territory. To travel without passports—that would be the ultimate in freedom!

But more passports were on their way—and more boundaries.

Lord Mountbatten, viceroy and governor-general-to-be, came for our Founder's Day and gave away the prizes. I had won a prize for something or the other, and mounted the rostrum to receive my book from this towering, handsome man in his pinstripe suit. Bishop Cotton's was then the premier school of India, often referred to as the 'Eton of the East'. Viceroys and governors had graced its functions. Many of its boys had gone on to eminence in the civil services and armed forces. There was one 'old boy' about whom they maintained a stolid silence—General Dyer, who had ordered the massacre at Amritsar and destroyed the trust that had been building up between Britain and India.

Now Mountbatten spoke of the momentous events that were happening all around us—the War had just come to an end, the United Nations held out the promise of a world living in peace and harmony, and India, an equal partner with Britain, would be among the great nations...

A few weeks later, Bengal and the Punjab provinces were bisected. Riots flared up across northern India, and there was a great exodus of people crossing the newly-drawn frontiers of Pakistan and India. Homes were destroyed, thousands lost their lives.

The common room radio and the occasional newspaper kept us abreast of events, but in our tunnel, Omar and I felt immune from all that was happening, worlds away from all the pillage, murder and revenge. And outside the tunnel, on the pine knoll below the school, there was fresh untrodden grass, sprinkled with clover and daisies; the only sounds we heard were the hammering of a woodpecker and the distant insistent call of the Himalayan Barbet. Who could touch us there?

'And when all the wars are done,' I said, 'a butterfly will still be beautiful.'

'Did you read that somewhere?'

'No, it just came into my head.'

'Already you're a writer.'

'No, I want to play hockey for India or football for Arsenal. Only winning teams!'

'You can't win forever. Better to be a writer.'

When the monsoon arrived, the tunnel was flooded, the drain choked with rubble. We were allowed out to the cinema to see Laurence Olivier's *Hamlet*, a film that did nothing to raise our spirits on a wet and gloomy afternoon; but it was our last picture that year, because communal riots suddenly broke out in Shimla's Lower Bazaar, an area that was still much as Kipling had described it—'a man who knows his way there can defy all the police of India's summer capital'—and we were confined to school indefinitely.

One morning after prayers in the chapel, the headmaster announced that the Muslim boys—those who had their homes in what was now Pakistan—would have to be evacuated, sent to their homes across the border with an armed convoy.

The tunnel no longer provided an escape for us. The bazaar was out of bounds. The flooded playing field was deserted. Omar and I sat on a damp wooden bench and talked about the future in vaguely hopeful terms, but we didn't solve any problems. Mountbatten and Nehru and Jinnah were doing all the solving.

It was soon time for Omar to leave—he left along with some fifty other boys from Lahore, Pindi and Peshawar. The rest of us—Hindus, Christians, Parsis—helped them load their luggage into the waiting trucks. A couple of boys broke down and wept. So did our departing school captain, a Pathan who had been known for his stoic and unemotional demeanour. Omar waved cheerfully to me and I waved back. We had vowed to meet again some day.

The convoy got through safely enough. There was only one casualty—the school cook, who had strayed into an off-limits area in the foothill town of Kalika and been set upon by a mob. He wasn't seen again.

Towards the end of the school year, just as we were all getting ready to leave for the school holidays, I received a letter from Omar. He told me something about his new school and how he missed my company and our games and our tunnel to freedom. I replied and gave him my home address, but I did not hear from him again.

Some seventeen or eighteen years later, I did get news of Omar, but in an entirely different context. India and Pakistan were at war, and in a bombing raid over Ambala, not far from Shimla, a Pakistani plane was shot down. Its crew died in the crash. One of them, I learnt later, was Omar.

Did he, I wonder, get a glimpse of the playing fields we knew so well as boys? Perhaps memories of his schooldays flooded back as he flew over the foothills. Perhaps he remembered the tunnel through which we were able to make our little escape to freedom.

But there are no tunnels in the sky.

The Night Train at Deoli

When I was at college I used to spend my summer vacations in Dehra, at my grandmother's place. I would leave the plains early in May and return late in July. Deoli was a small station about thirty miles from Dehra. It marked the beginning of the heavy jungles of the Indian terai.

The train would reach Deoli at about five in the morning when the station would be dimly lit with electric bulbs and oil lamps, and the jungle across the railway tracks would just be visible in the faint light of dawn. Deoli had only one platform, an office for the stationmaster and a waiting room. The platform boasted a tea stall, a fruit vendor and a few stray dogs; not much else because the train stopped there for only ten minutes before rushing on into the forests.

Why it stopped at Deoli, I don't know. Nothing ever happened there. Nobody got off the train and nobody got on. There were never any coolies on the platform. But the train would halt there a full ten minutes and then a bell would sound, the guard would blow his whistle, and presently Deoli would be left behind and forgotten.

I used to wonder what happened in Deoli behind the station walls. I always felt sorry for that lonely little platform and for the place that nobody wanted to visit. I decided that one day I would get off the train at Deoli and spend the day there just to please the town.

I was eighteen, visiting my grandmother, and the night train stopped at Deoli. A girl came down the platform selling baskets.

It was a cold morning and the girl had a shawl thrown across her shoulders. Her feet were bare and her clothes were old but she was a young girl, walking gracefully and with dignity.

When she came to my window, she stopped. She saw that I was looking at her intently, but at first she pretended not to notice. She had pale skin, set off by shiny black hair and dark, troubled eyes. And then those eyes, searching and eloquent, met mine.

She stood by my window for some time and neither of us said anything. But when she moved on, I found myself leaving my seat and going to the carriage door. I stood waiting on the platform looking the other way. I walked across to the tea stall. A kettle was boiling over a small fire, but the owner of the stall was busy serving tea somewhere on the train. The girl followed me behind the stall.

'Do you want to buy a basket?' she asked. 'They are very strong, made of the finest cane…'

'No,' I said, 'I don't want a basket.'

We stood looking at each other for what seemed a very long time, and she said, 'Are you sure you don't want a basket?'

'All right, give me one,' I said, and took the one on top and gave her a rupee, hardly daring to touch her fingers.

As she was about to speak, the guard blew his whistle. She said something, but it was lost in the clanging of the bell and the hissing of the engine. I had to run back to my compartment. The carriage shuddered and jolted forward.

I watched her as the platform slipped away. She was alone on the platform and she did not move, but she was looking at me and smiling. I watched her until the signal box came in the way and then the jungle hid the station. But I could still see her standing there alone…

I stayed awake for the rest of the journey. I could not rid my mind of the picture of the girl's face and her dark, smouldering eyes.

But when I reached Dehra the incident became blurred and distant, for there were other things to occupy my mind. It was only when I was making the return journey, two months later, that I remembered the girl.

I was looking out for her as the train drew into the station, and I felt an unexpected thrill when I saw her walking up the platform. I sprang off the footboard and waved to her.

When she saw me, she smiled. She was pleased that I remembered her. I was pleased that she remembered me. We were both pleased and it was almost like a meeting of old friends.

She did not go down the length of the train selling baskets but came straight to the tea stall. Her dark eyes were suddenly filled with light. We said nothing for some time but we couldn't have been more eloquent.

I felt the impulse to put her on the train there and then, and take her away with me. I could not bear the thought of having to watch her recede into the distance of Deoli station. I took the baskets from her hand and put them down on the ground. She put out her hand for one of them, but I caught her hand and held it.

'I have to go to Delhi,' I said.

She nodded. 'I do not have to go anywhere.'

The guard blew his whistle for the train to leave, and how I hated the guard for doing that.

'I will come again,' I said. 'Will you be here?'

She nodded again and, as she nodded, the bell clanged and the train slid forward. I had to wrench my hand away from the girl and run for the moving train.

This time I did not forget her. She was with me for the remainder of the journey and for long after. All that year she was a bright, living thing. And when the college term finished, I packed in haste and left for Dehra earlier than usual. My grandmother would be pleased at my eagerness to see her.

I was nervous and anxious as the train drew into Deoli, because I was wondering what I should say to the girl and what I should do. I was determined that I wouldn't stand helplessly before her, hardly able to speak or do anything about my feelings.

The train came to Deoli, and I looked up and down the platform but I could not see the girl anywhere.

I opened the door and stepped off the footboard. I was deeply disappointed and overcome by a sense of foreboding. I felt I had to do something and so I ran up to the stationmaster and said, 'Do you know the girl who used to sell baskets here?'

'No, I don't,' said the stationmaster. 'And you'd better get on the train if you don't want to be left behind.'

But I paced up and down the platform and stared over the railings at the station yard. All I saw was a mango tree and a dusty road leading into the jungle. Where did the road go? The train was moving out of the station and I had to run up the platform and jump for the door of my compartment. Then, as the train gathered speed and rushed through the forests, I sat brooding in front of the window.

What could I do about finding a girl I had seen only twice, who had hardly spoken to me, and about whom I knew nothing—absolutely nothing—but for whom I felt a tenderness and responsibility that I had never felt before?

My grandmother was not pleased with my visit after all, because I didn't stay at her place more than a couple of weeks. I felt restless and ill at ease. So I took the train back to the plains, meaning to ask further questions of the stationmaster at Deoli.

But at Deoli there was a new stationmaster. The previous man had been transferred to another post within the past week. The new man didn't know anything about the girl who sold baskets. I found the owner of the tea stall, a small, shrivelled-up man, wearing greasy clothes, and asked him if he knew anything about the girl with the baskets.

'Yes, there was such a girl here. I remember quite well,' he said. 'But she has stopped coming now.'

'Why?' I asked. 'What happened to her?'

'How should I know?' said the man. 'She was nothing to me.'

And once again I had to run for the train.

As Deoli platform receded, I decided that one day I would have to break journey there, spend a day in the town, make enquiries, and find the girl who had stolen my heart with nothing but a look from her dark, impatient eyes.

With this thought I consoled myself throughout my last term in college. I went to Dehra again in the summer and when, in the early hours of the morning, the night train drew into Deoli station, I looked up and down the platform for signs of the girl, knowing I wouldn't find her but hoping just the same.

Somehow, I couldn't bring myself to break journey at Deoli and spend a day there. (If it was all fiction or a film, I reflected, I would have got down and cleared up the mystery and reached a suitable ending to the whole thing.) I think I was afraid to do this.

I was afraid of discovering what really happened to the girl. Perhaps she was no longer in Deoli, perhaps she was married, perhaps she had fallen ill…

In the last few years I have passed through Deoli many times, and I always look out of the carriage window half expecting to see the same unchanged face smiling up at me. I wonder what happens in Deoli, behind the station walls. But I will never break my journey there. I prefer to keep hoping and dreaming and looking out of the window up and down that lonely platform, waiting for the girl with the baskets.

I never break my journey at Deoli but I pass through as often as I can.

Boy Scouts Forever!

I was a Boy Scout once, although I couldn't tell a slip knot from a granny knot, or a reef knot from a thief knot, except that a thief knot was supposed to be used to tie up a thief, should you happen to catch one. I have never caught a thief, and wouldn't know what to do with one since I can't tie a knot. Just let him go with a warning, I suppose. Tell him to become a Boy Scout.

'Be prepared!' That's the Boy Scout motto. And a good one, too. But I never seem to be well-prepared for anything, be it an exam or a journey or the roof blowing off my room. I get halfway through a speech and then forget what I have to say next. Or I get a new suit to attend a friend's wedding, and then turn up in my pyjamas.

So how did I, the most impractical of boys, become a Boy Scout? I was at boarding school in Shimla when it happened.

Well, it seems a rumour had gone around the junior school (I was still a junior then) that I was a good cook. I had never cooked anything in my life, but of course I had spent a lot of time in the tuck shop making suggestions and advising Chippu, who ran the tuck shop, and encouraging him to make more and better samosas, jalebis, tikkees and pakoras. For my unwanted advice he would favour me with an occasional free samosa, so naturally I looked upon him as a friend and benefactor. With this qualification I was given a cookery badge and put in charge of our troop's supply of rations.

There were about twenty of us in our troop, and during the summer break our Scoutmaster, Mr Oliver, took us on a camping expedition to Tara Devi, a temple-crowned mountain a few miles outside Shimla. That first night we were put to work, peeling potatoes, skinning onions, shelling peas and pounding masalas. These various ingredients being ready, I was asked—as the troop's cookery expert—what should be done with them.

'Put everything in that big *degchi*,' I ordered. 'Pour half a tin of ghee over the lot. Add some nettle leaves and cook for half an hour.'

When this was done, everyone had a taste, but the general opinion was that the dish lacked something.

'More salt,' I suggested.

More salt was added. It still lacked something.

'Add a cup of sugar,' I ordered.

Sugar was added to the concoction. But still it lacked something.

'We forgot to add tomatoes,' said Bimal, one of the Scouts.

'Never mind,' I said. 'We have tomato sauce. Add a bottle of tomato sauce!'

'How about some vinegar?' asked another boy. 'Just the thing,' I agreed. 'A cup of vinegar!'

'Now it's too sour,' said one of the tasters.

'What jam did we bring?' I asked.

'Gooseberry jam.'

'Just the thing. Empty the bottle!'

The dish was a great success. Everyone enjoyed it, including Mr Oliver, who had no idea what went into it.

'What's this called?' he asked.

'It's an all-Indian sweet-and-sour jam-potato curry,' I ventured.

'For short, just call it a Bond-bhujji,' said Bimal.

I had earned my cookery badge!

Poor Mr Oliver! He wasn't really cut out to be a Scoutmaster, any more than I was meant to be a Scout. The following day he announced that he would give us a lesson in tracking. He would take a half-hour start and walk into the forest, leaving behind him a trail of broken twigs, chicken feathers, pine cones and chestnuts, and we were to follow the trail until we found him.

Unfortunately, we were not very good trackers. We did follow

Mr Oliver's trail some way into the forest, but were distracted by a pool of clear water which looked very inviting. Abandoning our uniforms, we jumped into the pool and had a great time romping around or just lying on the grassy banks and enjoying the sunshine. A couple of hours later, feeling hungry, we returned to our campsite and set about preparing the evening meal. Bond-bhujji again, but with further variations.

It was growing dark, and we were beginning to worry about Mr Oliver's whereabouts when he limped into camp, assisted by a couple of local villagers. Having waited for us at the far end of the forest for a couple of hours, he had decided to come back by following his own trail, but in the gathering gloom he was soon lost. Some locals returning from the temple took charge of him and escorted him back to camp. He was very angry and made us all return our good-conduct and other badges, which he stuffed into his haversack. I had to give up my cookery badge too.

An hour later, when we were all preparing to get into our sleeping bags for the night, Mr Oliver called out: 'Where's dinner?'

'We've had ours,' said Bimal. 'Everything is finished, sir.'

'Where's Bond? He's supposed to be the cook. Bond, get up and make me an omelette.'

'Can't, sir.'

'Why not?'

'You have my badge. Not allowed to cook without it. Scout rule, sir.'

'Never heard of such a rule. But you can have your badges back, all of you. We return to school tomorrow.'

Mr Oliver returned to his tent in a huff. But I relented and made him an elaborate omelette, garnishing it with dandelion leaves and an extra chilli.

'Never had such an omelette before,' confessed Mr Oliver, blowing out his cheeks. 'A little too hot, but otherwise quite interesting.'

'Would you like another, sir?'

'Tomorrow, Bond, tomorrow. We'll breakfast early tomorrow.'

But we had to break up our camp very early the next day. In the early hours, a bear had strayed into our camp, entered the tent where our stores were kept, and created havoc with all our provisions, even rolling our biggest degchi down the hillside.

In the confusion and uproar that followed, the bear entered Mr Oliver's tent (he was already outside, fortunately) and came out entangled in Mr Oliver's dressing gown. It then made off in the direction of the forest.

A bear in a dressing gown? It was a comical sight.

And though we were a troop of brave little Scouts, we thought it better to let the bear keep the gown.

At Sea with Uncle Ken

With uncle Ken you always had to expect the unexpected. Even in the most normal circumstances, something unusual would happen to him and to those around him. He was a catalyst for confusion.

My mother should have known better than to ask him to accompany me to England the year after I'd finished school. She felt that a boy of sixteen was a little too young to make the voyage on his own; I might get lost or lose my money or fall overboard or catch some dreadful disease. She should have realized that Uncle Ken, her only brother (well spoilt by his five sisters), was more likely to do all these things.

Anyway, he was put in charge of me and instructed to deliver me safely to my aunt in England, after which he could either stay there or return to India, whichever he preferred. Granny had paid for his ticket; so in effect he was getting a free holiday which included a voyage on a posh P&O liner.

Our train journey to Bombay passed off without incident, although Uncle Ken did manage to misplace his spectacles, getting down at the station wearing someone else's. This left him a little short-sighted, which might have accounted for his mistaking the stationmaster for a porter and instructing him to look after our luggage.

We had two days in Bombay before boarding the *S.S. Strathnaver* and Uncle Ken vowed that we would enjoy ourselves. However, he was a little constrained by his budget and took me to a rather seedy hotel on Lamington Road, where we had to share a toilet with over twenty other people.

'Never mind,' he said. 'We won't spend much time in this dump.' So he took me to Marine Drive and the Gateway of India and to an Irani restaurant in Colaba, where we enjoyed a super dinner of curried prawns and scented rice. I don't know if it was the curry, the prawns or the scent, but Uncle Ken was up all night, running back and forth to that toilet, so that no one else had a chance to use it. Several dispirited travellers simply opened their windows and ejected into space, cursing Uncle Ken all the while.

He had recovered by morning and proposed a trip to the Elephanta Caves. After a breakfast of fish pickle, Malabar chilli chutney and sweet Gujarati puris, we got into a launch, accompanied by several other tourists and set off on our short cruise. The sea was rather choppy and we hadn't gone far before Uncle Ken decided to share his breakfast with the fishes of the sea. He was as green as a seaweed by the time we were ashore. Uncle Ken collapsed on the sand and refused to move, so we didn't see much of the caves. I brought him some coconut water and he revived a bit and suggested we go on a fast until it was time to board our ship.

We were safely on board the following morning, and the ship sailed majestically out from Ballard Pier, Bombay, and India receded into the distance, quite possibly forever as I wasn't sure that I would ever return. The sea fascinated me and I remained on deck all day, gazing at small crafts, passing steamers, sea birds, the distant shoreline, salt water smells, the surge of the waves and, of course, my fellow passengers. I could well understand the fascination it held for writers such as Conrad, Stevenson, Maugham and others.

Uncle Ken, however, remained confined to his cabin. The rolling of the ship made him feel extremely ill. If he had been looking green in Bombay, he was looking yellow at sea. I took my meals in the dining saloon, where I struck up an acquaintance with a well-known palmist and fortune teller who was on his way to London to make his fortune. He looked at my hand and told me I'd never be rich, but that I'd help other people get rich!

When Uncle Ken felt better (on the third day of the voyage), he struggled up on the deck, took a large lungful of sea air and subsided into a deck chair. He dozed the day away, but was suddenly wide awake when an attractive blonde strode past us on her way to the lounge. After some time we heard the tinkling of a piano. Intrigued, Uncle Ken rose and staggered into the lounge. The girl was at the piano, playing something classical which wasn't something that Uncle Ken normally enjoyed, but he was smitten by the girl's good looks and stood enraptured, his eyes brightly gleaming, his jaw sagging. With his nose pressed against the glass of the lounge door, he reminded me of a goldfish who had fallen in love with an angelfish that had just been introduced into the tank.

'What is she playing?' he whispered, aware that I had grown up on my father's classical record collection.

'Rachmaninoff,' I made a guess. 'Or maybe Rimsky Korsakov.'

'Something easier to pronounce,' he begged.

'Chopin,' I said.

'And what's his most famous composition?'

'*Polonaise in E flat.* Or maybe it's E minor.'

He pushed open the lounge door, walked in, and when the girl had finished playing, applauded loudly. She acknowledged his applause with a smile and then went on to play something else. When she had finished he clapped again and said, 'Wonderful! Chopin never sounded better!'

'Actually, it's Tchaikovsky,' said the girl. But she didn't seem to mind.

Uncle Ken would turn up at all her practice sessions and very soon they were strolling the decks together. She was Australian, on her way to London to pursue a musical career as a concert pianist. I don't know what she saw in Uncle Ken, but he knew all the right people. And he was quite good-looking in an effete sort of way.

Left to my own devices, I followed my fortune-telling friend around and watched him study the palms of our fellow passengers. He foretold romance, travel, success, happiness, health, wealth and longevity, but never predicted anything that might upset anyone.

As he did not charge anything (he was, after all, on holiday) he proved to be a popular passenger throughout the voyage. Later he was to become quite famous as a palmist and mind reader, an Indian 'Cheiro', much in demand in the capitals of Europe.

The voyage lasted eighteen days, with stops for passengers and cargo at Aden, Port Said and Marseilles, in that order. It was at Port Said that Uncle Ken and his friend went ashore, to look at the sights and do some shopping.

'You stay on the ship,' Uncle Ken told me. 'Port Said isn't safe for young boys.'

He wanted the girl all to himself, of course. He couldn't have shown off with me around. His 'man of the world' manner would not have been very convincing in my presence.

The ship was due to sail again that evening and passengers had to be back on board an hour before departure. The hours passed easily enough for me as the little library kept me engrossed. If there are books around, I am never bored. Towards evening, I went up on deck and saw Uncle Ken's friend coming up the gangway; but of Uncle Ken there was no sign.

'Where's Uncle?' I asked her.

'Hasn't he returned? We got separated in a busy marketplace and I thought he'd get here before me.'

We stood at the railings and looked up and down the pier, expecting to see Uncle Ken among the other returning passengers. But he did not turn up.

'I suppose he's looking for you,' I said. 'He'll miss the boat if he doesn't hurry.'

The ship's hooter sounded. 'All aboard!' called the captain on his megaphone. The big ship moved slowly out of the harbour. We were on our way! In the distance I saw a figure that looked like Uncle Ken running along the pier, frantically waving his arms. But there was no turning back.

A few days later my aunt met me at Tilbury Dock.

'Where's your Uncle Ken?' she asked.

'He stayed behind at Port Said. He went ashore and didn't get back in time.'

'Just like Ken. And I don't suppose he has much money with him. Well, if he gets in touch we'll send him a postal order.'

But Uncle Ken failed to get in touch. He was a topic of discussion for several days, while I settled down in my aunt's house and looked for a job. At sixteen, I was working in an office, earning a modest salary and contributing towards my aunt's housekeeping expenses. There was no time to worry about Uncle Ken's whereabouts.

My readers know that I longed to return to India, but it was nearly four years before that became possible. Finally I did come home and as the train drew into Dehra's little station, I looked out of the window and saw a familiar figure on the platform. It was Uncle Ken!

He made no reference to his disappearance at Port Said, and greeted me as though we had last seen each other the previous day.

'I've hired a cycle for you,' he said. 'Feel like a ride?'

'Let me get home first, Uncle Ken. I've got all this luggage.'

The luggage was piled into a tonga, I sat on top of everything and we went clip-clopping down an avenue of familiar litchi trees (all gone now, I fear). Uncle Ken rode behind the tonga, whistling cheerfully.

'When did you get back to Dehra?' I asked.

'Oh, a couple of years ago. Sorry I missed the boat. Was the girl upset?'

'She said she'd never forgive you.'

'Oh well, I expect she's better off without me. Fine piano player. Chopin and all that stuff.'

'Did Granny send you the money to come home?'

'No, I had to take a job working as a waiter in a Greek restaurant. Then I took tourists to look at the pyramids. I'm an expert on pyramids now. Great place, Egypt. But I had to leave when they found I had no papers or permit. They put me on a boat to Aden.

Stayed in Aden six months teaching English to the son of a shiekh. Shiekh's son went to England, I came back to India.'

'And what are you doing now, Uncle Ken?'

'Thinking of starting a poultry farm. Lots of space behind your Gran's house. Maybe you can help with it.'

'I couldn't save much money, Uncle.'

'We'll start in a small way. There is a big demand for eggs, you know. Everyone's into eggs—scrambled, fried, poached, boiled. Egg curry for lunch. Omelettes for dinner. Egg sandwiches for tea. How do you like your egg?'

'Fried,' I said. 'Sunny side up.'

'We shall have fried eggs for breakfast. Funny side up!'

The poultry farm never did happen, but it was good to be back in Dehra, with the prospect of limitless bicycle rides with Uncle Ken.

Gran's Kitchen

s kitchens went, it wasn't very big. What made it fabulous was all that came out of it. Gran's curries and kebabs, chocolate fudge and peanut toffee, jellies and gulab jamuns, meat pies and apple pies, stuffed chickens, stuffed eggplants, and even ham, stuffed with stuffed chicken! As far as I was concerned, Gran was the best cook in the world.

The town we lived in was called Dehradun. It's still there, though much bigger and more populous since India's independence. Gran had a large, rambling bungalow on the outskirts of town. On the grounds were many fruit trees—mangoes, litchis, guavas, bananas, papayas and lemons—there was room for all of them, including a giant jackfruit tree that threw its shadow on the walls of the house.

Gran had a saying,

'Blessed is the house upon whose walls

The shade of an old tree softly falls.'

She was right, hers was a good house to live in, especially for a ten-year-old boy with a tremendous appetite.

Every winter, when I came home from boarding school, I would spend at least a month with Gran before going over to my parents in Assam. My father managed a tea plantation there, and although the tea gardens were fun to play in, my parents couldn't cook. Like most colonials, they employed a Khansama, a professional cook, who made good mutton curry but little else. So I was always glad to spend half my holidays with Gran.

Gran was glad to have me too, because she lived alone most of the time. Not entirely alone, though. The gardener, his son Mohan and a mongrel dog named Crazy all lived in the compound. And sometimes there was Uncle Ken, a nephew of Gran's, who came to stay whenever he was out of a job (which was fairly often), or when he felt like enjoying some of Gran's cooking.

Gran didn't enjoy cooking just for herself; she liked to have someone to cook for. And although Uncle Ken sometimes appreciated her efforts, and Crazy loved her table scraps, a good cook likes a kid to feed, because kids are adventurous and ready to try even the most unusual dishes.

Whenever Gran tried out a new recipe on me, she would wait for my reaction, and then jot down some of my comments in a notebook. This was useful when she wanted to try the same dish on others.

'Do you like it?' she'd ask, after I'd taken a few mouthfuls.

'Yes, Gran.'

'Sweet enough?'

'Yes, Gran.'

'Not *too* sweet?'

'No, Gran.'

'Would you like some more?'

'Yes please, Gran.'

'Well, finish it off.'

'Mmmm…'

'Eat well, but don't overeat,' Gran used to tell me. And we did eat well, even though all those wonderful meals consisted of only one course followed by a sweet dish. It was Gran's cooking that turned a modest meal into a feast.

Roast duck was one of her specialties. The first time I had roast duck at Gran's place, Uncle Ken was there too. He'd just lost his job as a railway guard, and had come to stay with Gran until he could find something else.

Uncle Ken ate just as much as I did, but he never praised Gran's dishes and that annoyed me. He looked at the roast duck, his glasses slipping down to the edge of his nose. 'Hmmm… Duck again, Aunt May?'

'What do you mean by duck *again*? We haven't had duck since you were here last month!'

'That's what I mean,' said Uncle Ken. 'Somehow, one expects a little more variety.'

All the same, he took two large helpings and ate most of the stuffing before I could get at it. I got my revenge by emptying all the apple sauce onto my plate. Uncle Ken knew I loved stuffing, and I knew he was crazy about Gran's apple sauce. So we were even.

Gran was famous all over Dehra for her pickles. Green mangoes, pickled in oil, were always popular. So was her hot lime pickle. And she was adept at pickling turnips, carrots, cauliflowers, and chillies. She could pickle almost any fruit or vegetable—everything from nasturtium seeds to jackfruit.

One winter, when Gran's funds were low, Mohan and I went from house to house…selling pickles for her. Major Clarke, our neighbour across the road, was our first customer.

'And what have you got there?' he asked.

'Pickles, sir.'

'Pickles? Did you make them?'

'No, sir, they're my grandmother's. We're selling them so we can buy a turkey for Christmas.'

'Mrs Bond's pickles, eh? Well, I'm glad this is the first house on your route, because that basket will soon be empty. There's no one who can make a pickle like your grandmother! What have you this time? Stuffed chillies, I hope. She knows they're my favorite. I shall be deeply wounded if there are no stuffed chillies in that basket.'

There were, in fact, three bottles of stuffed red chillies in the basket, and Major Clarke bought all of them.

Further down the road, Dr Dutt bought several bottles of lime pickle, saying it was good for his liver. And Mr Hari, who owned a garage at the end of the road, purchased two bottles of pickled onions and begged us to bring another as soon as we could.

By the time we got home, the basket was empty, and Gran was richer by thirty rupees—enough, in those days, for a turkey.

Uncle Ken stayed for Christmas and ate most of the turkey.

A Week in the Jungle

Grandfather never hunted wild animals, he couldn't understand the pleasure some people obtained from killing the creatures of our forests. Birds and animals, he felt, had as much right to live as humans. We could kill them for food, he said, because even animals killed for food; but not for pleasure.

At the age of twelve I did not have the same high principles as Grandfather. Nevertheless, I disliked shooting. I found it boring.

Uncle Henry and some of his sporting friends once took me on a shikar expedition into the Terai jungles in the Shivalik range. The prospect of a week in the jungle, as camp-follower to several adults with guns, filled me with dismay. I knew that long, weary hours would be spent tramping behind these tall, professional-looking huntsmen who spoke in terms of bagging this tiger or that wild elephant, when all they ever got, if they were lucky, was a wild hare or a partridge. Tigers and excitement, it seemed, came only to Jim Corbett.

This particular expedition proved to be no different from others. There were four men with guns and at the end of the week all that they had shot were two miserable, underweight wildfowl. But I managed, on our second day in the jungle, to be left behind in the rest house. And, in the course of a morning's exploration of the old bungalow, I discovered a shelf of books half-hidden in a corner of the back verandah.

Who had left them there? A literary forest officer? A memsahib who had been bored by her husband's campfire boasting? Or someone who had no interest in the 'manly' sport of slaughtering wild animals and had brought his library along to pass the time?

He must have left it behind for others like him.

Or possibly the poor fellow had gone into the jungle one day, as a gesture to his more bloodthirsty companions, and been trampled by an elephant, or gored by a wild boar, or (more likely) accidentally shot by one of the shikaris—and his sorrowing friends had taken his remains away and left his books behind.

Anyway, there they were—a shelf of some thirty volumes, in different shapes, sizes, and colours. I wiped the thick dust off the covers and examined the titles. As my reading tastes had not yet formed, I was willing to try anything. The bookshelf was varied in its contents—and my own interests have since remained fairly universal.

On that second day in the forest rest house, I discovered P. G. Wodehouse and read his *Love Among the Chickens*, an early Ukridge story and still one of my favourites. By the time the perspiring hunters came home in the evening, with their spent cartridges and impressive excuses, I had made a start with M. R. James's *Ghost Stories of an Antiquary*. This kept me awake most of the night, until the oil in the kerosene lamp was exhausted.

Next morning, fresh and optimistic again, the shikaris set out for a different area, where they hoped to get a tiger. They had employed a party of villagers to beat the jungle, and all day I could hear the tom-toms throbbing in the distance. This did not prevent me from finishing M. R. James, or discovering a little book called *A Naturalist on the Prowl* by 'E. H. A'. It described the tremendous fun and interest to be had from studying the wildlife in one's own back garden—the grasshoppers, beetles, ants, butterflies and praying mantises, all living such fascinating lives just outside (and sometimes inside) our bedroom windows.

Before I had finished the book, I was looking for spiders in the corners of the old bungalow and stalking grasshoppers in the long grass of the compound. My concentration was disturbed only once, when I looked up and saw a spotted deer crossing the open space in front of the house. The deer disappeared among the sal trees and I returned to the verandah and my book.

Dusk had fallen when I heard the party returning from the hunt. The hunters were talking loudly and seemed excited. Perhaps they had got their tiger. I put down my book and came out of the house to meet them.

'Did you get the tiger?' I asked excitedly.

'No, laddie,' said Uncle Henry. 'I think we'll get it tomorrow. You should have been with us—we saw a spotted deer!'

There were three days left and I knew I would never get through the entire bookshelf. This I did not intend doing, as not all the authors on the shelf appealed to me. I chose at random *The Wind in the Willows*, *The Jungle Book*, and *David Copperfield*.

On the day I made the literary acquaintance of Mowgli, the wolf-boy, the shikaris shot the two wildfowl already mentioned. As the party had from the first intended living off the jungle, only some tinned foods had been brought along; but two lean birds were insufficient for a party of five, and once again the meal consisted mostly of corned meat and mustard.

Next day, while the grown-ups were looking for their tiger and I was learning wisdom from the Water Rat, Toad, and other river people of *The Wind in the Willows*, an event took place which disturbed my reading for a little while.

I had noticed, on the previous day, that a number of stray mongrels—belonging to watchmen, villagers and forest-guards—always hung about the house, waiting for scraps of food to be thrown away. It was ten o'clock in the morning (a time when wild animals seldom come into the open), when I heard a sudden yelp in the clearing. Looking up, I saw a full-grown panther making off into the jungle with one of the dogs held in its mouth. The panther had either been driven towards the house by the beaters, or had watched the party leave the bungalow and decided to help itself to a meal.

There was no one else about at the time. Since the dog was obviously dead within seconds of being seized, and the panther had disappeared, I saw no point in raising an alarm but returned to my book.

It was getting late when the shikaris returned. They were dirty, sweaty and, as usual, disappointed. This time their excuses held a note of defiance. They took their corned meat in silence. Next day, we were to return to 'civilization', and none of the hunters had anything to show for a week in the jungles of India.

'No game left in these jungles,' said the leading member of the party, famed for once having shot two man-eating tigers and a basking crocodile in rapid succession.

'It's the weather,' said another. 'No rain at all this winter.'

'Don't know what the country's coming to,' grumbled the third.

'I saw a panther this morning,' I said modestly.

In fact, I was altogether too modest. I might just as well have said, 'I saw a donkey this morning,' for all the impression I made.

'Did you really?' said the leading hunter. He glanced at the book lying beside me. 'Young Master Copperfield says he saw a panther!'

The others were only faintly amused. They did not have the energy to laugh.

'Too imaginative for his age,' said one of them. 'Comes from reading so much, I suppose.'

'If you were to get out of the house and into the jungle a little,' said Uncle Henry reproachfully, 'you might really see a panther.'

'Don't know what young fellows are coming to these days...'

'Why didn't you grab it, man, and take it to Grandfather?' And everyone laughed.

I went to bed early and left them to their tales of the 'good old days' when rhinos, cheetahs, and possibly even the legendary phoenix were still available for slaughter.

I came home with a poor reputation. My uncle's friends thought I was both a sissy and a liar. And Uncle Henry, poor man, seemed to think I was responsible for the failure of the entire expedition. He did not take me with him again. But Grandfather, when I told him all about the hunt, doubled up with laughter and said he wished he had been with us, if only to see the faces of Uncle Henry and his friends. As a measure of his delight, he bought me a copy of *David Copperfield*, for I had not been able to finish the one in the forest rest house. I finally got through it in the banyan tree, in the company of several squirrels and a very noisy cicada.

'Let's Go to the Pictures!'

My love affair with the cinema began when I was five and ended when I was about fifty. Not because I wanted it to, but because all my favourite cinema halls were closing down—being turned into shopping malls or garages or just disappearing altogether.

There was something magical about sitting in a darkened cinema hall, the audience silent, completely focused on the drama unfolding on the big screen. You could escape to a different world—run away to Dover with David Copperfield, sail away to a treasure island with Long John Silver, dance the light fantastic with Fred Astaire or Gene Kelly, sing with Saigal or Deanna Durbin or Nelson Eddy, fall in love with Madhubala or Elizabeth Taylor. And until the lights came on at the end of the show you were in their world, far removed from the troubles of one's own childhood or the struggles of early manhood.

Watching films on TV cannot be the same. People come and go, the power comes and goes, other viewers keep switching the channels, food is continually being served or consumed, family squabbles are ever present, and there is no escape from those dreaded commercials that are repeated every ten or fifteen minutes, or even between overs if you happen to be watching cricket.

No longer do we hear that evocative suggestion: 'Let's go to the pictures!'

Living in Mussoorie where there are no longer any functioning cinemas, the invitation is heard no more. I'm afraid there isn't half as much excitement in the words 'Let's put on the TV!'

For one thing, going to the pictures meant going out—on foot, or on a bicycle, or in the family car. When I lived on the outskirts of Mussoorie it took me almost an hour to climb the hill into town to see a film at one of our tiny halls—but walk I did, in hot sun or drenching rain or icy wind, because going to the pictures was an event in itself, a break from more mundane activities, quite often a social occasion. You would meet friends from other parts of the town, and after the show you would join them in a cafe for a cup of tea and the latest gossip. A stroll along the Mall and a visit to the local bookshop would bring the evening to a satisfying end. A long walk home under the stars, a drink before dinner, something to listen to on the radio... 'And then to bed,' as Mr Pepys would have said.

Not that everything went smoothly in our small-town cinemas. In Shimla, Mussoorie and other hill stations, the roofs were of corrugated tin sheets, and when there was heavy rain or a hailstorm it would be impossible to hear the soundtrack. You had then to imagine that you were back in the silent film era.

Mussoorie's oldest cinema, the Picture Palace, did in fact open early in the silent era. This was in 1912, the year electricity came to the town. Later, its basement floor was also turned into a cinema, the Jubilee, which probably made it India's first multiplex hall. Sadly, both closed down about five years ago, along with the Rialto, the Majestic and the Capitol (below Halman's Hotel).

In Shimla, we had the Ritz, the Regal and the Rivoli. This was when I was a schoolboy at Bishop Cotton's. How we used to look forward to our summer and autumn breaks. We would be allowed into town during these holidays, and we lost no time in tramping up to the Ridge to take in the latest films. Sometimes we'd arrive wet or perspiring, but the changeable weather did not prevent us from enjoying the film. One-and-a-half hours escape from the routine and discipline of boarding school life. Fast foods had yet to be invented, but roasted peanuts or *bhuttas* would keep us going. They were cheap too. The cinema ticket was just over a rupee. If you had five rupees in your pocket you could enjoy a pleasant few hours in the town.

It was during the winter holidays—three months of time on my hands—that I really caught up with the films of the day.

New Delhi, the winter of 1943. Second World War was still in progress. The halls were flooded with British and American movies. My father would return from Air Headquarters, where he'd been working on cyphers all day. 'Let's go to the pictures,' he'd say, and we'd be off to the Regal or Rivoli or Odeon or Plaza, only a short walk from our rooms on Atul Grove Road.

Comedies were my favourites. Laurel and Hardy, Abbott and Costello, George Formby, Harold Lloyd, the Marx Brothers... And sometimes we'd venture further afield, to the old Ritz at Kashmere Gate, to see Sabu in *The Thief of Baghdad* or *Cobra Woman*. These *Arabian Nights*-type entertainments were popular in the old city.

The Statesman, the premier newspaper of that era, ran ads for all the films in town, and I'd cut them out and stick them in a scrapbook. I could rattle off the cast of all the pictures I'd seen, and today, sixty years later, I can still name all the actors (and sometimes the director) of almost every 1940s film.

My father died when I was ten and I went to live with my mother and stepfather in Dehradun. Dehra too, was well served with cinemas, but I was a lonely picturegoer. I had no friends or companions in those years, and I would trudge off on my own to the Orient or Odeon or Hollywood, to indulge in a few hours of escapism. Books were there, of course, providing another and better form of escape, but books had to be read in the home, and sometimes I wanted to get away from the house and pursue a solitary other-life in the anonymous privacy of a darkened cinema hall.

It has gone now, the little Odeon cinema opposite the old Parade Ground in Dehra. Many of my age, and younger, will remember it with affection, for it was probably the most popular meeting place for English cinema buffs in the '40s and '50s. You could get a good idea of the popularity of a film by looking at the number of bicycles ranged outside. Dehra was a bicycle town. The scooter hadn't been invented, and cars were few. I belonged to a minority of walkers. I have walked all over the towns and cities I have lived in—Dehradun, New and Old Delhi, London, St Helier (in Jersey) and our hill stations. Those walks often ended at the cinema!

The Odeon was a twenty-minute walk from the Old Survey Road, where we lived at the time, and after the evening show I would walk home across the deserted parade ground, the starry night adding to my dreams of a starry world, where tap dancers, singing cowboys, swashbuckling swordsmen and glamorous women in sarongs reigned supreme in the firmament. I wasn't just a daydreamer; I was a star-dreamer.

During the intervals (five-minute breaks between the shorts and the main feature), the projectionist or his assistant would play a couple of gramophone records for the benefit of the audience. Unfortunately, the management had only two or three records, and the audience would grow restless listening to the same tunes at every show. I must have been compelled to listen to 'Don't Fence Me In' about a hundred times, and felt thoroughly fenced in.

At home, I had a good collection of gramophone records, passed on to me by relatives and neighbours who were leaving India around the time of Independence. I decided it would be a good idea to give some of them to the cinema's management so that we could be provided with a little more variety during the intervals. I made a selection of about twenty records—mostly dance music of the period—and presented them to the manager, Mr Suri.

Mr Suri was delighted. And to show me his gratitude, he presented me with a Free Pass which permitted me to see all the pictures I liked without having to buy a ticket! Any day, any show, for as long as Mr Suri was the manager! Could any ardent picturegoer have asked for more?

This unexpected bonanza lasted for almost two years with the result that during my school holidays, I saw a film every second day. Two days was the average run for most films. Except *Gone With the Wind*, which ran for a week, to my great chagrin. I found it so boring that I left in the middle.

Usually I did enjoy films based on famous or familiar books. Dickens was a natural for the screen. *David Copperfield, Oliver Twist, Great Expectations, Nicholas Nickleby, A Tale of Two Cities, Pickwick Papers, A Christmas Carol,* all made successful films, true to the originals. Daphne du Maurier's novels also transferred well to the screen. As did Somerset Maugham's works: *Of Human Bondage, The Razor's Edge, The Letter, Rain* and several others.

Occasionally I brought the management a change of records. Mr Suri was not a very communicative man, but I think he liked me (he knew something about my circumstances) and with a smile and a wave of the hand he would indicate that the freedom of the hall was mine.

Eventually, school finished, I was packed off to England, where my picture-going days went into a slight decline. No Free Passes any more. But on Jersey island, where I lived and worked for a year, I found an out-of-the-way cinema which specialized in showing old comedies, and here I caught up with many British film comedians such as Tommy Trinder, Sidney Howard, Max Miller, Will Hay, Old Mother Riley (a man in reality) and Gracie Fields. These artistes had been but names to me, as their films had never come to India. I was thrilled to be able to discover and enjoy their considerable talents. You would be hard put to find their films today; they have seldom been revived.

In London for two years I had an office job and most of my spare time was spent in writing (and rewriting) my first novel. All the same, I took to the streets and discovered the Everyman cinema in Hampstead, which showed old classics, including the films of Jean Renoir and Orson Welles. And the Academy in Leicester Square, which showed the best films from the continent. I also discovered a couple of seedy little cinemas in the East End, which appropriately showed the early gangster films of James Cagney and Humphrey Bogart.

I also saw the first Indian film to get a regular screening in London. It was called *Aan,* and was the usual extravagant mix of music and melodrama. But it ran for two or three weeks. Homesick Indians (which included me) flocked to see it. One of its stars was Nadira, who specialized in playing the scheming sultry villainess. A few years ago, she came out of retirement to take the part of Miss Mackenzie in a TV serial based on some of my short stories set in Mussoorie. A sympathetic role for a change. And she played it to perfection.

It was four years before I saw Dehra again. Mr Suri had gone elsewhere. The little cinema had closed down and was about to be demolished, to make way for a hotel and a block of shops.

We must move on, of course. There's no point in hankering after distant pleasures and lost picture palaces. But there's no harm in indulging in a little nostalgia. What is nostalgia, after all, but an attempt to preserve that which was good in the past?

And last year I was reminded of that golden era of the silver screen. I was rummaging around in a *kabari* shop in one of Dehradun's bazaars where I came across a pile of old 78 RPM records, all looking a little the worse for wear. And on a couple of them I found my name scratched on the labels. 'Pennies from Heaven' was the title of one of the songs. It had certainly saved me a few rupees. That and the goodwill of Mr Suri, the Odeon's manager, all those years ago.

I bought the records. Can't play them now. No wind-up gramophone! But I am a sentimental fellow and I keep them among my souvenirs as a reminder of the days when I walked home alone across the silent, moonlit parade ground, after the evening show was over.

The Bar That Time Forgot

'Cockroaches!' exclaimed Her Highness the Maharani. 'Cockroaches everywhere! Can't put down my glass without finding a cockroach beneath it!'

'Cockroaches have a special liking for this room,' observed Colonel Wilkie, from his corner by the disused fireplace. 'For one thing, our Melaram there,' and he indicated the bartender with a tilt of his double chin, 'never washes the glasses properly. And there are sandwich remains all over the place. Last week's sandwiches, I might add. From that party of yours, Krishan.'

Krishan, former Test cricketer, now forty and with a forty-three-inch waist, turned to the Colonel. 'You should see the kitchen. A pigsty. The cook is seldom sober.'

'*We* are seldom sober,' said Suresh Mathur, income-tax lawyer, from his favourite bar stool.

'Speak for yourself,' snapped H.H. 'Simon, fetch me another whisky.'

Simon Lee, secretary-companion to Her Highness, rose dutifully from his chair and took her glass over to the bar counter.

'Indian whisky or scotch, sir?' asked the bartender in a loud voice, knowing the Maharani was too mean to buy scotch.

'Whisky will do,' said Simon, 'and a beer for me,' just then he felt like spiking the Maharani's whisky with something really lethal, and being free of her for the rest of his days. Years of loyalty and companionship had given way to abject slavery, and there was nothing he could do about it. Nearing seventy, unqualified and unworldly, he could hardly set about creating any sort of career for himself.

'And what are *you* having?' he asked Suresh Mathur, who had just put away his first drink.

'I am never vague, I ask for Haig!' Suresh replied, chuckling at his clever rhyme. None of the others thought it amusing, but this was usual. 'When they stop giving me credit, I'll try the local stuff.'

'Good on you!' called Colonel Wilkie from his corner. 'But there's nothing to beat Solan No. 1. Don't trust these single malts—they always give one gout!'

'I've never seen you move from that chair,' said Krishan. 'No wonder you suffer from gout.'

'Played cricket once, like you,' said the Colonel. 'Made a few runs. But they always made me twelfth man. Got fed up of carrying out the drinks, or fielding when the star batsman felt indisposed. Gave up cricket. Indoor games are better. Why don't we have a dartboard in here? In England, every respectable pub has a dartboard.'

I'd been listening to the conversation from a small table behind a potted palm. I was sixteen, just out of school, and I wasn't supposed to be in the bar, even if I wasn't drinking. The large potted palm separated the bar-room from the outer lounge; it was neutral territory.

'I have a dartboard!' I piped up, and every head turned towards me. Most of them had been unaware of my presence. They knew, of course, that I was the son of the lady who managed the hotel.

Suresh Mathur, the most literary-inclined of the lot, said: 'Young Copperfield has a dartboard!'

'I'll go and fetch it,' I said, only too ready to justify my presence in the bar.

I dashed down the corridor to my room and collided with my mother who was doing her nightly round of the hotel.

'What are you doing here? You mustn't hang around the bar,' she said sharply. 'You have a radio in your room, apart from all your books.'

The radio had been given to me the previous year by a guest who was now wanted by the police (on suspicion of being a serial killer), but I did not feel in any way guilty about possessing it; the guest had been very friendly and generous.

'Darts,' I told my mother. 'They want to play darts. That's what a pub is for, isn't it?' And I charged into my room, picked up my old dartboard and set of darts, and returned breathless to the bar-room.

My arrival was greeted by cheers, and Krishan helped me find a place for the dartboard, just below a framed picture of winged cherubs sporting about on some unlikely clouds.

'Whoever gets the highest score gets a free drink,' announced Krishan.

'Who pays for it?' asked Suresh Mathur.

'We all do—income-tax lawyers included.'

'He never saved anyone a rupee of tax,' declared the Maharani. 'But come on, let's have a game.'

'Would you like to start the proceedings, H.H.?'

'No, I'll wait till everyone's finished. You can start with Colonel Wilkie.'

'Age before beauty,' said Krishan. 'Come on, Colonel, we know you have a steady hand.'

Colonel Wilkie's hand was far from steady. His hands were always trembling. But he struggled out of his chair and took up his position at a point indicated by Krishan. Only one of his darts struck the board, earning him fifteen points. The others were near misses. Two darts bounced off the picture on the wall.

'The old fool's aiming at those naked cherubs,' crowed H.H. 'Go on, Simon, see if you can win a free drink for me.'

Simon did his best, but scored a meagre thirty points.

'Idiot!' cried H.H. 'And you always said you were a good darts player.'

'Out of practice,' Simon mumbled.

Meanwhile, someone had opened up the old radiogram and placed a record on the turntable. The cheeky voice of Maurice Chevalier filled the room:

All I want is just one girl,
But I have to have one girl
All I want is one
For a start!

The evening was livening up. Suresh Mathur scored a few points, but it was Krishan who hit the bullseye and claimed a drink on the house.

'Not until I've had my turn,' shouted H.H., and made a grab for the darts.

She flung them at the board at random, missing wildly—so much so that one dart lodged itself in Colonel Wilkie's old felt hat which was hanging from a peg, while another streaked across the room and narrowly missed the Roman nose of Reggie Bhowmik, ex-actor, who had just entered the room accompanied by his demure little wife.

Between ex-actor Reggie and former cricketer Krishan, there was no love lost. Both middle aged and no longer in demand, they were rivals in failure. One spoke of the prejudice and incompetence of the cricket selectors, the other of jealousy in the film industry and his subsequent neglect. Both lived in the past—Krishan recalling the one outstanding innings he had played for the country (before being dropped after a series of failures), Reggie living on memories of his one great romantic role before a sagging waistline and alcohol-coarsened features had led to a rapid decline in his popularity. Somehow they had drifted into the backwater that was Dehra in 1950.

There are some places, no matter how dull or lacking in opportunity, which nevertheless take a grip on the individual, especially the more easy-going types, and hold him in thrall, rendering him unfit for life in a larger, more competitive milieu. Dehra was one such place.

The bar at Green's Hotel was their refuge and their strength. Here they could reminisce, hark back to glory days, even speak optimistically of the future. Colonel Wilkie, Suresh Mathur, Krishan Kapoor, Reggie Bhowmik, H.H.—the Maharani—and Simon Lee, were all dropouts, failures in their own way. Had they been busy and successful, they would not have found their way to Green's every evening.

Reggie Bhowmik liked making dramatic entrances, but the Maharani was just as fond of being the centre of attention, and wasn't about to give up centre stage to a fading actor.

'A double whisky for Krishan!' she declared. 'He's the only one here who still has a steady hand.'

'You haven't felt *my* hand,' said Reggie, bearing down on her. 'You missed my nose by a whisker.'

'You'd look better with a scar running down your face,' said H.H. 'Then you might get a role as Frankenstein or the phantom of the opera.'

This touched a raw nerve, as Reggie had been having some difficulty in getting a decent role in recent months. But he snapped back: 'I'll play the phantom on condition that you're cast as the fat soprano—then I shall take great pleasure in strangling you.'

'Let's change the subject,' said his wife Ruby, always ready to pour oil on troubled waters. She moved over to Colonel Wilkie's table and asked: 'How have you been, Colonel?'

'Like an old bus just about moving, and badly in need of spare parts.'

'Well, have a beer with us—and some French fries if we can get any.'

'Cook's on strike,' said Krishan. 'Only liquid diet today.' I saw my opportunity, and piped up again from behind the potted palm. 'I can boil some eggs for you if you like!' There was a stunned silence, broken by Suresh Mathur who said, sounding a little incredulous, 'Young Master Copperfield can boil an egg!'

Everyone clapped, and Krishan said, 'Copperfield has certainly saved the day for us. First he produces a dartboard, and now he's about to save us from starvation. Go to it, Copperfield!'

Off I went, then, not to boil eggs—there weren't any in the kitchen—but to find Sitaram, the room-boy, who was the only person of my age in the hotel. I found him in my room, listening to 'Binaca Geetmala', the popular musical request programme, on my radio.

'We need some eggs,' I told him. 'Boiled.'

'Egg-man comes tomorrow,' he said. 'Cook finished the rest. Made himself an omelette, got drunk, and took off!'

'Well, let's go down to the bazaar and buy some eggs. I've got enough money on me.'

So off we went, and near the clock tower found a street vendor selling boiled eggs. We bought a dozen and hurried back to the bar-room, where Krishan and Reggie were having a heated argument on the relative merits of cricket and football. Reggie didn't think much of cricket, and Krishan didn't think much of football.

'And what's *your* favourite game?' asked Ruby of Suresh Mathur.

'Snakes and ladders,' he said, chuckling, and returned to his drink.

'Boiled eggs!' I announced. 'On the house!'

Sitaram produced saucers, and distributed the eggs among the guests—two each, exactly.

'Do I have to peel my own egg?' asked the Maharani querulously, staring down at the two eggs rolling about on her plate. 'Peel them for me, Simon!'

Simon dutifully cracked one of the eggs and began peeling it for her. 'Not that way, you fool. You're leaving all the skin on it.' And seizing the half-peeled egg from her companion, she flung it across the room, narrowly missing the bartender.

'Good throw!' exclaimed Krishan. 'You'd be great fielding on the boundary.'

'Better at baseball,' said Reggie.

'Snakes and ladders,' said Suresh again, now quite drunk.

Colonel Wilkie, equally drunk, gave a loud belch.

The Maharani got up to leave. 'Well, I'm not going to sit here to be insulted by everyone. Come on, Simon, drive me home!' And she marched out of the room with an attempt at majesty, but tripped over the hotel cat, an ugly, striped creature who had sensed that there was food around and had come looking for it. The cat caterwauled, H.H. screamed and cursed, Reggie cheered, and Suresh Mather pronounced, 'When two cats are fighting they make a hideous sound.'

Not to be outdone in nastiness, the Maharani went up to Suresh, looked him up and down, and said, 'It's easy to tell you're a single man.'

'I'm not homosexual,' said Suresh defensively. (The word 'gay' had yet to be used in any sense other than 'happy' in those days.)

'No,' the Maharani smiled wickedly. 'You're single because you are so damn ugly!'

And on that triumphant note she left the room, followed by the obedient Simon.

'Pay no attention to her, Suresh,' said Krishan generously. 'You're better-looking than that old lapdog who follows her around.'

'I understand she's leaving him her fortunes,' said Reggie. 'I could do with some of it myself. Perhaps I could interest her in producing a film.'

'She's tight-fisted,' said Krishan. 'If you look closely at Simon you'll notice he's wearing the late Maharaja's smoking jacket and deerstalker cap. The old Maharaja loved dressing up like Sherlock Holmes.'

Colonel Wilkie came out of his reverie. 'When I was in Jamnagar—' he began.

'We've heard that a hundred times,' said Krishan.

'*I* haven't,' said Ruby.

'When I was in Jamnagar,' continued Colonel Wilkie, 'I saw Duleep Singh ji make a hundred. That was against Lord Tennyson's team.'

'Yesterday you said Ranjit Singh ji,' remarked Krishan.

'I'm not that old,' said Colonel Wilkie, struggling to his feet. 'But old enough to want to go to bed. I'll toddle off now.' Locating his walking-stick, he found his way to the door, wishing everyone goodnight as he passed them. They heard the tap of his walking stick as he walked away down the corridor.

'Shouldn't someone go with him?' asked Ruby. 'It's very late and he isn't too steady on his feet.'

'Oh, he'll find his way home,' said Suresh nonchalantly. 'Lives just around the corner, in rented rooms near the Club.'

'Why doesn't he join the Club?'

'Can't afford it. Neither can I.'

'Neither can I,' said Krishan.

'Neither can we,' added Ruby, sadly. 'And anyway, it's more homely here. Even when the Maharani is around.'

'*She* can afford the Club,' said Suresh. 'But they won't let her in. Created a disturbance once too often. Insulted the secretary and emptied a dish of chicken biryani on his head.'

'Not done,' said Krishan. 'Not cricket.'

'I don't believe it,' said Reggie. 'Can't be true.'

'Calling me a liar?' asked Suresh, bristling.

Ruby poured oil on troubled waters again. 'Interesting if true,' she said. 'And if not true, still interesting.'

'Mark Twain.'

My mother came along the corridor just as Krishan had shown off his knowledge of literature, and found me behind the palms listening to all this fascinating talk.

'Time you went to your room, young man,' she said.

'I'm waiting for everyone to go home,' I said. 'Then I'll help Sitaram tidy up. There's no cook, as you know.'

'Let him stay,' called Suresh from his bar stool. 'It's all part of his education. And he's old enough for a glass of beer. How old are you, sonny?'

'Sixteen,' I said.

'Well, enjoy yourself. It's later than you think.'

But I wasn't thinking of beer just then. I knew there were sausages in the fridge, and I had every intention of polishing them off as soon as all the guests had gone. I wanted to be a writer, but

I had no intention of starving in a garret. However, all thoughts of food vanished when I looked across the room and saw Colonel Wilkie framed in the opposite doorway. He was staring at us through the glass. The glass door then opened of its own volition, and Colonel Wilkie stepped into the room. We all looked up, and Reggie said, 'Back again, Colonel? Still feeling thirsty?' But Colonel Wilkie ignored the jibe, and walked slowly across the room to the table where he had been sitting. This was close to where I was standing. He bent down and picked up his pipe from the table. He'd forgotten it when he'd left the bar-room. Shoving the pipe into his pocket, he turned and retraced his steps, leaving the room by the door from which he had entered.

'Well, I'm blowed,' said Krishan. 'I thought he was sleepwalking.'

'Never goes anywhere without his pipe,' said Suresh. 'A perfect example of single-mindedness.'

'Didn't say a word.'

'The pipe was all that mattered.'

'Like a favourite cricket bat,' said Krishan.

'Maybe I'll come back for mine when I'm dead.'

A silence fell upon the room. The mention of death had a sobering effect upon the small group. And come to think of it, Colonel Wilkie on his return to the bar-room had something of the zombie about him—the walking dead.

There was a commotion in the passageway, and my mother burst into the room, followed by the night-watchman.

'Colonel Wilkie's dead,' said my mother. 'He collapsed on his steps about half an hour ago.'

'But he was here five minutes ago,' said Krishan.

'No, sir,' said Gopal the watchman. 'I went home with him when he left here some time back. Madam said to keep an eye on him. When we got to his place, he began climbing his steps with some difficulty. I helped him to the top step, and then he collapsed. I dragged him into his room and then ran for Dr Bhist. He is there now.'

There was silence for a couple of minutes, and then Ruby said, 'We all saw him. Colonel Wilkie.'

'We saw his ghost,' Krishan murmured.

'He came for his pipe,' said Suresh quietly. 'I told you he wouldn't go anywhere without it.'

Colonel Wilkie was buried the next day, and we made sure his pipe was buried with him. We did not want him turning up from time to time, looking for it. It could be a bit unnerving for the customers.

In all the excitement I'd forgotten about the sausages, but decided they would keep until after the funeral.

All the regular barflies turned up for the funeral. H.H. was quite sloshed when she arrived and had to be extricated from an open grave into which she had slipped, the ground being soft and yielding after recent rain. She blamed secretary Simon for the mishap and called him an *ullu ka patha*—son of an owl—but he was quite used to such broadsides and took them in his stride. Was it love or loyalty or dependence that kept him in abeyance? Or was it, as some said, the prospect of becoming her heir? If so, he was paying a heavy price well in advance of such a prospect. Not everyone relishes being abused and kicked around in public by a half-crazed maharani.

When Colonel Wilkie's coffin was lowered into the grave, we all said 'Cheers!' He would have liked that. We then returned to Green's for an early opening of the bar. Alcoholics Unanimous held a subdued but not too melancholy meeting.

But bad news was in store for everyone. A day or two later, I heard the owner, our Sardarji, inform my mother that the hotel had been sold and that she'd have to leave at the end of the month. She'd been expecting something like this, and had already accepted a matron's job at one of the schools in the valley. As for me, I was to be packed off to England to my aunt's home in Jersey. The prospect did not thrill me, but I was more or less resigned to it. And there did not appear to be much future for me in Dehra.

Even before the month was out, workers had begun pulling down parts of the building. It was to be rebuilt as a cinema hall, and would show the latest hits from Bombay. It was even rumoured that Dilip Kumar, the biggest star of that era, would inaugurate the new cinema when it was ready to open.

The spirit and character of a building lasts only while the building lasts. Remove the roof-beams, pull down the walls, smash the stairways, and you are left with nothing but memories. Even the ghosts have nowhere to go.

An old hotel that once had a personality of its own was now dismantled with startling rapidity. It had gone up slowly, brick by brick; it came down like a house of cards. No treasures cascaded from its walls; no skeletons were discovered. In two or three days the demolishers had wiped out the past, removed Green's Hotel from the face of the earth so effectively that it might never have existed.

Searching through the ruins one day, I found a bottle-opener lying in the dust, and kept it as a souvenir.

The bar had been the only common factor in the lives of those disparate individuals who had come there so regularly—drawn to the place rather than to each other.

Now they went their different ways—Suresh Mathur to the Club, the Maharani to her card table and private bar, Krishan to a public school as a cricket coach, Reggie Bhowmik and Ruby to Darjeeling to make a documentary… Sitaram continued to work for my mother, so I had his company whenever he was free.

The cinema came up quite rapidly, but I had left for England before it opened. When I returned five years later, it was showing Madhubala and Guru Dutt in a romantic comedy, *Mr & Mrs 55.*

Then I moved to Delhi.

In recent years, some of the old single cinemas have been closing down, giving way to multiplexes. The other day, passing through Dehra, I saw that 'our' cinema hall was being pulled down. 'What now?' I asked my taxi driver. 'A multiplex?' 'No, sir. A shopping mall!'

And such is progress.

I think I'm the only one around who is old enough to remember the old Green's Hotel, its dusty corridors, shabby bar-room, and oddball customers. All have gone. All forgotten! Not even footprints in the sands of time. But by putting down this memoir of an evening or two at that forgotten watering place, I think I have cheated Time just a little.

The School among the Pines

1

A leopard, lithe and sinewy, drank at the mountain stream, and then lay down on the grass to bask in the late February sunshine. Its tail twitched occasionally and the animal appeared to be sleeping. At the sound of distant voices it raised its head to listen, then stood up and leapt lightly over the boulders in the stream, disappearing among the trees on the opposite bank.

A minute or two later, three children came walking down the forest path. They were a girl and two boys, and they were singing in their local dialect an old song they had learnt from their grandparents.

Five more miles to go!
We climb through rain and snow.
A river to cross...
A mountain to pass...
Now we've four more miles to go!

Their school satchels looked new, their clothes had been washed and pressed. Their loud and cheerful singing startled a Spotted Forktail. The bird left its favourite rock in the stream and flew down the dark ravine.

'Well, we have only three more miles to go,' said the bigger boy, Prakash, who had been this way hundreds of times. 'But first we have to cross the stream.'

He was a sturdy twelve-year-old with eyes like raspberries and a mop of bushy hair that refused to settle down on his head. The girl and her small brother were taking this path for the first time.

'I'm feeling tired, Bina,' said the little boy.

Bina smiled at him, and Prakash said, 'Don't worry, Sonu, you'll get used to the walk. There's plenty of time.' He glanced at the old watch he'd been given by his grandfather. It needed constant winding. 'We can rest here for five or six minutes.'

They sat down on a smooth boulder and watched the clear water of the shallow stream tumbling downhill. Bina examined the old watch on Prakash's wrist. The glass was badly scratched and she could barely make out the figures on the dial. 'Are you sure it still gives the right time?' she asked.

'Well, it loses five minutes every day, so I put it ten minutes forward at night. That means by morning it's quite accurate! Even our teacher, Mr Mani, asks me for the time. If he doesn't ask, I tell him! The clock in our classroom keeps stopping.'

They removed their shoes and let the cold mountain water run over their feet. Bina was the same age as Prakash. She had pink cheeks, soft brown eyes, and hair that was just beginning to lose its natural curls. Hers was a gentle face, but a determined little chin showed that she could be a strong person. Sonu, her younger brother, was ten. He was a thin boy who had been sickly as a child but was now beginning to fill out. Although he did not look very athletic, he could run like the wind.

Bina had been going to school in her own village of Koli, on the other side of the mountain. But it had been a primary school, finishing at Class Five. Now, in order to study in the Sixth, she would have to walk several miles every day to Nauti, where there was a high school going up to the Eighth. It had been decided that Sonu would also shift to the new school, to give Bina company. Prakash, their neighbour in Koli, was already a pupil at the Nauti school. His mischievous nature, which sometimes got him into trouble, had resulted in his having to repeat a year.

But this didn't seem to bother him. 'What's the hurry?' he had told his indignant parents. 'You're not sending me to a foreign land when I finish school. And our cows aren't running away, are they?'

'You would prefer to look after the cows, wouldn't you?' asked Bina, as they got up to continue their walk.

'Oh, school's all right. Wait till you see old Mr Mani. He always gets our names mixed up, as well as the subjects he's supposed to be teaching. At our last lesson, instead of maths, he gave us a geography lesson!'

'More fun than maths,' said Bina.

'Yes, but there's a new teacher this year. She's very young, they say, just out of college. I wonder what she'll be like.'

Bina walked faster and Sonu had some trouble keeping up with them. She was excited about the new school and the prospect of different surroundings. She had seldom been outside her own village, with its small school and single ration shop. The day's routine never varied—helping her mother in the fields or with household tasks like fetching water from the spring or cutting grass and fodder for the cattle. Her father, who was a soldier, was away for nine months in the year and Sonu was still too small for the heavier tasks.

As they neared Nauti village, they were joined by other children coming from different directions. Even where there were no major roads, the mountains were full of little lanes and short cuts. Like a game of snakes and ladders, these narrow paths zigzagged around the hills and villages, cutting through fields and crossing narrow ravines until they came together to form a fairly busy road along which mules, cattle and goats joined the throng.

Nauti was a fairly large village, and from here a broader but dustier road started for Tehri. There was a small bus, several trucks and (for part of the way) a road-roller. The road hadn't been completed because the heavy diesel roller couldn't take the steep climb to Nauti. It stood on the roadside halfway up the road from Tehri.

Prakash knew almost everyone in the area, and exchanged greetings and gossip with other children as well as with muleteers, bus drivers, milkmen and labourers working on the road. He loved telling everyone the time, even if they weren't interested.

'It's nine o'clock,' he would announce, glancing at his wrist. 'Isn't your bus leaving today?'

'Off with you!' the bus driver would respond, 'I'll leave when I'm ready.'

As the children approached Nauti, the small flat school buildings came into view on the outskirts of the village, fringed with a line of long-leaved pines. A small crowd had assembled on the playing field. Something unusual seemed to have happened. Prakash ran forward to see what it was all about. Bina and Sonu stood aside, waiting in a patch of sunlight near the boundary wall.

Prakash soon came running back to them. He was bubbling over with excitement.

'It's Mr Mani!' he gasped. 'He's disappeared! People are saying a leopard must have carried him off!'

2

Mr Mani wasn't really old. He was about fifty-five and was expected to retire soon. But for the children, adults over forty seemed ancient! And Mr Mani had always been a bit absent-minded, even as a young man.

He had gone out for his early morning walk, saying he'd be back by eight o'clock, in time to have his breakfast and be ready for class. He wasn't married, but his sister and her husband stayed with him. When it was past nine o'clock his sister presumed he'd stopped at a neighbour's house for breakfast (he loved tucking into other people's breakfast) and that he had gone on to school from there. But when the school bell rang at ten o'clock, and everyone but Mr Mani was present, questions were asked and guesses were made.

No one had seen him return from his walk and enquiries made in the village showed that he had not stopped at anyone's house. For Mr Mani to disappear was puzzling; for him to disappear without his breakfast was extraordinary.

Then a milkman returning from the next village said he had seen a leopard sitting on a rock on the outskirts of the pine forest. There had been talk of a cattle-killer in the valley, of leopards and other animals being displaced by the construction of a dam. But as yet no one had heard of a leopard attacking a man. Could Mr Mani have been its first victim? Someone found a strip of red cloth entangled in a blackberry bush and went running through the village showing it to everyone. Mr Mani had been known to wear red pyjamas. Surely, he had been seized and eaten! But where were his remains? And why had he been in his pyjamas?

Meanwhile, Bina and Sonu and the rest of the children had followed their teachers into the school playground. Feeling a little lost, Bina looked around for Prakash. She found herself facing a dark slender young woman wearing spectacles, who must have been in her early twenties—just a little too old to be another student. She had a kind expressive face and she seemed a little concerned by all that had been happening.

Bina noticed that she had lovely hands; it was obvious that the new teacher hadn't milked cows or worked in the fields!

'You must be new here,' said the teacher, smiling at Bina. 'And is this your little brother?'

'Yes, we've come from Koli village. We were at school there.'

'It's a long walk from Koli. You didn't see any leopards, did you? Well, I'm new too. Are you in the Sixth class?'

'Sonu is in the Third. I'm in the Sixth.'

'Then I'm your new teacher. My name is Tania Ramola. Come along, let's see if we can settle down in our classroom.'

Mr Mani turned up at twelve o'clock, wondering what all the fuss was about. No, he snapped, he had not been attacked by a leopard; and yes, he had lost his pyjamas and would someone kindly return them to him?

'How did you lose your pyjamas, sir?' asked Prakash.

'They were blown off the washing line!' snapped Mr Mani.

After much questioning, Mr Mani admitted that he had gone further than he had intended, and that he had lost his way coming back. He had been a bit upset because the new teacher, a slip of a girl, had been given charge of the Sixth, while he was still with the Fifth, along with that troublesome boy Prakash, who kept on reminding him of the time! The headmaster had explained that as Mr Mani was due to retire at the end of the year, the school did not wish to burden him with a senior class. But Mr Mani looked upon the whole thing as a plot to get rid of him. He glowered at Miss Ramola whenever he passed her. And when she smiled back at him, he looked the other way!

Mr Mani had been getting even more absent-minded of late—putting on his shoes without his socks, wearing his homespun waistcoat inside out, mixing up people's names and, of course, eating other people's lunches and dinners. His sister had made a special mutton broth (*pai*) for the postmaster, who was down with flu and had asked Mr Mani to take it over in a thermos. When the postmaster opened the thermos, he found only a few drops of broth at the bottom—Mr Mani had drunk the rest somewhere along the way.

When sometimes Mr Mani spoke of his coming retirement, it was to describe his plans for the small field he owned just behind the house. Right now, it was full of potatoes, which did not require much looking after; but he had plans for growing dahlias, roses, French beans, and other fruits and flowers.

The next time he visited Tehri, he promised himself, he would buy some dahlia bulbs and rose cuttings. The monsoon season would be a good time to put them down. And meanwhile, his potatoes were still flourishing.

3

Bina enjoyed her first day at the new school. She felt at ease with Miss Ramola, as did most of the boys and girls in her class. Tania

Ramola had been to distant towns such as Delhi and Lucknow—places they had only read about—and it was said that she had a brother who was a pilot and flew planes all over the world. Perhaps he'd fly over Nauti some day!

Most of the children had, of course, seen planes flying overhead, but none of them had seen a ship, and only a few had been on a train. Tehri mountain was far from the railway and hundreds of miles from the sea. But they all knew about the big dam that was being built at Tehri, just forty miles away.

Bina, Sonu and Prakash had company for part of the way home, but gradually the other children went off in different directions. Once they had crossed the stream, they were on their own again.

It was a steep climb all the way back to their village. Prakash had a supply of peanuts which he shared with Bina and Sonu, and at a small spring they quenched their thirst.

When they were less than a mile from home, they met a postman who had finished his round of the villages in the area and was now returning to Nauti.

'Don't waste time along the way,' he told them. 'Try to get home before dark.'

'What's the hurry?' asked Prakash, glancing at his watch. 'It's only five o'clock.'

'There's a leopard around. I saw it this morning, not far from the stream. No one is sure how it got here. So don't take any chances. Get home early.'

'So there really is a leopard,' said Sonu.

They took his advice and walked faster, and Sonu forgot to complain about his aching feet.

They were home well before sunset.

There was a smell of cooking in the air and they were hungry.

'Cabbage and roti,' said Prakash gloomily. 'But I could eat anything today.' He stopped outside his small slate-roofed house, and Bina and Sonu waved him goodbye, then carried on across a couple of ploughed fields until they reached their small stone house.

'Stuffed tomatoes,' said Sonu, sniffing just outside the front door.

'And lemon pickle,' said Bina, who had helped cut, sun and salt the lemons a month previously.

Their mother was lighting the kitchen stove. They greeted her with great hugs and demands for an immediate dinner. She was a good cook who could make even the simplest of dishes taste delicious. Her favourite saying was, 'Homemade pai is better than chicken soup in Delhi,' and Bina and Sonu had to agree.

Electricity had yet to reach their village, and they took their meal by the light of a kerosene lamp. After the meal, Sonu settled down to do a little homework, while Bina stepped outside to look at the stars.

Across the fields, someone was playing a flute. *It must be Prakash*, thought Bina. *He always breaks off on the high notes.* But the flute music was simple and appealing, and she began singing softly to herself in the dark.

4

Mr Mani was having trouble with the porcupines. They had been getting into his garden at night and digging up and eating his potatoes. From his bedroom window—left open, now that the mild-April weather had arrived—he could listen to them enjoying the vegetables he had worked hard to grow. Scrunch, scrunch! *Katar, katar*, as their sharp teeth sliced through the largest and juiciest of potatoes. For Mr Mani it was as though they were biting through his own flesh. And the sound of them digging industriously as they rooted up those healthy, leafy plants made him tremble with rage and indignation. The unfairness of it all!

Yes, Mr Mani hated porcupines. He prayed for their destruction, their removal from the face of the earth. But, as his friends were quick to point out, 'Bhagwan protected porcupines too,' and in any case you could never see the creatures or catch them; they were completely nocturnal.

Mr Mani got out of bed every night, torch in one hand, a stout stick in the other, but as soon as he stepped into the garden the crunching and digging stopped and he was greeted by the most infuriating of silences. He would grope around in the dark, swinging wildly with the stick, but not a single porcupine was to be seen or heard. As soon as he was back in bed—the sounds would start all over again. Scrunch, scrunch, *katar, katar...*

Mr Mani came to his class tired and dishevelled, with rings beneath his eyes and a permanent frown on his face. It took some time for his pupils to discover the reason for his misery, but when they did, they felt sorry for their teacher and took to discussing ways and means of saving his potatoes from the porcupines.

It was Prakash who came up with the idea of a moat or waterditch. 'Porcupines don't like water,' he said knowledgeably.

'How do you know?' asked one of his friends.

'Throw water on one and see how it runs! They don't like getting their quills wet.'

There was no one who could disprove Prakash's theory, and the class fell in with the idea of building a moat, especially as it meant getting most of the day off.

'Anything to make Mr Mani happy,' said the headmaster, and the rest of the school watched with envy as the pupils of Class Five, armed with spades and shovels collected from all parts of the village, took up their positions around Mr Mani's potato field and began digging a ditch.

By evening the moat was ready, but it was still dry and the porcupines got in again that night and had a great feast.

'At this rate,' said Mr Mani gloomily, 'there won't be any potatoes left to save.'

But next day Prakash and the other boys and girls managed to divert the water from a stream that flowed past the village. They had the satisfaction of watching it flow gently into the ditch. Everyone went home in a good mood. By nightfall, the ditch had overflowed, the potato field was flooded, and Mr Mani found himself trapped inside his house. But Prakash and his friends had won the day. The porcupines stayed away that night!

A month had passed, and wild violets, daisies and buttercups now sprinkled the hill slopes, and on her way to school Bina gathered enough to make a little posy. The bunch of flowers fitted easily into an old inkwell. Miss Ramola was delighted to find this little display in the middle of her desk.

'Who put these here?' she asked in surprise.

Bina kept quiet, and the rest of the class smiled secretively. After that, they took turns bringing flowers for the classroom.

On her long walks to school and home again, Bina became aware that April was the month of new leaves. The oak leaves were bright green above and silver beneath, and when they rippled in the breeze they were like clouds of silvery green. The path was strewn with old leaves, dry and crackly. Sonu loved kicking them around.

Clouds of white butterflies floated across the stream. Sonu was chasing a butterfly when he stumbled over something dark and repulsive. He went sprawling on the grass. When he got to his feet, he looked down at the remains of a small animal.

'Bina! Prakash! Come quickly!' he shouted.

It was part of a sheep, killed some days earlier by a much larger animal.

'Only a leopard could have done this,' said Prakash.

'Let's get away, then,' said Sonu. 'It might still be around!'

'No, there's nothing left to eat. The leopard will be hunting elsewhere by now. Perhaps it's moved on to the next valley.'

'Still, I'm frightened,' said Sonu. 'There may be more leopards!'

Bina took him by the hand. 'Leopards don't attack humans!' she said.

'They will, if they get a taste for people!' insisted Prakash.

'Well, this one hasn't attacked any people as yet,' said Bina, although she couldn't be sure. Hadn't there been rumours of a leopard attacking some workers near the dam? But she did not want Sonu to feel afraid, so she did not mention the story. All she said was, 'It has probably come here because of all the activity near the dam.'

All the same, they hurried home. And for a few days, whenever they reached the stream, they crossed over very quickly, unwilling to linger too long at that lovely spot.

5

A few days later, a school party was on its way to Tehri to see the new dam that was being built.

Miss Ramola had arranged to take her class, and Mr Mani, not wishing to be left out, insisted on taking his class as well. That meant there were about fifty boys and girls taking part in the outing. The little bus could only take thirty. A friendly truck driver agreed to take some children if they were prepared to sit on sacks of potatoes. And Prakash persuaded the owner of the diesel roller to turn it round and head it back to Tehri—with him and a couple of friends up on the driving seat.

Prakash's small group set off at sunrise, as they had to walk some distance in order to reach the stranded road roller. The bus left at 9.00 a.m. with Miss Ramola and her class, and Mr Mani and some of his pupils. The truck was to follow later.

It was Bina's first visit to a large town and her first bus ride.

The sharp curves along the winding, downhill road made several children feel sick. The bus driver seemed to be in a tearing hurry. He took them along at rolling, rollicking speed, which made Bina feel quite giddy. She rested her head on her arms and refused to look out of the window. Hairpin bends and cliff edges, pine forests and snowcapped peaks, all swept past her, but she felt too ill to want to look at anything. It was just as well—those sudden drops, hundreds of feet to the valley below, were quite frightening. Bina began to wish that she hadn't come—or that she had joined Prakash on the road roller instead!

Miss Ramola and Mr Mani didn't seem to notice the lurching and groaning of the old bus. They had made this journey many times. They were busy arguing about the advantages and disadvantages of large dams—an argument that was to continue on and off for much of the day; sometimes in Hindi, sometimes in English, sometimes in the local dialect!

Meanwhile, Prakash and his friends had reached the roller. The driver hadn't turned up, but they managed to reverse it and get it going in the direction of Tehri. They were soon overtaken by both the bus and the truck but kept moving along at a steady chug. Prakash spotted Bina at the window of the bus and waved cheerfully. She responded feebly.

Bina felt better when the road levelled out near Tehri. As they crossed an old bridge over the wide river, they were startled by a loud bang which made the bus shudder. A cloud of dust rose above the town.

'They're blasting the mountain,' said Miss Ramola.

'End of a mountain,' said Mr Mani mournfully.

While they were drinking cups of tea at the bus stop, waiting for the potato truck and the road roller, Miss Ramola and Mr Mani continued their argument about the dam. Miss Ramola maintained that it would bring electric power and water for irrigation to large areas of the country, including the surrounding area. Mr Mani declared that it was a menace, as it was situated in an earthquake zone. There would be a terrible disaster if the dam burst! Bina found it all very confusing. *And what about the animals in the area,* she wondered. *What would happen to them?*

The argument was becoming quite heated when the potato truck arrived. There was no sign of the road roller, so it was decided that Mr Mani should wait for Prakash and his friends while Miss Ramola's group went ahead.

Some eight or nine miles before Tehri the road roller had broken down, and Prakash and his friends were forced to walk. They had not gone far, however, when a mule train came along—five or six mules that had been delivering sacks of grain in Nauti. A boy rode on the first mule, but the others had no loads.

'Can you give us a ride to Tehri?' called Prakash.

'Make yourselves comfortable,' said the boy.

There were no saddles, only gunny sacks strapped on to the mules with rope. They had a rough but jolly ride down to the Tehri bus stop. None of them had ever ridden mules; but they had saved at least an hour on the road.

Looking around the bus stop for the rest of the party, they could find no one from their school. And Mr Mani, who should have been waiting for them, had vanished.

6

Tania Ramola and her group had taken the steep road to the hill above Tehri. Half an hour's climbing brought them to a little plateau which overlooked the town, the river and the dam site.

The earthworks for the dam were only just coming up, but a wide tunnel had been bored through the mountain to divert the river into another channel. Down below, the old town was still spread out across the valley and from a distance it looked quite charming and picturesque.

'Will the whole town be swallowed up by the waters of the dam?' asked Bina.

'Yes, all of it,' said Miss Ramola. 'The clock tower and the old palace. The long bazaar, and the temples, the schools and the jail, and hundreds of houses, for many miles up the valley. All those people will have to go—thousands of them! Of course, they'll be resettled elsewhere.'

'But the town's been here for hundreds of years,' said Bina. 'They were quite happy without the dam, weren't they?'

'I suppose they were. But the dam isn't just for them—it's for the millions who live further downstream, across the plains.'

'And it doesn't matter what happens to this place?'

'The local people will be given new homes, somewhere else.' Miss Ramola found herself on the defensive and decided to change the subject. 'Everyone must be hungry. It's time we had our lunch.'

Bina kept quiet. She didn't think the local people would want to go away. And it was a good thing, she mused, that there was only a small stream and not a big river running past her village. To be uprooted like this—a town and hundreds of villages—and put down somewhere on the hot, dusty plains—seemed to her unbearable.

'Well, I'm glad I don't live in Tehri,' she said.

She did not know it, but all the animals and most of the birds had already left the area. The leopard had been among them.

They walked through the colourful, crowded bazaar, where fruit sellers did business beside silversmiths, and pavement vendors sold everything from umbrellas to glass bangles. Sparrows attacked sacks of grain, monkeys made off with bananas, and stray cows and dogs rummaged in refuse bins, but nobody took any notice. Music blared from radios. Buses blew their horns. Sonu bought a whistle to add to the general din, but Miss Ramola told him to put it away. Bina had kept ten rupees aside, and now she used it to buy a cotton head scarf for her mother.

As they were about to enter a small restaurant for a meal, they were joined by Prakash and his companions; but of Mr Mani there was still no sign.

'He must have met one of his relatives,' said Prakash. 'He has relatives everywhere.'

After a simple meal of rice and lentils, they walked the length of the bazaar without seeing Mr Mani. At last, when they were about to give up the search, they saw him emerge from a bylane, a large sack slung over his shoulder.

'Sir, where have you been?' asked Prakash. 'We have been looking for you everywhere.'

On Mr Mani's face was a look of triumph.

'Help me with this bag,' he said breathlessly.

'You've bought more potatoes, sir,' said Prakash.

'Not potatoes, boy. Dahlia bulbs!'

7

It was dark by the time they were all back in Nauti. Mr Mani had refused to be separated from his sack of dahlia bulbs, and had been forced to sit in the back of the truck with Prakash and most of the boys.

Bina did not feel so ill on the return journey. Going uphill was definitely better than going downhill! But by the time the bus reached Nauti it was too late for most of the children to walk back to the more distant villages. The boys were put up in different homes, while the girls were given beds in the school verandah.

The night was warm and still. Large moths fluttered around the single bulb that lit the verandah. Counting moths, Sonu soon fell asleep. But Bina stayed awake for some time, listening to the sounds of the night. A nightjar went *tonk-tonk* in the bushes, and somewhere in the forest an owl hooted softly. The sharp call of a barking deer travelled up the valley, from the direction of the stream. Jackals kept howling. It seemed that there were more of them than ever before.

Bina was not the only one to hear the barking deer. The leopard, stretched full length on a rocky ledge, heard it too. The leopard raised its head and then got up slowly. The deer was its natural prey. But there weren't many left, and that was why the leopard, robbed of its forest by the dam, had taken to attacking dogs and cattle near the villages.

As the cry of the barking deer sounded nearer, the leopard left its lookout point and moved swiftly through the shadows towards the stream.

8

In early June the hills were dry and dusty, and forest fires broke out, destroying shrubs and trees, killing birds and small animals. The resin in the pines made these trees burn more fiercely, and the wind would take sparks from the trees and carry them into the dry grass and leaves, so that new fires would spring up before the old ones had died out. Fortunately, Bina's village was not in the pine belt; the fires did not reach it. But Nauti was surrounded by a fire that raged for three days, and the children had to stay away from school.

And then, towards the end of June, the monsoon rains arrived and there was an end to forest fires. The monsoon lasts three months and the lower Himalayas would be drenched in rain, mist and cloud for the next three months.

The first rain arrived while Bina, Prakash and Sonu were returning home from school. Those first few drops on the dusty path made them cry out with excitement. Then the rain grew heavier and a wonderful aroma rose from the earth.

'The best smell in the world!' exclaimed Bina.

Everything suddenly came to life. The grass, the crops, the trees, the birds. Even the leaves of the trees glistened and looked new.

That first wet weekend, Bina and Sonu helped their mother plant beans, maize and cucumbers. Sometimes, when the rain was very heavy, they had to run indoors. Otherwise they worked in the rain, the soft mud clinging to their bare legs.

Prakash now owned a black dog with one ear up and one ear down. The dog ran around getting in everyone's way, barking at cows, goats, hens and humans, without frightening any of them. Prakash said it was a very clever dog, but no one else seemed to think so. Prakash also said it would protect the village from the leopard, but others said the dog would be the first to be taken— he'd run straight into the jaws of Mr Spots!

In Nauti, Tania Ramola was trying to find a dry spot in the

quarters she'd been given. It was an old building and the roof was leaking in several places. Mugs and buckets were scattered about the floor in order to catch the drip.

Mr Mani had dug up all his potatoes and presented them to the friends and neighbours who had given him lunches and dinners. He was having the time of his life, planting dahlia bulbs all over his garden.

'I'll have a field of many-coloured dahlias!' he announced. 'Just wait till the end of August!'

'Watch out for those porcupines,' warned his sister. 'They eat dahlia bulbs too!'

Mr Mani made an inspection tour of his moat, no longer in flood, and found everything in good order. Prakash had done his job well.

Now, when the children crossed the stream, they found that the water level had risen by about a foot. Small cascades had turned into waterfalls. Ferns had sprung up on the banks. Frogs chanted.

Prakash and his dog dashed across the stream. Bina and Sonu followed more cautiously. The current was much stronger now and the water was almost up to their knees. Once they had crossed the stream, they hurried along the path, anxious not to be caught in a sudden downpour.

By the time they reached school, each of them had two or three leeches clinging to their legs. They had to use salt to remove them. The leeches were the most troublesome part of the rainy season. Even the leopard did not like them. It could not lie in the long grass without getting leeches on its paws and face.

One day, when Bina, Prakash and Sonu were about to cross the stream they heard a low rumble, which grew louder every second. Looking up at the opposite hill, they saw several trees shudder, tilt outwards and begin to fall. Earth and rocks bulged out from the mountain, then came crashing down into the ravine.

'Landslide!' shouted Sonu.

'It's carried away the path,' said Bina. 'Don't go any further.'

There was a tremendous roar as more rocks, trees and bushes fell away and crashed down the hillside.

Prakash's dog, who had gone ahead, came running back, tail between his legs.

They remained rooted to the spot until the rocks had stopped falling and the dust had settled. Birds circled the area, calling wildly. A frightened barking deer ran past them.

'We can't go to school now,' said Prakash. 'There's no way around.'

They turned and trudged home through the gathering mist.

In Koli, Prakash's parents had heard the roar of the landslide. They were setting out in search of the children when they saw them emerge from the mist, waving cheerfully.

9

They had to miss school for another three days, and Bina was afraid they might not be able to take their final exams. Although Prakash was not really troubled at the thought of missing exams, he did not like feeling helpless just because their path had been swept away. So he explored the hillside until he found a goat track going around the mountain. It joined up with another path near Nauti. This made their walk longer by a mile, but Bina did not mind. It was much cooler now that the rains were in full swing.

The only trouble with the new route was that it passed close to the leopard's lair. The animal had made this area its own since being forced to leave the dam area.

One day Prakash's dog ran ahead of them, barking furiously. Then he ran back, whimpering.

'He's always running away from something,' observed Sonu. But a minute later he understood the reason for the dog's fear.

They rounded a bend and Sonu saw the leopard standing in their way. They were struck dumb—too terrified to run. It was a strong, sinewy creature. A low growl rose from its throat. It seemed ready to spring.

They stood perfectly still, afraid to move or say a word. And the leopard must have been equally surprised. It stared at them for a few seconds, then bounded across the path and into the oak forest.

Sonu was shaking. Bina could hear her heart hammering. Prakash could only stammer: 'Did you see the way he sprang? Wasn't he beautiful?'

He forgot to look at his watch for the rest of the day.

A few days later Sonu stopped and pointed to a large outcrop of rock on the next hill.

The leopard stood far above them, outlined against the sky. It looked strong, majestic. Standing beside it were two young cubs.

'Look at those little ones!' exclaimed Sonu.

'So it's a female, not a male,' said Prakash.

'That's why she was killing so often,' said Bina. 'She had to feed her cubs too.'

They remained still for several minutes, gazing up at the leopard and her cubs. The leopard family took no notice of them.

'She knows we are here,' said Prakash, 'but she doesn't care. She knows we won't harm them.'

'We are cubs too!' said Sonu.

'Yes,' said Bina. 'And there's still plenty of space for all of us. Even when the dam is ready there will still be room for leopards and humans.'

10

The school exams were over. The rains were nearly over too. The landslide had been cleared, and Bina, Prakash and Sonu were once again crossing the stream.

There was a chill in the air, for it was the end of September.

Prakash had learnt to play the flute quite well, and he played on the way to school and then again on the way home. As a result he did not look at his watch so often.

One morning they found a small crowd in front of Mr Mani's house.

'What could have happened?' wondered Bina. 'I hope he hasn't got lost again.'

'Maybe he's sick,' said Sonu.

'Maybe it's the porcupines,' said Prakash.

But it was none of these things.

Mr Mani's first dahlia was in bloom, and half the village had turned out to look at it! It was a huge red double dahlia, so heavy that it had to be supported with sticks. No one had ever seen such a magnificent flower!

Mr Mani was a happy man. And his mood only improved over the coming week, as more and more dahlias flowered—crimson, yellow, purple, mauve, white—button dahlias, pompom dahlias, spotted dahlias, striped dahlias... Mr Mani had them all! A dahlia even turned up on Tania Romola's desk—he got on quite well with her now—and another brightened up the headmaster's study.

A week later, on their way home—it was almost the last day of the school term—Bina, Prakash and Sonu talked about what they might do when they grew up.

'I think I'll become a teacher,' said Bina. 'I'll teach children about animals and birds, and trees and flowers.'

'Better than maths!' said Prakash.

'I'll be a pilot,' said Sonu. 'I want to fly a plane like Miss Ramola's brother.'

'And what about you, Prakash?' asked Bina.

Prakash just smiled and said, 'Maybe I'll be a flute player,' and he put the flute to his lips and played a sweet melody.

'Well, the world needs flute players too,' said Bina, as they fell into step beside him.

The leopard had been stalking a barking deer. She paused when she heard the flute and the voices of the children. Her own young ones were growing quickly, but the girl and the two boys did not look much older.

They had started singing their favourite song again:

Five more miles to go!
We climb through rain and snow.
A river to cross...
A mountain to pass...
Now we've four more miles to go!

The leopard waited until they had passed, before returning to the trail of the barking deer.

OF ADULTHOOD

My Two Years in London

I was lonely in London.

Living alone in a big city, working in an office from nine to five, and coming back to a gas-fire in an empty bed-sitting room, was not what I wanted out of life. I'd go out to eat in a small café, then return to my room, put a sheet of paper into my small portable typewriter, and type out a page or two of my novel. It was into its second draft. And there would be a third before it finally found favour with its eventual publisher.

Diana Athill, my publisher's editor, was kind and helpful. The people in the Photax Office, where I worked, were kind and friendly. My landlady was kind and solicitous. Or I should say landladies, because I had at least three of them, one after another—Belsize Park, Haverstock Hill, Swiss Cottage—all Jewish landladies, widows I think, who never troubled or scolded me if I came in late or played my radio too loudly. One of them gave me breakfast in my room. Scrambled eggs, occasionally with peppers. This helped sustain me, because for lunch—at a snackbar near the office—it was almost always baked beans on toast, the cheapest item on their menu.

> People were kind,
> But I was lonely,
> I had no companions of my own age.

So I went to the pictures. And once a month to the theatre. And I dropped at Foyles and bought old books. And I came home to my empty room, lit the gas-fire and worked on my book.

After about six months on my own, I found I was losing vision in my right eye. It was as though I was looking at the world through a shifting cloud. I took vitamins, they had been 'discovered' only recently—and experimented with various eye-drops—but the cloud only got darker and denser. So I went to a doctor, who said it needed further investigation and got me admitted to the Hampstead General Hospital. There, various specialists came to see me. One said I was suffering from malnutrition; true enough. Another said I had Eales' disease, a rare condition of the retina. A third felt it had something to do with a sluggish liver. (I'd suffered from jaundice in the past.) Tests showed that my intestines were full of amoebiasis, no doubt brought with me from India, and I was put on a course of emetine injections, which made me feel awful. Then my eye, or rather retina, was photographed by a high intensity camera, and the resultant picture appeared in a medical journal. (Not my picture, only the eye's; I had to wait a few years before my own mugshot appeared in a newspaper.)

Once the amoeba had been vanquished, I (or rather my sick eye), was given cortisone injections, cortisone then being the wonder drug that was supposed to clear up all sorts of intractable conditions. This left my poor eye looking rather bloody and fierce, prompting one fellow patient to remark that I could have passed for *The Phantom of the Opera*.

Weakened by the emitine and various laxatives, I found myself too weak to even get up in order to visit the loo, so I was given the privilege of having a bed-pan. This occasioned some raillery from the others in the ward (it was a general ward with about twenty beds), who labelled me the B-P Superman—the Bed-pan Superman, after the British Petroleum Superman who was on all the hoardings.

I did improve rapidly, and was soon making the rounds of the ward, interviewing the other patients like a doctor on the rounds, quizzing them on their ailments and recommending purgatives and the bed-pan.

The book trolley came the rounds every day, and I read a book a day, discovering the stories of William Saroyan (*My Name is Aram* and *The Humans Comedy*), Denton Welch (*A Voice Through a Cloud*) and Josephine Tey (*The Daughter of Time*).

Saroyan had grown up in an Armenian immigrant community in California, and in his stories he captured the essence of small-town life in his part of the world. He won the Pulitzer Prize for his play *The Time of Your Life*, and was very popular in the 1940s and '50s, but most of his work is now out of print.

Denton Welch was a promising young English writer who had a tragic accident while riding his bicycle on a country road. He was knocked down and run over by a lorry. For over a year, he lingered between life and death, and during this period he managed to write his very moving account of his struggle to recover. He succumbed to his many injuries. I hope *A Voice Through a Cloud* is reprinted some day. His earlier travel book, *Maiden Voyage,* should also be revisted.

Josephine Tey wrote several detective novels during her short life. In *The Daughter of Time,* the novel I read in my hospital bed, her detective, Inspector Grant, finds himself in a hospital bed and passes the time by trying to reconstruct the murder of the princes in the tower, and with the help of his research assistant proves that it was King Henry VII and not King Richard III who was responsible for their deaths. A historical who-done-it, resolved without moving from the hospital bed. No fast-paced action, but suspenseful all the same.

How sad it is that such fine writers have been neglected or forgotten. Time and changing fashions take their toll on the best talents. Only a handful survive.

Sometimes short stories have a better chance of survival, because the good ones get picked up for inclusions in anthologies, and then get selected again and again. One of my earliest short stories, 'The Eyes Have It', is still turning up in anthologies and school readers, fifty years after it was first written. But once a novel goes out of print, it is hard to revive it. And novels date very quickly. Sometimes too much extraneous matter goes into them, whereas the best short stories stick to the essentials.

When I wrote *The Room on the Roof* I had published only two or three short stories, so what was I, still a pimply and skinny youth, doing, trying to write a novel?

In a way it was a mistake, because in writing it I used up all the experience I had of life and was left with nothing for a second novel!

But it had to be written.

That last year in Dehra, before I left for England, was now so ingrained in me, so much a part of my emotional make-up, that it had to be expressed in the way I knew best—the written word. The journal had become a novel, and some, Krishan, Meena and the rest stayed alive for me on the printed page. Though it might never have been published and I couldn't be sure of this during the four years that various drafts shuttled between me and Andre Deutsch's editor, Diana Athill, the thing had been done, the catharsis had completed, and I could think of other people, other loves, and try something different.

My editor, Diana Athill, was then a young woman in her thirties. Many years later she was to become quite a celebrity, the author of several successful autobiographies, which were frank, revealing and beautifully written. But when I knew her she hadn't done any writing (or none that I know of), although she was very busy assessing and introducing the work of many promising young writers, novelists such as Jack Kerouac and V.S. Naipaul. Although she did not (could not) teach me how to write (I stubbornly refused to temper my addiction to semi-commas and certain Indianisms), she made me feel that I was part of her literary world, giving me gossip about others writers and telling me about the books they were publishing. I visited her at her flat in Regent's Park quite often, and even took her to see an Indian picture, *Aan* (the first to get a commercial release in London) but it was a terrible let-down, a very silly film, the sort of Bombay extravaganza that gave a completely misleading and over-romanticized conception of Indians. I felt more at ease introducing her to paan at a little Indian restaurant near

Fitzroy Square, but I'm afraid she didn't care much for paan either. My efforts to make Diana an Indophile were not very successful. But she liked my book. 'I can see why you love India,' she said, 'It's so easy to make friends.'

But my first appearance in print (in London, that is) really came about as a result of my lengthy stay in the Hampstead General Hospital. A fellow patient, an English boy of about my age (perhaps a little younger) turned out to be a good reader, and when he was discharged he gave me a copy of a magazine for teenagers called *Young Elizabethan.* A couple of months later, when I was back at my typewriter, I sent them one of my short stories. It was published, and paid for. And even after I had returned to India I continued to write for the *Elizabethan*, and several of my early stories appeared in it—'The Thief,' 'The Long Day', 'The Big Race,' 'The Stolen Daffodils,' among others—until it closed down around 1959.

And while still in that hospital bed, I had written a piece called 'My Two Homes'—about an English boy growing up in an Indian home—and this became a talk that I gave on BBC Radio. The BBC's Home Service also ran a weekly short story programme, and when I returned to India and started freelancing, many of my early stories found a home with them. 'The Night Train at Deoli', 'The Woman on Platform 8' and many others were read by Robert Rietti, a fine actor in radio plays. Back in Dehra, I would drop in on a friend who had a short-wave radio, and listened spellbound to my stories being beamed to me from distant London.

So my two years in London were a good preparation for the years of struggle that lay ahead, when I returned to India. Although my job was a dull one, I did find time to write, to read, to visit the theatre, to wander about the streets of London (getting to know that city fairly well), and so banishing the loneliness that awaited me whenever I returned to cold bed-sitting room.

And there were friends too. Students, mostly, who came in and out of my life at random.

Praveen, a Gujarati boy who was a little younger than me; he liked visiting pubs and night clubs! I had no idea what he was studying—I never saw him with a book—but he was the recipient of regular remittances from his father in Bombay.

Thanh, a Vietnamese, who cultivated me because he wanted to 'improve his English', he dropped me when he discovered I spoke English with an Indian accent.

Vu-phuong, also Vietnamese, who used to tell me my fortune with tea-leaves. When you finish drinking your tea, you let the tea-leaves settle naturally, and the pattern they form gives you an indication of what to expect in the future. This was great fun, because it meant sharing innumerable cups of tea with Vu, with whom I fell in love. But when I asked her to marry me, she said it was not in the tea-leaves.

Just as well, perhaps. If I'd been married in England (or Vietnam), I might never have returned to India.

And returning to India was still very much my first priority.

But first I had to save a little money, publish my novel, and try to see a little better with my right eye.

The best way to get to know a city is to walk all over the place. So I walked all over Soho and the West End; I walked from Primrose Hill down to Baker Street, looking for Sherlock Holmes, but couldn't find him; I walked all over the East End, looking for places described by Dickens in *Oliver Twist* and *Our Mutual Friend,* but they looked very different from what I'd imagined; I walked around Kensington Gardens, looking for Peter Pan, but he must have been away in Neverland. So I went to Kew Gardens, and felt quite at home in a big glass hothouse, surrounded by tropical plants of every description, after that, whenever I felt homesick, I went down to Kew—not just in lilac time, but any time...

Andre Deutsch finally gave me a £50 advance for *The Room on the Roof.* I did not wait for it to be published, but bought a ticket to Bombay for £40; gave a week's notice to my kind employers, who presented me with a travel bag; and boarded the *M.S. Batory* at Southampton, accompanied by said travel bag and an old suitcase bulging with books and a few clothes. It was March, 1955, and I was twenty-one years old. I had left India to seek my fortune in the West; and now I was returning to the East to find, if not fortune, at least fulfilment of a sort.

Although I was over twenty, and had been earning my own living for over three years, in many ways I was still a boy, with a boy's thoughts and dreams—dreams of romance, high adventure and good companionship. And I was still a lonely boy, alone on that big ship—passengers and crew all strangers to me—sailing into an uncertain future.

I had two books with me—Thoreau's *Walden* and Richard Jefferies' *The Story of My Heart*—both reflecting my burgeoning interest in the natural world—but during the day the cabin was hot and stuffy, and the decks too crowded, so I postponed most of my reading until the journey was over. But at night, when it was cool on the deck, and most of the passengers were down below, watching a film or drinking Polish vodka (the Batory was a Polish ship), I would sit out under the stars while the ship ploughed on through the Red Sea, bringing me home to India. There was no sound but the dull thunder of the ship's screws and the faint tinkle of music from an open porthole.

And as I sat there, pondering over my future, a line from Thoreau kept running through my head. 'Lonely! Why should I feel lonely? Is not our planet in the Milky Way?'

Wherever I went, the stars were there to keep me company. And I knew that as long as I connected, in both a physical and mystical way, with the natural world—sea, sun, earth, moon and stars—I would never feel lonely upon this planet.

Calypso Christmas

My first Christmas in London had been a lonely one. My small bed-sitting-room near Swiss Cottage had been cold and austere, and my landlady had disapproved of any sort of revelry. Moreover, I hadn't the money for the theatre or a good restaurant. That first English Christmas was spent sitting in front of a lukewarm gas-fire, eating beans on toast, and drinking cheap sherry. My one consolation was the row of Christmas cards on the mantelpiece—most of them from friends in India.

But the following year I was making more money and living in a bigger, brighter, homelier room. The new landlady approved of my bringing friends—even girls—to the house, and had even made me a plum pudding so that I could entertain my guests. My friends in London included a number of Indian and Commonwealth students, and through them I met George, a friendly, sensitive person from Trinidad.

George was not a student. He was over thirty. Like thousands of other West Indians, he had come to England because he had been told that jobs were plentiful, that there was a free health scheme and national insurance, and that he could earn anything from ten to twenty pounds a week—far more than he could make in Trinidad or Jamaica. But, while it was true that jobs were to be had in England, it was also true that sections of local labour resented outsiders filling these posts. There were also those, belonging chiefly to the lower-middle classes, who were prone to various prejudices, and though these people were a minority, they were still capable of making themselves felt and heard.

In any case, London is a lonely place, especially for the stranger.

And for the happy-go-lucky West Indian, accustomed to sunshine, colour and music, London must be quite baffling.

As though to match the grey-green fogs of winter, Londoners wore sombre colours, greys and browns. The West Indians couldn't understand this. Surely, they reasoned, during a grey season the colours worn should be vivid reds and greens—colours that would defy the curling fog and uncomfortable rain? But Londoners frowned on these gay splashes of colour; to them it all seemed an expression of some sort of barbarism. And then again Londoners had a horror of any sort of loud noise, and a blaring radio could (quite justifiably) bring in scores of protests from neighbouring houses. The West Indians, on the other hand, liked letting off steam; they liked holding parties in their rooms at which there was much singing and shouting. They had always believed that England was their mother country, and so, despite rain, fog, sleet and snow, they were determined to live as they had lived back home in Trinidad. And it is to their credit, and even to the credit of indigenous Londoners, that this is what they succeeded in doing.

George worked for British Railways. He was a ticket collector at one of the underground stations. He liked his work, and received about ten pounds a week for collecting tickets. A large, stout man, with huge hands and feet, he always had a gentle, kindly expression on his mobile face. Among other accomplishments, he could play the piano, and as there was an old, rather dilapidated piano in my room, he would often come over in the evenings to run his fat, heavy fingers over the keys, playing tunes that ranged from hymns to jazz pieces. I thought he would be a nice person to spend Christmas with, so I asked him to come and share the pudding my landlady had made, and a bottle of sherry I had procured.

Little did I realize that an invitation to George would be interpreted as an invitation to all of George's friends and relations—in fact, anyone who had known him in Trinidad—but this was the way he looked at it, and at eight o'clock on Christmas Eve, while a chilly wind blew dead leaves down from Hampstead

Heath, I saw a veritable army of West Indians marching down Belsize Avenue, with George in the lead.

Bewildered, I opened my door to them; and in streamed George, George's cousins, George's nephews and George's friends. They were all smiling and they all shook hands with me, making complimentary remarks about my room ('Man, that's some piano!', 'Hey, look at that crazy picture!', 'This rocking chair gives me fever!') and took no time at all to feel and make themselves at home. Everyone had brought something along for the party. George had brought several bottles of beer. Eric, a flashy, coffee-coloured youth, had brought cigarettes and more beer. Marian, a buxom woman of thirty-five, who called me 'darling' as soon as we met, and kissed me on the cheeks saying she adored pink cheeks, had brought bacon and eggs. Her daughter Lucy, who was sixteen and in the full bloom of youth, had brought a gramophone, while the little nephews carried the records. Other friends and familiars had also brought beer; and one enterprising fellow produced a bottle of Jamaican rum.

Then everything began to happen at once.

Lucy put a record on the gramophone, and the strains of 'Basin Street Blues' filled the room. At the same time, George sat down at the piano to hammer out an accompaniment to the record. His huge hands crushed down on the keys as though he were chopping up hunks of meat. Marian had lit the gas-fire and was busy frying bacon and eggs. Eric was opening beer bottles. In the midst of the noise and confusion I heard a knock on the door—a very timid, hesitant sort of knock—and opening it, found my landlady standing on the threshold.

'Oh, Mr Bond, the neighbours—' she began, and glancing into the room was rendered speechless.

'It's only tonight,' I said. 'They'll all go home after an hour. Remember, it's Christmas!'

She nodded mutely and hurried away down the corridor, pursued by something called 'Be Bop A-Lula'. I closed the door and drew all the curtains in an effort to stifle the noise; but everyone was stamping about on the floorboards, and I hoped fervently that the downstairs people had gone to the theatre. George had started playing calypso music, and Eric and Lucy were strutting and stomping in the middle of the room, while the two nephews were improvising on their own. Before I knew what was happening, Marian had taken me in her strong arms and was teaching me to do the calypso. The song playing, I think, was 'Banana Boat Song'.

Instead of the party lasting an hour, it lasted three hours. We ate innumerable fried eggs and finished off all the beer. I took turns dancing with Marian, Lucy and the nephews. There was a peculiar expression they used when excited. 'Fire!' they shouted. I never knew what was supposed to be on fire, or what the exclamation implied, but I too shouted 'Fire!' and somehow it seemed a very sensible thing to shout.

Perhaps their hearts were on fire, I don't know; but for all their excitability and flashiness and brashness they were lovable and sincere friends, and today, when I look back on my two years in London, that Christmas party is the brightest, most vivid memory of all, and the faces of George and Marian, Lucy and Eric, are the faces I remember best.

At midnight someone turned out the light. I was dancing with Lucy at the time, and in the dark she threw her arms around me and kissed me full on the lips. It was the first time I had been kissed by a girl, and when I think about it, I am glad that it was Lucy who kissed me.

When they left, they went in a bunch, just as they had come. I stood at the gate and watched them saunter down the dark, empty street. The buses and tubes had stopped running at midnight, and George and his friends would have to walk all the way back to their rooms at Highgate and Golders Green.

After they had gone, the street was suddenly empty and silent, and my own footsteps were the only sounds I could hear. The cold came clutching at me, and I turned up my collar. I looked up at the windows of my house, and at the windows of all the other houses in the street. They were all in darkness. It seemed to me that we were the only ones who had really celebrated Christmas.

The India I Carried with Me

I am now going back in time, to a period when I was caught between East and West, and had to make up my mind just where I belonged. I had been away from India for barely a month before I was longing to return. The insularity of the place where I found myself (Jersey, in the Channel Islands) had something to do with it, I suppose. There was little there to remind me of India or the East, not one brown face to be seen in the streets or on the beaches. I'm sure it's a different sort of place now; but fifty years ago it had nothing to offer by way of companionship or good cheer to a lonely, sensitive boy who had left home and friends in search of a 'better future'.

I had come to England with a dream of sorts, and I was to return to India with another kind of dream; but in between there were to be four years of dreary office work, lonely bed-sitting rooms, shabby lodging houses, cheap snack bars, hospital wards, and the struggle to write my first book and find a publisher for it.

I started work in a large departmental store called *Le Riche*. At eight in the morning, when I walked to the store, it was dark. At six in the evening, when I walked home, it was dark again. Where were all those sunny beaches Jersey was famous for? I would have to wait for summer to see them, and a Saturday afternoon to take a dip in the sea.

Occasionally, after an early supper, I would walk along the deserted seafront. If the tide was in and the wind was approaching gale-force, the waves would climb the sea wall and drench me with their cold salt spray. My aunt, with whom I was staying, thought I was quite mad to take this solitary walk; but I have always been at one with nature, even in its wilder moments, and the wind and the crashing waves gave me a sense of freedom, strengthened my determination to escape from the island and go my own way.

When I wasn't walking along the seafront, I would sit at the portable typewriter in my small attic room, and hammer out the rough chapters of the book that was to become my first novel. These were characters and incidents based on the journal I had kept during my last year in India. It was 1951, recalled in late 1952. An eighteen-year-old looking back on incidents in the life of a seventeen-year-old! Nostalgia and longing suffused those pages. How I longed to be back with my friends in the small town of Dehradun—a leafy place, sunny, fruit-laden, easy-going, every familiar corner etched clearly in my memory. Somehow, it had been that last year in Dehra that had brought me closer to the India that I had so far only taken for granted. An India of close and sometimes sentimental friendships. Of striking contrasts: a small cinema showing English pictures (a George Formby comedy or an American musical) and only a couple of hours away thousands taking a dip in the sacred water of the Ganga. Or outside the station, hundreds of pony-drawn tongas waiting to pick up passengers, while the more affluent climbed into their Ford Convertibles, Morris Minors, Baby Austins or flashy Packards and Daimlers.

But of course Dehra in the 1950s was a town of bicycles. Students, shopkeepers, Army cadets, office workers, all used them. The scooter (or Lambretta) had only just been invented, and it would be several years before it took over from the bicycle. It was still unaffordable for the great majority.

I was awkward on a bicycle and frequently fell off, breaking my arm on one occasion. But this did not prevent me from joining my friends on cycle rides to the sulphur springs, or to Premnagar (where the Military Academy was situated) or along the Haridwar road and down to the riverbed at Lachhiwala.

In Jersey, I found an old cycle belonging to my cousin, and I rode from St Helier, where we lived, to St Brelade's Bay, at the other end of the island. But returning after dark, I was hauled up for riding without lights. I had no idea that cycles had also to be equipped with lights. Back in Dehra, we never used them!

The attic room had no view, so one of my favourite occupations, gazing out of windows, came to a stop. But perhaps this was helpful in that it made me concentrate on the sheet of paper in my typewriter. After about six months, I had a book of sorts ready for submission to any publisher who was prepared to look at it. Meanwhile, I had been through at least three jobs and had even been offered a post in the Jersey Civil Service, having successfully taken the local civil service exam—something I had done out of sheer boredom, as I had no intention of settling permanently on the island.

I had been keeping a diary of sorts and in some of the entries I had expressed my desire to get back to India, and my discontent at having to stay with relatives who were unsympathetic, not only to my feelings for India but also to my ambitions to become a writer. The diary fell into my uncle's hands. He read it, and was naturally upset. We had a row. I was contrite; but a few days later I packed my suitcases (all two of them) and stepped on to the ferry that was to take me to Southampton and then to London. Lesson one: don't leave your personal diaries lying around!

But perhaps it was all for the best, otherwise I might have hung around in Jersey for another year or two, to the detriment of my personal happiness and my writing ambitions.

I arrived in London in the middle of a thick yellow November fog—those were the days of the killer London fogs—and after a search found the Students' Hostel where I was given a cubicle to myself. But I did not stay there very long; the available food was awful. As soon as I got an office job—not too difficult in the 1950s—I rented an attic room in Belsize Park, the first of many bed-sitters that I was to live in during my three-year sojourn in London.

From Belsize Park I was to move to Haverstock Hill (close to

Hampstead Heath), then to South London for a short time, and finally to Swiss Cottage. Most of my landladies were Jewish—refugees from persecution in pre-War Europe—and I too was a refugee of sorts, still very unsure of where I belonged. Was it England, the land of my father, or India, the land of my birth? But my father had also been born in India, had grown up and made a living there, visiting *his* father's land, England, only a couple of times during his life.

The link with Britain was tenuous, based on heredity rather than upbringing. It was more in the mind. It was a literary England I had been drawn to, not a physical England. And in fact, I took several exploratory walks around 'literary' London, visiting houses or streets where famous writers had once lived; in particular the East End and Dockland, for I had grown up on the novels and stories of Dickens, Smollett, Captain Marryat, and W.W. Jacobs. But I did not make many English friends. If they were a reserved race, I was even more reserved. Always shy, I waited for others to take the initiative. In India, people will take the initiative, they lose no time in getting to know you. Not so in England. They were too polite to look at you. And in that respect, I was more English than the English.

The gentleman who lived on the floor below me occasionally went so far as to greet me with the observation, 'Beastly weather, isn't it?'

And I would respond by saying, 'Oh, perfectly beastly,' and pass on.

How different it was when I bumped into a Gujarati boy, Praveen, who lived on the basement floor. He gave me a winning smile, and I remember saying, 'Oh, to be in Bombay now that winter's here,' and immediately we were friends.

He was only seventeen, a year or two younger than me, and he was studying at one of the polytechnics with a view to getting into the London School of Economics. At that time, most of the Indians in London were students, the great immigration rush was still a long way off, and racial antagonisms were directed more at the recently arrived West Indians than at Asians.

Praveen took me on the rounds of the coffee bars, then proliferating all over London, and introduced me to other students, among them a Vietnamese called Thanh, who cultivated my friendship because, as he said, 'I want to speak English.' When he discovered that my accent was very un-English (you could have called it Welsh with an Anglo-Indian interaction), he dropped me like a hot brick. He was very frank; he was not interested in friendship, he said, only in improving his accent. I heard later that he'd attached himself to a young journalist from up north, who spoke Broad Yorkshire.

Most evenings I remained in my room and worked on my novel. From being a journal it had become a first person narrative, and now I was turning it into fiction in the third person. The title had also undergone a few changes, but finally I settled on *The Room on the Roof.*

Into it, I put all the love and affection I felt for the friends I had left behind in Dehra. It was more than nostalgia, it was a recreation of the people, places and incidents of that last year in India. I did not want it to fade away. The riverbanks at Haridwar, the mango-groves of the Doon, the poinsettias and bougainvillaea, the games on the parade ground, the chaat shops near the Clock Tower, the summer heat, the monsoon downpours, romping naked in the rain, sitting on railway platforms, gnawing at a stick of sugar cane, listening to street cries... All this and more came crowding upon me as I sat writing before the gas fire in my little room.

When it grew very cold, I used an old overcoat given to me by Diana Athill, the junior partner at Andre Deutsch, who had promised to publish *The Room* if I rewrote it as a novel. Another who encouraged me was a BBC producer, Prudence Smith, who got me to give a couple of talks on Radio's Third Programme. I felt I was getting somewhere; and when I found myself confined to the Hampstead General Hospital for almost a month, with a mysterious disease that had affected the vision in my right eye, I used the left to catch up on my reading and to write a couple of short stories.

A nurse brought a tray of books around the ward every afternoon, and thanks to this courtesy, I was able to discover the delightful stories of William Saroyan and Denton Welch's sensitive first novel *Maiden Voyage*. Saroyan, a Pulitzer Prize winner for his play *The Time of Your Life*, was then very successful and popular. Denton's promising career had been cut short by a terrible accident. Out cycling on a country road, he had been knocked down by a speeding motorist. He had lived for several years, struggling against crippling injuries and almost completing his sensitive autobiography *A Voice in the Clouds*. He was thirty-one when he died. Towards the end, he could only work for three or four minutes at a time. Complications set in, and the left side of his heart started failing. Even then he made a terrific effort to finish his book. His friend Eric wrote—'Denton was upheld by the high courage which seemed somehow the fruit of his rare intelligence.'

The work of these writers, together with the bottle of Guinness I was given every day as a tonic (they had found me somewhat undernourished), meant that I walked out of the hospital with a spring in my step and a determination to succeed.

But Andre Deutsch was still dithering over my book. The firm was doing well, but he didn't like taking risks. No publisher likes losing money. And he wasn't going to make much out of my novel, a subjective and unsensational work.

But I resented his indecision. So I returned the small amount he'd paid me by way of an option, and demanded the return of my manuscript. Back came an apologetic letter and an advance (then £50) against publication.

Today, almost fifty years later, the firm of Andre Deutsch has gone, but *The Room on the Roof* is still in print, still making friends. This is not something that I gloat over, it only goes to show that books are unpredictable commodities, and that the most successful authors and publishers often fall by the wayside. Publishers go out of business, writers fade from the public mind. Even Saroyan is forgotten now. I'll be forgotten too, someday.

There were to be further delays before *The Room* was published, and I was back in India when it did come out. By then I'd almost forgotten about the book! But it picked up the John Llewellyn Rhys Prize, an award that also went to V.S. Naipaul a year later, for his first book. It was then worth only £50. There were no big sponsors in those days. It is now sponsored by a British newspaper and is worth £5,000. This was turned down last year by another Indian writer, who disagreed with the paper's policies.

Meanwhile, in London, there were other distractions. I loved stage musicals, and if I had a little money to spare I went to the theatre, taking in such productions as *Porgy and Bess*, *Paint Your Wagon*, *Pal Joey*, *Teahouse of the August Moon*, and the occasional review. And of course the annual presentation of *Peter Pan* at the Scala Theatre, not far from where I worked. I had grown up on Peter Pan, first read to me by my father in distant Jamnagar, and at school I had read Barrie's other plays and been charmed by them; but, like operetta, they had gone out of fashion and only the ageless Peter remained. 'Do you believe in fairies?' he asks in the play. And to save Tinker Bell from extinction, I clapped with the rest of the audience. But did I really believe in fairies? I looked for them in Kensington Gardens, where Peter Pan's statue stood, and found a few mothers pushing their perambulators, but no fairies. And I looked in Hyde Park, but found only courting couples. And I looked all over Leicester Square, but instead of fairies I found prostitutes soliciting business. As I was still looking for romance, I crept back to my room and my portable typewriter—I would have to create my own romance.

The small portable had been in the windows of a Jersey department store, and every time I passed the store I glanced at the window to see if the typewriter was still there. It seemed to be waiting for me to come in and take it away. I longed to buy it, partly because I had to type out the final drafts of my book, and also because it looked very dainty and attractive. It was definitely out to seduce me. Finally, with the help of a loan from Mr Bromley, a kindly senior clerk, I bought the machine. It cost only £12, but that was three month's wages at the time. It accompanied me to London, and then a couple of years later to India, giving me good service in Dehradun, New Delhi, and then Mussoorie where it finally succumbed to the damp monsoon climate.

My worldly possessions had increased, not only by the typewriter, but also by a record player that I had bought second-hand from a Thai student. I had become an ardent fan of the Black singer Eartha Kitt and had bought all her records; but they were no good without a player until the Thai boy came to my rescue. Then the sensual, throaty voice of Eartha reverberated through the lodging house, bringing complaints from the landlady and the gentleman downstairs. I had to keep the volume low, which wasn't much fun.

I was also fond of the clarinet (turj) playing of an Indian musician, Master Ibrahim, and I had some of his recordings, which transported me back to the streets and bazaars of small-town India. Light, lilting and tuneful, I preferred this sort of flute music to the warblings of the more popular songsters.

Praveen liked gangster films and wanted me to accompany him to anything which featured Humphrey Bogart, James Cagney, George Raft and other tough guys. Praveen wanted to be a tough guy himself and often struck a Bogart-like pose, cigarette dangling from the side of his mouth. There was nothing tough about Praveen, who was really rather delicate, but his affectations were charming and risible.

One day he announced that he was returning to India for a few months, as his ailing mother was anxious to see him. He asked me to come along too, to give him company during the three week voyage. To do so, I would have to throw up my job, but I had already thrown up several jobs. They were simply stop-gaps until I could establish myself as a writer. I hadn't the slightest intention or ambition of being a senior clerk or even an executive for the firm in which I was working. The only problem in leaving England then was that I would have to leave my book in limbo, as there was still no guarantee that Deutsch would publish it. But it was time I went on to write other things; time to strike out on my own, to take a chance with India. The ships were full of British and Anglo-Indian families coming to England, to make a 'better future' for themselves. I would do the opposite, go into reverse, and make my future, for good or ill, in the land of my birth.

My passport was in order, and I had only to give a week's notice to my employers. I had saved up about £200, and of this £50 went on the cost of my passage, London to Bombay. Praveen and I boarded the *S.S. Balory*, a Polish liner with a reputation for running into trouble. We had no difficulty in securing berths in tourist class. Praveen had every intention of returning to England to complete his studies. My own intentions were very vague. I knew there would be no job for me in India, but I was quietly confident that I could make a living from writing, and that too in the English language.

The *Balory* lived up to its reputation. Some of the crew went missing at Gibraltar. A passenger fell overboard in the Red Sea. Lifeboats were lowered, but he could not be found.

Praveen fell in love with an Egyptian girl who disembarked at Aden. He followed her ashore, and I had to run after him and get him back to the ship. As we docked at Ballard Pier, a fire broke out in one of the holds, but by then we were safely ashore. Praveen was swamped by relatives who carried him off to the suburbs of Bombay. I made my way to Victoria Terminus and boarded the Dehradun Express. It was a slow passenger train, which went chugging through several states in the general direction of northern India. Two days and two nights later we crawled through the eastern Doon. It was early March. The mango trees were in blossom, the peacocks were calling, and Belsize Park was far away.

Friends of My Youth

1
SUDHEER

Friendship is all about doing things together. It may be climbing a mountain, fishing in a mountain stream, cycling along a country road, camping in a forest clearing, or simply travelling together and sharing the experiences that a new place can bring.

On at least two of these counts, Sudheer qualified as a friend, albeit a troublesome one, given to involving me in his adolescent escapades.

I met him in Dehra soon after my return from England. He turned up at my room saying he'd heard I was a writer and asking if I had any comics to lend him.

'I don't write comics,' I said; but there were some comics lying around, left over from my own boyhood collection so I gave these to the lanky youth who stood smiling in the doorway, and he thanked me and said he'd bring them back. From my window I saw him cycling off in the general direction of Dalanwala.

He turned up again a few days later and dumped a large pile of new-looking comics on my desk. 'Here are all the latest,' he announced. 'You can keep them for me. I'm not allowed to read comics at home.'

It was only weeks later that I learnt he was given to pilfering comics and magazines from the town's bookstores. In no time at all, I'd become a receiver of stolen goods!

My landlady had warned me against Sudheer and so had one or two others. He had acquired a certain notoriety for having been expelled from his school. He had been in charge of the library, and before a consignment of newly acquired books could be registered and library stamped, he had sold them back to the bookshop from which they had originally been purchased. Very enterprising but not to be countenanced in a very *pukka* public school. He was now studying in a municipal school too poor to afford a library.

Sudheer was an amoral scamp all right, but I found it difficult to avoid him, or to resist his undeniable and openly affectionate manner. He could make you laugh. And anyone who can do that is easily forgiven for a great many faults.

One day he produced a couple of white mice from his pockets and left them on my desk.

'You keep them for me,' he said. 'I'm not allowed to keep them at home.'

There were a great many things he was not allowed to keep at home. Anyway, the white mice were given a home in an old cupboard, where my landlady kept unwanted dishes, pots and pans, and they were quite happy there, being fed on bits of bread or *chapatti*, until one day I heard shrieks from the storeroom, and charging into it, found my dear stout landlady having hysterics as one of the white mice sought refuge under her blouse and the other ran frantically up and down her back.

Sudheer had to find another home for the white mice. It was that or finding another home for myself.

Most young men, boys and quite a few girls used bicycles. There was a cycle hire shop across the road, and Sudheer persuaded me to hire cycles for both of us. We cycled out of town, through tea gardens and mustard fields, and down a forest road until we discovered a small, shallow river where we bathed and wrestled on the sand. Although I was three or four years older than Sudheer, he was much the stronger, being about six feet tall and broad in the shoulders. His parents had come from Bhanu, a rough-and-ready district on the North West Frontier, as a result of the partition of the country. His father ran a small press situated behind the Sabzi Mandi and brought out a weekly newspaper called *The Frontier Times.*

We came to the stream quite often. It was Sudheer's way of playing truant from school without being detected in the bazaar or at the cinema. He was sixteen when I met him, and eighteen when we parted, but I can't recall that he ever showed any interest in his school work.

He took me to his home in the Karanpur bazaar, then a stronghold of the Bhanu community. The Karanpur boys were an aggressive lot and resented Sudheer's friendship with an *angrez.* To avoid a confrontation, I would use the back alleys and side streets to get to and from the house in which they lived. Sudheer had been overindulged by his mother, who protected him from his father's wrath. Both parents felt I might have an 'improving' influence on their son, and encouraged our friendship. His elder sister seemed more doubtful. She felt he was incorrigible, beyond redemption, and that I was not much better, and she was probably right.

The father invited me to his small press and asked me if I'd like to work with him. I agreed to help with the newspaper for a couple of hours every morning. This involved proofreading and editing news agency reports. Uninspiring work, but useful.

Meanwhile, Sudheer had got hold of a pet monkey, and he carried it about in the basket attached to the handlebar of his bicycle. He used it to ingratiate himself with the girls. 'How sweet! How pretty!' they would exclaim, and Sudheer would get the monkey to show them its tricks.

After some time, however, the monkey appeared to be infected by Sudheer's amorous nature, and would make obscene gestures that were not appreciated by his former admirers. On one occasion, the monkey made off with a girl's *dupatta.* A chase ensued, and the dupatta was retrieved, but the outcome of it all was that Sudheer was accosted by the girl's brothers and given a black eye and a bruised cheek. His father took the monkey away and returned it to the itinerant juggler who had sold it to the young man.

Sudheer soon developed an insatiable need for money. He wasn't getting anything at home, apart from what he pinched from his mother and sister, and his father urged me not to give the boy any money. After paying for my boarding and lodging I had very little to spare, but Sudheer seemed to sense when a money order or cheque arrived, and would hang around, spinning tall tales of great financial distress until, in order to be rid of him, I would give him five to ten rupees. (In those days, a magazine payment seldom exceeded fifty rupees.)

He was becoming something of a trial, constantly interrupting me in my work, and even picking up confectionery from my landlady's small shop and charging it to my account. I had stopped going for bicycle rides. He had wrecked one of the cycles and the shopkeeper held me responsible for repairs.

The sad thing was that Sudheer had no other friends. He did not go in for team games or for music or other creative pursuits which might have helped him to move around with people of his own age group. He was a loner with a propensity for mischief. Had he entered a bicycle race, he would have won easily. Forever eluding a variety of pursuers, he was extremely fast on his bike. But we did not have cycle races in Dehra.

And then, for a blessed two or three weeks, I saw nothing of my unpredictable friend.

I discovered later that he had taken a fancy to a young schoolteacher, about five years his senior, who lived in a hostel up at Rajpur. His cycle rides took him in that direction. As usual, his charm proved irresistible, and it wasn't long before the teacher and the acolyte were taking rides together down lonely forest roads. This was all right by me, of course, but it wasn't the norm with the middle-class matrons of small-town India, at least not in 1957. Hostel wardens, other students, and naturally Sudheer's parents, were all in a state of agitation. So I wasn't surprised when Sudheer turned up in my room to announce that he was on his way to Nahan to study at an Inter College there.

Nahan was a small hill town about sixty miles from Dehra.

Sudheer was banished to the home of his *mama*, an uncle who was a sub-inspector in the local police force. He had promised to see that Sudheer stayed out of trouble.

Whether he succeeded or not, I could not tell, for a couple of months later I gave up my rooms in Dehra and left for Delhi. I lost touch with Sudheer's family, and it was only several years later, when I bumped into an old acquaintance, that I was given news of my erstwhile friend.

He had apparently done quite well for himself. Taking off for Calcutta, he had used his charm and his fluent English to land a job as an assistant on a tea estate. Here he had proved quite efficient, earning the approval of his manager and employers. But his roving eye soon got him into trouble. The women working in the tea gardens became prey to his amorous and amoral nature. Keeping one mistress was acceptable. Keeping several was asking for trouble. He was found dead early one morning with his throat cut.

2

THE ROYAL CAFE SET

Dehra was going through a slump in those days, and there wasn't much work for anyone—least of all for my neighbour Suresh Mathur, an income tax lawyer, who was broke for two reasons. To begin with, there was not much work going around, as those with taxable incomes were few and far between. Apart from that, when he did get work, he was slow and half-hearted about getting it done. This was because he seldom got up before eleven in the morning, and by the time he took a bus down from Rajpur and reached his own small office (next door to my rooms), or the income tax office a little further on, it was lunchtime and all the tax officials were out. Suresh would then repair to the Royal Cafe for a beer or two (often at my expense) and this would stretch into a gin and tonic, after which he would stagger up to his first-floor office and collapse on the sofa for an afternoon nap.

He would wake up at six, after the income tax office had closed.

I occupied two rooms next to his office, and we were on friendly terms, sharing an enthusiasm for the humorous works of P.G. Wodehouse. I think he modelled himself on Bertie Wooster, for he would often turn up wearing mauve or yellow socks, or a pink shirt and a bright green tie—enough to make anyone in his company feel quite liverish. Unlike Bertie Wooster, he did not have a Jeeves to look after him and get him out of various scrapes. I tried not to be too friendly, as Suresh was in the habit of borrowing lavishly from all his friends, conveniently forgetting to return the amounts. I wasn't well off and could ill afford the company of a spendthrift friend. Sudheer was trouble enough.

Dehra, in those days, was full of people living on borrowed money or no money at all. Hence, the large number of disconnected telephone and electric lines. I did not have electricity myself, simply because the previous tenant had taken off, leaving me with outstandings of over a thousand rupees, then a princely sum. My monthly income seldom exceeded 500 rupees. No matter. There was plenty of kerosene available, and the oil lamp lent a romantic glow to my literary endeavours.

Looking back, I am amazed at the number of people who were quite broke. There was William Matheson, a Swiss journalist, whose remittances from Zurich never seemed to turn up; my landlady, whose husband had deserted her two years previously; Mr Madan, who dealt in second-hand cars that no one wanted; the owner of the corner restaurant, who sat in solitary splendour surrounded by empty tables; and the proprietor of the Ideal Book Depot, who was selling off his stock of unsold books and becoming a departmental store. We complain that few people buy or read books today, but I can assure you that there were even fewer customers in the fifties and sixties. Only doctors, dentists and the proprietors of English schools were making money.

Suresh spent whatever cash came his way, and borrowed more. He had an advantage over the rest of us—he owned an old bungalow, inherited from his father, up at Rajpur in the foothills, where he lived alone with an old manservant. And owning a property gave him some standing with his creditors. The grounds boasted of a mango and litchi orchard, and these he gave out on contract every year, so that his friends did not even get to enjoy some of his produce. The proceeds helped him to pay his office rent in town, with a little left over to give small amounts on account to the owner of the Royal Cafe.

If a lawyer could be hard up, what chance had a journalist? And yet, William Matheson had everything going for him from the start, when he came out to India as an assistant to Von Hesseltein, correspondent for some of the German papers. Von Hesseltein passed on some of the assignments to William, and for a time, all went well. William lived with Von Hesseltein and his family, and was also friendly with Suresh, often paying for the drinks at the Royal Cafe. Then William committed the folly (if not the sin) of having an affair with Von Hesseltein's wife. Von Hesseltein was not the understanding sort. He threw William out of the house and stopped giving him work.

William hired an old typewriter and set himself up as a correspondent in his own right, living and working from a room in the Doon Guest House. At first he was welcome there, having paid a three-month advance for room and board. He bombarded the Swiss and German papers with his articles, but there were very few takers. No one in Europe was really interested in India's five-year plans, or Corbusier's Chandigarh, or the Bhakra Nangal Dam. Book publishing in India was confined to textbooks, otherwise William might have published a vivid account of his experiences in the French Foreign Legion. After two or three rums at the Royal Cafe, he would regale us with tales of his exploits in the Legion, before and after the siege of Dien Bien Phu. Some of his stories had the ring of truth, others (particularly his sexual exploits) were obviously tall tales; but I was happy to pay for the beer or coffee in order to hear him spin them out.

Those were glorious days for an unknown freelance writer. I was realizing my dream of living by my pen, and I was doing it from a small town in North India, having turned my back on both London and New Delhi. I had no ambitions to be a great writer, or even a famous one, or even a rich one. All I wanted to do was *write*. And I wanted a few readers and the occasional cheque so I could carry on living my dream.

The cheques came along in their own desultory way—fifty rupees from the *Weekly*, or thirty-five from *The Statesman* or the same from *Sport and Pastime*, and so on—just enough to get by, and to be the envy of Suresh Mathur, William Matheson, and a few others, professional people who felt that I had no business earning more than they did. Suresh even declared that I should have been paying tax, and offered to represent me, his other clients having gone elsewhere.

And there was old Colonel Wilkie, living on a small pension in a corner room of the White House Hotel. His wife had left him some years before, presumably because of his drinking, but he claimed to have left her because of her obsession with moving the furniture—it seems she was always shifting things about, changing rooms, throwing out perfectly sound tables and chairs and replacing them with fancy stuff picked up here and there. If he took a liking to a particular easy chair and showed signs of settling down in it, it would disappear the next day to be replaced by something horribly ugly and uncomfortable.

'It was a form of mental torture,' said Colonel Wilkie, confiding in me over a glass of beer on the White House verandah. 'The sitting room was cluttered with all sorts of ornamental junk and flimsy side tables, so that I was constantly falling over the damn things. It was like a minefield! And the mines were never in the same place. You've noticed that I walk with a limp?'

'First World War?' I ventured. 'Wounded at Ypres? Or was it Flanders?'

'Nothing of the sort,' snorted the Colonel. 'I did get one or two flesh wounds but they were nothing as compared to the damage inflicted on me by those damned shifting tables and chairs. Fell over a coffee table and dislocated my shoulder. Then broke an ankle negotiating a stool that was in the wrong place. Bookshelf fell on me. Tripped on a rolled-up carpet. Hit by a curtain rod. Would you have put up with it?'

'No,' I had to admit.

'Had to leave her, of course. She went off to England. Send her an allowance. Half my pension! All spent on furniture!'

'It's a superstition of sorts, I suppose. Collecting things.'

The Colonel told me that the final straw was when his favourite spring bed had suddenly been replaced by a bed made up of hard wooden slats. It was sheer torture trying to sleep on it, and he had left his house and moved into the White House Hotel as a permanent guest.

Now he couldn't allow anyone to touch or tidy up anything in his room. There were beer stains on the tablecloth, cobwebs on his family pictures, dust on his books, empty medicine bottles on his dressing table, and mice nesting in his old, discarded boots. He had gone to the other extreme and wouldn't have anything changed or moved in his room.

I didn't see much of the room because we usually sat out on the verandah, waited upon by one of the hotel bearers, who came over with bottles of beer that I dutifully paid for, the Colonel having exhausted his credit. I suppose he was in his late sixties then. He never went anywhere, not even for a walk in the compound. He blamed this inactivity on his gout, but it was really inertia and an unwillingness to leave the precincts of the bar, where he could cadge the occasional drink from a sympathetic guest. I am that age now, and not half as active as I used to be, but there are people to live for and tales to tell, and I keep writing. It is important to keep writing.

Colonel Wilkie had given up on life. I suppose he could have gone off to England, but he would have been more miserable there, with no one to buy him a drink (since he wasn't likely to reciprocate) and the possibility of his wife turning up again to rearrange the furniture.

3

BIBIJI

My landlady was a remarkable woman, and this little memoir of Dehra in the 1950s would be incomplete without a sketch of hers.

She would often say, 'Ruskin, one day you must write my life story,' and I would promise to do so. And although she really deserves a book to herself, I shall try to do justice to her in these few pages.

She was, in fact, my Punjabi stepfather's first wife. Does that sound confusing? It was certainly complicated. And you might well ask, why on earth were you living with your stepfather's first wife instead of your stepfather and mother?

The answer is simple. I got on rather well with this rotund, well-built lady, and sympathized with her predicament. She had been married at a young age to my stepfather, who was something of a playboy, and who ran the photographic saloon he had received as part of her dowry. When he left her for my mother, he sold the saloon and gave his first wife part of the premises. In order to sustain herself and two small children, she started a small provision store and thus became Dehra's first lady shopkeeper.

I had just started freelancing from Dehra and was not keen on joining my mother and stepfather in Delhi. When 'Bibiji'—as I called her—offered me a portion of her flat on very reasonable terms, I accepted without hesitation and was to spend the next two years above her little shop on Rajpur Road. Almost fifty years later, the flat is still there, but it is now an ice cream parlour! Poetic justice, perhaps.

Bibiji sold the usual provisions. Occasionally, I lent a helping hand and soon learnt the names of the various lentils arrayed before us—*moong, malka, masoor, arhar, channa, rajma,* etc. She bought her rice, flour and other items wholesale from the *mandi*, and sometimes I would accompany her on an early morning march to the mandi (about two miles distant) where we would load a handcart with her purchases. She was immensely strong and could lift sacks of wheat or rice that left me gasping. I can't say I blame my rather skinny stepfather for staying out of her reach.

She had a helper, a Bihari youth, who would trundle the cart back to the shop and help with the loading and unloading. Before opening the shop (at around 8 a.m.) she would make our breakfast—*parathas* with my favourite *shalgam* pickle, and in winter, a delicious *kanji* made from the juice of red carrots. When the shop opened, I would go upstairs to do my writing while she conducted the day's business.

Sometimes she would ask me to help her with her accounts, or in making out a bill, for she was barely literate. But she was an astute shopkeeper; she knew instinctively who was good for credit and who was strictly *nakad* (cash). She would also warn me against friends who borrowed money without any intention of returning it; warnings that I failed to heed. Friends in perpetual need there were aplenty—Sudheer, William, Suresh and a couple of others—and I am amazed that I didn't have to borrow, too, considering the uncertain nature of my income. Those little cheques and money orders from magazines did not always arrive in time. But sooner or later something *did* turn up. I was very lucky.

Bibiji had a friend, a neighbour, Mrs Singh, an attractive woman in her thirties who smoked a hookah and regaled us with tales of ghosts and *chudails* from her village near Agra. We did not see much of her husband who was an excise inspector. He was busy making money.

Bibiji and Mrs Singh were almost inseparable, which was quite understandable in view of the fact that both had absentee husbands. They were really happy together. During the day Mrs Singh would sit in the shop, observing the customers. And afterwards she would entertain us with clever imitations of the more odd or eccentric among them. At night, after the shop was closed, Bibiji and her friend would make themselves comfortable on the same cot (creaking beneath their combined weights), wrap themselves in a *razai* or blanket and invite me to sit on the next *charpai* and listen to their yarns or tell them a few of my own. Mrs Singh had a small son, not very bright, who was continually eating laddoos, jalebis, *barfis* and other sweets. Quite appropriately, he was called Laddoo. And I believe he grew into one.

Bibiji's son and daughter were then at a residential school. They came home occasionally. So did Mr Singh, with more sweets for his son. He did not appear to find anything unusual in his wife's intimate relationship with Bibiji. His mind was obviously on other things.

Bibiji and Mrs Singh both made plans to get me married. When I protested, saying I was only twenty-three, they said I was old enough. Bibiji had an eye on an Anglo-Indian schoolteacher who sometimes came to the shop, but Mrs Singh turned her down, saying she had very spindly legs. Instead, she suggested the daughter of the local padre, a glamorous-looking, dusky beauty, but Bibiji vetoed the proposal, saying the young lady used too much make-up and already displayed too much fat around the waistline. Both agreed that I should marry a plain-looking girl who could cook, use a sewing machine and speak a little English.

'And be strong in the legs,' I added, much to Mrs Singh's approval.

They did not know it, but I was enamoured of Kamla, a girl from the hills, who lived with her parents in quarters behind the flat. She was always giving me mischievous glances with her dark, beautiful, expressive eyes. And whenever I passed her on the landing, we exchanged pleasantries and friendly banter; it was as though we had known each other for a long time. But she was already betrothed, and that too to a much older man, a widower, who owned some land outside the town. Kamla's family was poor, her father was in debt, and it was to be a marriage of convenience. There was nothing much I could do about it—landless and without prospects—but after the marriage had taken place and she had left for her new home, I befriended her younger brother and through him sent her my good wishes from time to time. She is just a distant memory now, but a bright one, like a forget-me-not blooming on a bare rock. Would I have married her, had I been able to? She was simple, unlettered; but I might have taken the chance.

Those two years on Rajpur Road were an eventful time, what with the visitations of Sudheer, the company of William and Suresh, the participation in Bibiji's little shop, the evanescent friendship with Kamla. I did a lot of writing and even sold a few stories here and there; but the returns were modest, barely adequate. Everyone was urging me to try my luck in Delhi. And so I bid goodbye to sleepy little Dehra (as it then was) and took a bus to the capital. I did no better there as a writer, but I found a job of sorts and that kept me going for a couple of years.

But to return to Bibiji, I cannot just leave her in limbo. She continued to run her shop for several years, and it was only failing health that forced her to close it. She sold the business and went to live with her married daughter in New Delhi. I saw her from time to time. In spite of high blood pressure, diabetes and eventually blindness, she lived on into her eighties. She was always glad to see me, and never gave up trying to find a suitable bride for me.

The last time I saw her, shortly before she died, she said, 'Ruskin, there is this widow—lady who lives down the road and comes over sometimes. She has two children but they are grown up. She feels lonely in her big house. If you like, I'll talk to her. It's time you settled down. And she's only sixty.'

'Thanks, Bibiji,' I said, holding both ears. 'But I think I'll settle down in my next life.'

A Love of Long Ago

Last week, as the taxi took me to Delhi, I passed through the small town in the foothills where I had lived as a young man.

Well, it's the only road to Delhi and one must go that way, but I seldom travel beyond the foothills. As the years go by, my visits to the city—any city—are few and far between. But whenever I am on that road, I look out of the window of my bus or taxi, to catch a glimpse of the first-floor balcony where a row of potted plants lend colour to an old and decrepit building. Ferns, a palm, a few bright marigolds, zinnias and nasturtiums—they made that balcony stand out from others; it was impossible to miss it.

But last week, when I looked out of the taxi window, the balcony garden had gone. A few broken pots remained; but the ferns had crumpled into dust, the palm had turned brown and yellow, and of the flowers nothing remained.

All these years I had taken that balcony garden for granted, and now it had gone. It jerked me upright in my seat. I looked back at the building for signs of life, but saw none. The taxi sped on. On my way back, I decided, I would look again. But it was as though a part of my life had come to an abrupt end; a part that I had almost come to take for granted. The link between youth and middle age, the bridge that spanned that gap, had suddenly been swept away.

And what had happened to Kamla, I wondered. Kamla, who had tended those plants all these years, knowing I would be looking out for them even though I might not see her, even though she might never see me.

Chance gives, and takes away, and gives again. But I would have to look elsewhere now, for the memories of my love, my young love, the girl who came into my life for a few blissful weeks and then went out of it for the remainder of our lives.

Was it almost thirty years ago that it all happened? How old was I then? Twenty-two at the most! And Kamla could not have been more than seventeen.

She had a laughing face, mischievous, always ready to break into a smile or peals of laughter. Sparkling brown eyes. How can I ever forget those eyes? Peeping at me from behind a window curtain, following me as I climbed the steps to my room—the room that was separated from her quarters by a narrow wooden landing that creaked loudly if I tried to move quietly across it. The trick was to dash across, as she did so neatly on her butterfly feet.

She was always on the move—flitting about on the verandah, running errands of no consequence, dancing on the steps, singing on the rooftop as she hung out the family washing. Only once was she still. That was when we met on the steps in the dark, and I stole a kiss, a sweet phantom kiss. She was very still then, very close, a butterfly drawing out nectar, and then she broke away from me and ran away laughing.

'What is your work?' she asked me one day.

'I write stories.'

'Will you write one about me?'

'Some day.'

I was living in a room above Moti-Bibi's grocery shop near the cinema. At night I could hear the soundtrack from the films. The songs did not help me much with my writing, nor with my affair, for Kamla could not come out at night. We met in the afternoons when the whole town took a siesta and expected us to do the same. Kamla had a young brother who worked for Moti-Bibi (a widow who was also my landlady) and it was through the boy that I had first met Kamla.

Moti-Bibi always a sent me a glass of kanji or sugar-cane juice or lime-juice (depending on the season) around noon. Usually the boy brought me the drink, but one day I looked up from my typewriter to see what at first I thought was an apparition hovering over me. She seemed to shimmer before me in the hot sunlight that came slashing through the open door. I looked up into her face and our eyes met over the rim of the glass. I forgot to take it from her.

What I liked about her was her smile. It dropped over her face slowly, like sunshine moving over brown hills. She seemed to give out some of the glow that was in her face. I felt it pour over me. And this golden feeling did not pass when she left the room. That was how I knew she was going to mean something special to me.

They were poor, but in time I was to realize that I was even poorer. When I discovered that plans were afoot to marry her to a widower of forty, I plucked up enough courage to declare that I would marry her myself. But my youth was no consideration. The widower had land and a generous gift of money for Kamla's parents. Not only was this offer attractive; it was customary. What had I to offer? A small rented room, a typewriter and a precarious income of two to three hundred rupees a month from freelancing. I told the brother that I would be famous one day, that I would be rich, that I would be writing bestsellers! He did not believe me. And who can blame him? I never did write bestsellers or become rich. Nor did I have parents or relatives to speak on my behalf.

I thought of running away with Kamla. When I mentioned it to her, her eyes lit up. She thought it would be great fun. Women in love can be more reckless than men! But I had read too many stories about runaway marriages ending in disaster, and I lacked the courage to go through with such an adventure. I must have known instinctively that it would not work. Where would we go, and how would we live? There would be no home to crawl back to, for either of us.

Had I loved more passionately, more fiercely, I might have felt compelled to elope with Kamla, regardless of the consequences. But it never became an intense relationship. We had so few moments together. Always stolen moments—on the stairs, on the roof, in the deserted junkyard behind the shops. She seemed to enjoy every moment of this secret affair. I fretted and longed for something more permanent. Her responses, so sweet and generous, only made my longing greater. But she seemed content with the immediate moment and what it offered.

And so the marriage took place, and she did not appear to be too dismayed about her future. But before she left for her husband's house, she asked me for some of the plants that I had owned and nourished on my small balcony.

'Take them all,' I said. 'I am leaving, anyway.'

'Where are you going?'

'To Delhi—to find work. But I shall come this way sometimes.'

'My husband's house is on the Delhi road. You will pass that way. I will keep these flowers where you can see them.'

We did not touch each other in parting. Her brother came and collected the plants. Only the cacti remained. Not a lover's plant, the cactus! I gave the cacti to my landlady and went to live in Delhi.

And whenever I passed through the old place, summer or winter, I looked out of the window of my bus or taxi and saw the garden flourishing on Kamla's balcony; leaf and fern abounded, and the flowers grew rampant on the sunny ledge.

Once I saw her, leaning over the balcony railing. I stopped the taxi and waved to her. She waved back, smiling like the sun breaking through clouds. She called to me to come up, but I said I would come another time. I never did visit her home, and I never saw her husband. Her parents had gone back to their village, her brother had vanished into the great grey spaces of India.

In recent years, after leaving Delhi and making my home in the hills, I have passed through the town less often; but the flowers have always been there, bright and glowing in their increasingly shabby surroundings. Except on this last journey of mine...

And on the return trip, only yesterday, I looked again, but the house was empty and desolate. I got out of the car and looked up at the balcony and called Kamla's name—called it after so many years—but there was no answer.

I asked questions in the locality. The old man had died, his wife had gone away, probably to her village. There had been no children. Would she return? No one could say. The house had been sold; it would be pulled down to make way for a block of flats.

I glanced once more at the deserted balcony, the withered, drooping plants. A butterfly flitted about the railing, looking in vain for a flower on which to alight. It settled briefly on my hand, before opening its wings and fluttering away into the blue.

The Last Time I Saw Delhi

I'd had this old and faded negative with me for a number of years and had never bothered to make a print from it. It was a picture of my maternal grandparents. I remembered my grandmother quite well, because a large part of my childhood had been spent in her house in Dehra after she had been widowed; but although everyone said she was fond of me, I remembered her as a stern, somewhat aloof person, of whom I was a little afraid.

I hadn't kept many family pictures and this negative was yellow and spotted with damp.

Then last week, when I was visiting my mother in hospital in Delhi, while she awaited her operation, we got talking about my grandparents, and I remembered the negative and decided I'd make a print for my mother.

When I got the photograph and saw my grandmother's face for the first time in twenty-five years, I was immediately struck by my resemblance to her. I have, like her, lived a rather spartan life, happy with my one room, just as she was content to live in a room of her own while the rest of the family took over the house! And like her, I have lived tidily. But I did not know the physical resemblance was so close—the fair hair, the heavy build, the wide forehead. She looks more like me than my mother!

In the photograph she is seated on her favourite chair, at the top of the verandah steps, and Grandfather stands behind her in the shadows thrown by a large mango tree which is not in the picture. I can tell it was a mango tree because of the pattern the leaves make on the wall. Grandfather was a slim, trim man, with a drooping moustache that was fashionable in the 1920s. By all accounts he had a mischievous sense of humour, although he looks unwell in the picture. He appears to have been quite swarthy. No wonder he was so successful in dressing up 'native' style and passing himself off as a street vendor. My mother tells me he even took my grandmother in on one occasion, and sold her a basketful of bad oranges. His character was in strong contrast to my grandmother's rather forbidding personality and Victorian sense of propriety; but they made a good match.

So here's the picture, and I am taking it to show my mother who lies in the Lady Hardinge Hospital, awaiting the removal of her left breast.

It is early August and the day is hot and sultry. It rained during the night, but now the sun is out and the sweat oozes through my shirt as I sit in the back of a stuffy little taxi taking me through the suburbs of Greater New Delhi.

On either side of the road are the houses of well-to-do Punjabis who came to Delhi as refugees in 1947 and now make up more than half the capital's population. Industrious, flashy, go-ahead people. Thirty years ago, fields extended on either side of this road as far as the eye could see. The Ridge, an outcrop of the Aravallis, was scrub jungle, in which the black buck roamed. Feroz Shah's fourteenth century hunting lodge stood here in splendid isolation. It is still here, hidden by petrol pumps and lost in the sounds of buses, cars, trucks and scooter rickshaws. The peacock has fled the forest, the black buck is extinct. Only the jackal remains. When, a thousand years from now, the last human has left this contaminated planet for some other star, the jackal and the crow will remain, to survive for years on all the refuse we leave behind.

It is difficult to find the right entrance to the hospital, because for about a mile along the Panchkuian Road the pavement has been obliterated by tea shops, furniture shops, and piles of accumulated junk. A public hydrant stands near the gate, and dirty water runs across the road.

I find my mother in a small ward. It is a cool, dark room, and a ceiling fan whirrs pleasantly overhead. A nurse, a dark, pretty girl from the South, is attending to my mother. She says, 'In a minute,' and proceeds to make an entry on a chart.

My mother gives me a wan smile and beckons me to come nearer. Her cheeks are slightly flushed, due possibly to fever, otherwise she looks her normal self. I find it hard to believe that the operation she will have tomorrow will only give her, at the most, another year's lease on life.

I sit at the foot of her bed. This is my third visit since I flew back from Jersey, using up all my savings in the process; and I will leave after the operation, not to fly away again, but to return to the hills which have always called me back.

'How do you feel?' I ask.

'All right. They say they will operate in the morning. They've stopped my smoking.'

'Can you drink? Your rum, I mean?'

'No. Not until a few days after the operation.'

She has a fair amount of grey in her hair, natural enough at fifty-four. Otherwise she hasn't changed much; the same small chin and mouth, lively brown eyes. Her father's face, not her mother's.

The nurse has left us. I produce the photograph and hand it to my mother.

'The negative was lying with me all these years. I had it printed yesterday.'

'I can't see without my glasses.'

The glasses are lying on the locker near her bed. I hand them to her. She puts them on and studies the photograph.

'Your grandmother was always very fond of you.'

'It was hard to tell. She wasn't a soft woman.'

'It was her money that got you to Jersey, when you finished school. It wasn't much, just enough for the ticket.'

'I didn't know that.'

'The only person who ever left you anything. I'm afraid I've nothing to leave you, either.'

'You know very well that I've never cared a damn about money. My father taught me to write. That was inheritance enough.'

'And what did I teach you?'

'I'm not sure… Perhaps you taught me how to enjoy myself now and then.'

She looked pleased at this. 'Yes, I've enjoyed myself between troubles. But your father didn't know how to enjoy himself. That's why we quarrelled so much. And finally separated.'

'He was much older than you.'

'You've always blamed me for leaving him, haven't you?'

'I was very small at the time. You left us suddenly. My father had to look after me, and it wasn't easy for him. He was very sick. Naturally, I blamed you.'

'He wouldn't let me take you away.'

'Because you were going to marry someone else.'

I break off; we have been over this before. I am not here as my father's advocate, and the time for recrimination has passed.

And now it is raining outside, and the scent of wet earth comes through the open doors, overpowering the odour of medicines and disinfectants. The dark-eyed nurse comes in again and informs me that the doctor will soon be on his rounds. I can come again in the evening or early morning before the operation.

'Come in the evening,' says my mother. 'The others will be here then.'

'I haven't come to see the others.'

'They are looking forward to seeing you.' 'They' being my stepfather and half-brothers.

'I'll be seeing them in the morning.'

'As you like…'

And then I am on the road again, standing on the pavement, on the fringe of a chaotic rush of traffic, in which it appears that every vehicle is doing its best to overtake its neighbour. The blare of horns can be heard in the corridors of the hospital, but everyone is conditioned to the noise and pays no attention to it. Rather, the sick and the dying are heartened by the thought that people are still well enough to feel reckless, indifferent to each other's safety! In Delhi, there is a feverish desire to be first in line, the first to get anything… This is probably because no one ever gets round to dealing with second-comers.

When I hail a scooter rickshaw and it stops a short distance away, someone elbows his way past me and gets in first. This epitomizes the philosophy and outlook of the Delhiwallah.

So I stand on the pavement waiting for another scooter, which doesn't come. In Delhi, to be second in the race is to be last.

I walk all the way back to my small hotel, with a foreboding of having seen my mother for the last time.

Letter to My Father

My Dear Dad,

Last week I decided to walk from the Dilaram Bazaar to Rajpur, a walk I hadn't undertaken for many years. It's only about five miles, along straight tree-lined road, houses most of the way, but here and there are open spaces where there are fields and patches of sal forest. The road hasn't changed much, but there is far more traffic than there used to be, which makes it noisy and dusty, detracting from the sylvan surroundings. All the same I enjoyed the walk—enjoyed the cool breeze that came down from the hills, the rich variety of trees, the splashes of colour where bougainvillea trailed over porches and enjoyed the passing cyclists and bullock carts, for they were reminders of the old days when cars, trucks and buses were the exception rather than the rule.

A little way above the Dilaram Bazaar, just where the canal goes under the road, stands the old house we used to know as Melville Hall, where three generations of Melvilles had lived. It is now a government office and looks dirty and neglected. Beside it still stands the little cottage, or guest house, where you stayed for a few weeks while the separation from my mother was being made legal. Then I went to live with you in Delhi.

At the time you were a guest of the Melvilles, I was in boarding school, so I did not share the cottage with you, although I was to share a number of rooms, tents and RAF hutments with you during the next two or three years. But of course I knew the Melvilles; I would visit them during school holidays in the years after you died, and they always spoke affectionately of you. One of the sisters was particularly kind to me; I think it was she who gave you the use of the cottage. This was Mrs Chill—she'd lost her husband to cholera during their honeymoon, and never married again. But I always found her cheerful and good-natured, loading me with presents on birthdays and at Christmas. The kindest people are often those who have come through testing personal tragedies.

A young man on a bicycle stops beside me and asks if I remember him. 'Not with that terrible moustache,' I confess. 'Romi from Sisters Bazaar.' Yes, of course. And I do remember him, although it must be about ten years since we last met; he was just a schoolboy then. Now, he tells me, he's a teacher. Not very well paid, as he works in a small private school. But better than being unemployed, he says. I have to agree.

'You're a good teacher, I'm sure, Romi. And it's still a noble profession…'

He looks pleased as he cycles away. When I see boys on bicycles I am always taken back to my boyhood days in Dehra. The roads in those uncrowded days were ideal for cyclists. Semi on his bicycle, riding down this very road in the light spring rain, provided me with the opening scene for my very first novel, *Room on the Roof,* written a couple of years after I'd said goodbye to Semi and Dehra and even, for a time, India.

That's how I remember him best—on his bicycle, wearing shorts, turban slightly askew, always a song on his lips. He was just fifteen. I was a couple of years older, but wasn't much of a bicycle rider, always falling off the machine when I was supposed to dismount gracefully. On one occasion I went sailing into a buffalo cart and fractured my forearm. Last year when Dr Murti, a senior citizen of the Doon, met me at a local function, he recalled how he had set my arm forty years ago. He was so nice to me that I forbore from telling him that my arm was still crooked.

Strictly an earth man, I have never really felt at ease with my feet off the ground. That's why I've been a walking person for most of my life. In planes, on ships, even in lifts, panic sets in.

As it did on that occasion when I was four or five, and you, Dad, decided to give me a treat by taking me on an Arab dhow across the Gulf of Kutch. Five minutes on that swinging, swaying sailing ship, was enough for me; I became so hysterical that I had to be taken off and rowed back to port. Not that the rowing boat was much better.

And then my mother thought I should go up with her in one those four-winged aeroplanes, a Tiger Moth I think—there's a photograph of it somewhere among my mementos—one of those contraptions that fell out of the sky without much assistance during the first World War. I think you could make them at home. Anyway, in this too I kicked and screamed with such abandon that the poor pilot had to be content with taxiing around the airfield and dropping me off at the first opportunity. That same plane with the same pilot crashed a couple of months later, only reinforcing my fears about machines that could not stay anchored to the ground.

To return to Somi, he was one of those friends I never saw again as an adult, so he remains transfixed in my memory as eternal youth, bright and forever loving… Meeting boyhood friends again after long intervals can often be disappointing, even disconcerting. Mere survival leaves its mark. Success is even more disfiguring. Those who climb to the top of a profession, or who seek the pinnacles of power, usually have to pay a heavy price for it, both physically and spiritually. It sounds like a cliche but it's true that money can't buy good health or a serene state of mind—especially the latter. You can fly to the ends of the earth in search of the best climate or the best medical treatment and the chances are that you will have to keep flying! Poverty is not ennobling—far from it—but it does at least teach you to make the most out of every rule.

I have often dreamt of Somi, and it is always the same dream, year after year, for over forty years. We meet in a fairground, set up on Dehra's old parade-ground which has seen better days. In the dream I am a man but he is still a boy. We wander through the fairground, enjoying all that it has to offer, and when the dream ends we are still in that fairground which probably represents heaven.

Heaven. Is that the real heaven—the perfect place with the perfect companion? And if you and I meet again, Dad, will you look the same, and will I be a small boy or an old man?

In my dreams of you I meet you on a busy street, after many lost years, and you receive me with the same old warmth, but where were you all those missing years? A traveller in another dimension, perhaps, returning occasionally just to see if I am all right.

Ruskin Bond

Tribute to a Dead Friend

Now that Thanh is dead, I suppose it is not too treacherous of me to write about him. He was only a year older than I. He died in Paris, in his twenty-second year, and Pravin wrote to me from London and told me about it. I will get more details from Pravin when he returns to India next month. Just now I only know that Thanh is dead.

It is supposed to be in very bad taste to discuss a person behind his back and to discuss a dead person is most unfair, for he cannot even retaliate. But Thanh had this very weakness of criticizing absent people and it cannot hurt him now if I do a little to expose his colossal ego.

Thanh was a fraud all right but no one knew it. He had beautiful round eyes, a flashing smile and a sweet voice and everyone said he was a charming person. He was certainly charming but I have found that charming people are seldom sincere. I think I was the only person who came anywhere near to being his friend for he had cultivated a special loneliness of his own and it was difficult to intrude on it.

I met him in London in the summer of '54. I was trying to become a writer while I worked part-time at a number of different jobs. I had been two years in London and was longing for the hills and rivers of India. Thanh was Vietnamese. His family was well-to-do and though the Communists had taken their home town of Hanoi, most of the family was in France, well established in the restaurant business. Thanh did not suffer from the same financial distress as other students whose homes were in Northern Vietnam. He wasn't studying anything in particular but practised assiduously on the piano, though the only thing he could play fairly well was Chopin's Funeral March.

My friend Pravin, a happy-go-lucky, very friendly Gujarati boy, introduced me to Thanh. Pravin, like a good Indian, thought all Asians were superior people, but he didn't know Thanh well enough to know that Thanh didn't like being an Asian.

At first, Thanh was glad to meet me. He said he had for a long time been wanting to make friends with an Englishman, a real Englishman, not one who was a Pole, a Cockney or a Jew; he was most anxious to improve his English and talk like Mr Glendenning of the BBC. Pravin, knowing that I had been born and bred in India, that my parents had been born and bred in India, suppressed his laughter with some difficulty. But Thanh was soon disillusioned. My accent was anything but English. It was a pronounced *chi-chi* accent.

'You speak like an Indian!' exclaimed Thanh, horrified. 'Are you an Indian?'

'He's Welsh,' said Pravin with a wink.

Thanh was slightly mollified. Being Welsh was the next best thing to being English. Only he disapproved of the Welsh for speaking with an Indian accent.

Later, when Pravin had gone, and I was sitting in Thanh's room drinking Chinese tea, he confided in me that he disliked Indians.

'Isn't Pravin your friend?' I asked.

'I don't trust him,' he said. 'I have to be friendly but I don't trust him at all. I don't trust any Indians.'

'What's wrong with them?'

'They are too inquisitive,' complained Thanh. 'No sooner have you met one of them than he is asking you who your father is, and what your job is, and how much money you have in the bank.'

I laughed and tried to explain that in India inquisitiveness is a sign of a desire for friendship, and that he should feel flattered when asked such personal questions. I protested that I was an Indian myself and he said if that was so he wouldn't trust me either.

But he seemed to like me and often invited me to his rooms. He could make some wonderful Chinese and French dishes. When we had eaten, he would sit down at his second-hand piano and play Chopin. He always complained that I didn't listen properly.

He complained of my untidiness and my unwarranted self-confidence. It was true that I appeared most confident when I was not very sure of myself. I boasted of an intimate knowledge of London's geography but I was an expert at losing my way and then blaming it on someone else.

'You are a useless person,' said Thanh, while with chopsticks I stuffed my mouth with delicious pork and fried rice. 'You cannot find your way anywhere. You cannot speak English properly. You do not know any people except Indians. How are you going to be a writer?'

'If I am as bad as all that,' I said, 'why do you remain my friend?'

'I want to study your stupidity,' he said.

That was why he never made any real friends. He loved to work out your faults and examine your imperfections. There was no such thing as a real friend, he said. He had looked everywhere but he could not find the perfect friend.

'What is your idea of a perfect friend?' I asked him. 'Does he have to speak perfect English?'

But sarcasm was only wasted on Thanh—he admitted that perfect English was one of the requisites of a perfect friend!

Sometimes, in moments of deep gloom, he would tell me that he did not have long to live.

'There is a pain in my chest,' he complained. 'There is something ticking there all the time. Can you hear it?'

He would bare his bony chest for me and I would put my ear to the offending spot. But I could never hear any ticking. 'Visit the hospital,' I advised. 'They'll give you an X-ray and a proper check-up.'

'I have had X-rays,' he lied. 'They never show anything.' Then he would talk of killing himself. This was his theme song: he had no friends, he was a failure as a musician, there was no other career open to him, he hadn't seen his family for five years, and he couldn't go back to Indo-China because of the Communists. He magnified his own troubles and minimized other people's troubles. When I was in hospital with an old acquaintance, amoebic dysentery, Pravin came to see me every day. Thanh, who was not very busy, came only once and never again. He said the hospital ward depressed him.

'You need a holiday,' I told him when I was out of hospital. 'Why don't you join the students' union and work on a farm for a week or two? That should toughen you up.'

To my surprise, the idea appealed to him and he got ready for the trip. Suddenly, he became suffused with goodwill towards all mankind. As evidence of his trust in me, he gave me the key of his room to keep (though he would have been secretly delighted if I had stolen his piano and chopsticks, giving him the excuse to say 'never trust an Indian or an Anglo-Indian'), and introduced me to a girl called Vu-Phuong, a small, very pretty Annamite girl who was studying at the Polytechnic. Miss Vu, Thanh told me, had to leave her lodgings next week and would I find somewhere else for her to stay? I was an experienced hand at finding bed-sitting rooms, having changed my own abode five times in six months (that sweet, nomadic London life!). As I found Miss Vu very attractive, I told her I would get her a room, one not far from my own, in case she needed any further assistance.

Later, in confidence, Thanh asked me not to be too friendly with Vu-Phuong as she was not to be trusted.

But as soon as he left for the farm, I went round to see Vu in her new lodgings which were one tube-station away from my own. She seemed glad to see me and as she too could make French and Chinese dishes I accepted her invitation to lunch. We had chicken noodles, soya sauce and fried rice. I did the washing-up. Vu said: 'Do you play cards, Ruskin?' She had a sweet, gentle voice that brought out all the gallantry in a man. I began to feel protective and hovered about her like a devoted cocker spaniel.

'I'm not much of a card-player,' I said.

'Never mind, I'll tell your fortune with them.'

She made me shuffle the cards. Then scattered them about on the bed in different patterns. I would be very rich, she said. I would travel a lot and I would reach the age of forty. I told her I was comforted to know it.

The month was June and Hampstead Heath was only ten minutes walk from the house. Boys flew kites from the hill and little painted boats scurried about on the ponds. We sat down on the grass, on the slope of the hill, and I held Vu's hand.

For three days I ate with Vu and we told each other our fortunes and lay on the grass on Hampstead Heath and on the fourth day I said, 'Vu, I would like to marry you.'

'I will think about it,' she said.

Thanh came back on the sixth day and said, 'You know, Ruskin, I have been doing some thinking and Vu is not such a bad girl after all. I will ask her to marry me. That is what I need—a wife!'

'Why didn't you think of it before?' I said. 'When will you ask her?'

'Tonight,' he said. 'I will come to see you afterwards and tell you if I have been successful.'

I shrugged my shoulders resignedly and waited. Thanh left me at six in the evening and I waited for him till ten o'clock, all the time feeling a little sorry for him. More disillusionment for Thanh! Poor Thanh…

He came in at ten o'clock, his face beaming. He slapped me on the back and said I was his best friend.

'Did you ask her?' I said.

'Yes. She said she would think about it. That is the same as "yes".'

'It isn't,' I said, unfortunately for both of us. 'She told me the same thing.'

Thanh looked at me as though I had just stabbed him in the back. Et tu Ruskin, was what his expression said.

We took a taxi and sped across to Vu's rooms. The uncertain nature of her replies was too much for both of us. Without a definite answer neither of us would have been able to sleep that night.

Vu was not at home. The landlady met us at the door and told us that Vu had gone to the theatre with an Indian gentleman.

Thanh gave me a long, contemptuous look.

'Never trust an Indian,' he said.

'Never trust a woman,' I replied.

At twelve o'clock I woke Pravin. Whenever I could not sleep, I went to Pravin. He knew the remedy for all ailments.

As on previous occasions, he went to the cupboard and produced a bottle of Cognac. We got drunk. He was seventeen and I was nineteen and we were both quite decadent.

Three weeks later I returned to India. Thanh went to Paris to help in his sister's restaurant. I did not hear of Vu-Phuong again.

And now, a year later, there is the letter from Pravin. All he can tell me is that Thanh died of some unknown disease. I wonder if it had anything to do with the ticking in his chest or with his vague threats of suicide. I doubt if I will ever know. And I will never know how much I hated Thanh, and how much I loved him, or if there was any difference between hating and loving him.

From Small Beginnings

And the last puff of the day-wind brought from the unseen villages, the scent of damp wood-smoke, hot cakes, dripping undergrowth, and rotting pine cones. That is the true smell of the Himalayas, and if once it creeps into the blood of a man, that man will at the last, forgetting all else, return to the hills to die.

—Rudyard Kipling

On the first clear September day, towards the end of the rains, I visited the pine knoll, my place of peace and power.

It was months since I'd last been there. Trips to the plains, a crisis in my affairs, involvements with other people and their troubles, and an entire monsoon had come between me and the grassy, pine-topped slope facing the Hill of Fairies (Pari Tibba to the locals). Now I tramped through late monsoon foliage—tall ferns, bushes festooned with flowering convolvulus—crossed the stream by way of its little bridge of stones and climbed the steep hill to the pine slope.

When the trees saw me, they made as if to turn in my direction. A puff of wind came across the valley from the distant snows. A long-tailed blue magpie took alarm and flew noisily out of an oak tree. The cicadas were suddenly silent. But the trees remembered me. They bowed gently in the breeze and beckoned me nearer, welcoming me home. Three pines, a straggling oak and a wild cherry. I went among them and acknowledged their welcome with a touch of my hand against their trunks—the cherry's smooth and polished; the pine's patterned and whorled; the oak's rough, gnarled, full of experience. He'd been there longest, and the wind had bent his upper branches and twisted a few, so that he looked shaggy and undistinguished. But like the philosopher who is careless about his dress and appearance, the oak has secrets, a hidden wisdom. He has learnt the art of survival!

While the oak and the pines are older than me and have been here many years, the cherry tree is exactly seven years old. I know because I planted it.

One day I had this cherry seed in my hand, and on an impulse I thrust it into the soft earth, and then went away and forgot all about it. A few months later I found a tiny cherry tree in the long grass. I did not expect it to survive. But the following year it was two feet tall. And then some goats ate its leaves, and a grass cutter's scythe injured the stem, and I was sure it would wither away. But it renewed itself, sprang up even faster, and within three years it was a healthy, growing tree, about five feet tall.

I left the hills for two years—forced by circumstances to make a living in Delhi—but this time I did not forget the cherry tree. I thought about it fairly often, sent telepathic messages of encouragement in its direction. And when, a couple of years ago, I returned in the autumn, my heart did a somersault when I found my tree sprinkled with pale pink blossom. (The Himalayan cherry flowers in November.) And later, when the fruit was ripe, the tree was visited by finches, tits, bulbuls and other small birds, all come to feast on the sour, red cherries.

Last summer I spent a night on the pine knoll, sleeping on the grass beneath the cherry tree. I lay awake for hours, listening to the chatter of the stream and the occasional tonk-tonk of a nightjar, and watching, through the branches overhead, the stars turning in the sky; I felt the power of the sky and earth, and the power of a small cherry seed...

And so when the rains are over, this is where I come, that I might feel the peace and power of this place. It's a big world and momentous events are taking place all the time. But this is where I have seen it happen.

This is where I will write my stories. I can see everything from here—my cottage across the valley; behind and above me, the town and the bazaar straddling the ridge; to the left, the high mountains and the twisting road to the source of the great river; below me, the little stream and the path to the village; ahead, the Hill of Fairies, the fields beyond; the wide valley below, and then another range of hills and then the distant plains. I can even see Prem Singh in the garden, putting the mattresses out in the sun.

From here he is just a speck on the far hill, but I know it is Prem by the way he stands. A man may have a hundred disguises, but in the end it is his posture that gives him away. Like my grandfather, who was a master of disguise and successfully roamed the bazaars as fruit vendor or basket maker; but we could always recognize him because of his pronounced slouch.

Prem Singh doesn't slouch, but he has this habit of looking up at the sky (regardless of whether it's cloudy or clear), and at the moment he's looking at the sky.

Eight years with Prem! He was just a sixteen-year-old boy when I first saw him, and now he has a wife and child.

I had been in the cottage for just over a year… He stood on the landing outside the kitchen door. A tall boy, dark, with good teeth and brown, deep-set eyes; dressed smartly in white drill—his only change of clothes. Looking for a job. I liked the look of him, but—

'I already have someone working for me,' I said.

'Yes, sir. He is my uncle.'

In the hills, everyone is a brother or an uncle.

'You don't want me to dismiss your uncle?'

'No, sir. But he says you can find a job for me.'

'I'll try. I'll make inquiries. Have you just come from your village?'

'Yes. Yesterday I walked ten miles to Pauri. There I got a bus.'

'Sit down. Your uncle will make some tea.'

He sat down on the steps, removed his white keds, wriggled his toes. His feet were both long and broad, large feet, but not ugly. He was unusually clean for a hill boy. And taller than most.

'Do you smoke?' I asked.

'No, sir.'

'It is true,' said his uncle, 'he does not smoke. All my nephews smoke, but this one, he is a little peculiar, he does not smoke—neither beedi nor hookah.'

'Do you drink?'

'It makes me vomit.'

'Do you take bhang?'

'No, sahib.'

'You have no vices. It's unnatural.'

'He is unnatural, sahib,' said his uncle.

'Does he chase girls?'

'They chase him, sahib.'

'So he left the village and came looking for a job.' I looked at him. He grinned, then looked away, began rubbing his feet.

'Your name is?'

'Prem Singh.'

'All right, Prem, I will try to do something for you.'

I did not see him for a couple of weeks. I forgot about finding him a job. But when I met him again, on the road to the bazaar, he told me that he had got a temporary job in the Survey, looking after the surveyor's tents.

'Next week we will be going to Rajasthan,' he said.

'It will be very hot. Have you been in the desert before?'

'No, sir.'

'It is not like the hills. And it is far from home.'

'I know. But I have no choice in the matter. I have to collect some money in order to get married.'

In his region there was a bride price, usually of two thousand rupees.

'Do you have to get married so soon?'

'I have only one brother and he is still very young. My mother is not well. She needs a daughter-in-law to help her in the fields and with the cows and in the house. We are a small family, so the work is greater.'

Every family has its few terraced fields, narrow and stony, usually perched on a hillside above a stream or river. They grow rice, barley, maize, potatoes—just enough to live on. Even if their produce is sufficient for marketing, the absence of roads makes it difficult to get the produce to the market towns. There is no money to be earned in the villages, and money is needed for clothes, soap, medicines, and for recovering the family jewellery from the moneylenders. So the young men leave their villages to find work, and to find work they must go to the plains. The lucky ones get into the army. Others enter domestic service or take jobs in garages, hotels, wayside tea shops, schools...

In Mussoorie the main attraction is the large number of schools, which employ cooks and bearers. But the schools were full when Prem arrived. He'd been to the recruiting centre at Roorkee, hoping to get into the army; but they found a deformity in his right foot, the result of a bone broken when a landslip carried him away one dark monsoon night; he was lucky, he said, that it was only his foot and not his head that had been broken.

He came to the house to inform his uncle about the job and to say goodbye. I thought: another nice person I probably won't see again; another ship passing in the night, the friendly twinkle of its lights soon vanishing in the darkness. I said 'come again', held his smile with mine so that I could remember him better, and returned to my study and my typewriter. The typewriter is the repository of a writer's loneliness. It stares unsympathetically back at him every day, doing its best to be discouraging. Maybe I'll go back to the old-fashioned quill pen and marble inkstand;

then I can feel like a real writer, Balzac or Dickens, scratching away into the endless reaches of the night... Of course, the days and nights are seemingly shorter than they need to be! They must be, otherwise why do we hurry so much and achieve so little, by the standards of the past...

Prem goes, disappears into the vast faceless cities of the plains, and a year slips by, or rather I do, and then here he is again, thinner and darker and still smiling and still looking for a job. I should have known that hill men don't disappear altogether. The spirit-haunted rocks don't let their people wander too far, lest they lose them forever.

I was able to get him a job in the school. The Headmaster's wife needed a cook. I wasn't sure if Prem could cook very well but I sent him along and they said they'd give him a trial. Three days later the Headmaster's wife met me on the road and started gushing all over me. She was the type who gushes.

'We're so grateful to you! Thank you for sending me that lovely boy. He's so polite. And he cooks very well. A little too hot for my husband, but otherwise delicious—just delicious! He's a real treasure—a lovely boy.' And she gave me an arch look—the famous look that she used to captivate all the good-looking young prefects who became prefects, it was said, only if she approved of them.

I wasn't sure that she didn't want something more than a cook, and I only hoped that Prem would give every satisfaction.

He looked cheerful enough when he came to see me on his off-day.

'How are you getting on?' I asked.

'Lovely,' he said, using his mistress's favourite expression.

'What do you mean—lovely? Do they like your work?'

'The memsahib likes it. She strokes me on the cheek whenever she enters the kitchen. The sahib says nothing. He takes medicine after every meal.'

'Did he always take medicine—or only now that you're doing the cooking?'

'I am not sure. I think he has always been sick.'

He was sleeping in the Headmaster's verandah and getting sixty rupees a month. A cook in Delhi got a hundred and sixty. And a cook in Paris or New York got ten times as much. I did not say as much to Prem. He might ask me to get him a job in New York. And that would be the last I saw of him! He, as a cook, might well get a job making curries off Broadway; I, as a writer, wouldn't get to first base. And only my Uncle Ken knew the secret of how to make a living without actually doing any work. But then, of course, he had four sisters. And each of them was married to a fairly prosperous husband. So Uncle Ken divided his year among them. Three months with Aunt Ruby in Nainital. Three months with Aunt Susie in Kashmir. Three months with my mother (not quite so affluent) in Jamnagar. And three months in the Vet Hospital in Bareilly, where Aunt Mabel ran the hospital for her veterinary husband. In this way, he never overstayed his welcome. A sister can look after a brother for just three months at a time and no more. Uncle Ken had it worked out to perfection.

But I had no sisters and I couldn't live forever on the royalties of a single novel. So I had to write others. So I came to the hills.

The hill men go to the plains to make a living. I had to come to the hills to try and make mine.

'Prem,' I said, 'why don't you work for me?'

'And what about my uncle?'

'He seems ready to desert me any day. His grandfather is ill, he says, and he wants to go home.'

'His grandfather died last year.'

'That's what I mean—he's getting restless. And I don't mind if he goes. These days he seems to be suffering from a form of sleeping sickness. I have to get up first and make his tea…'

Sitting here under the cherry tree, whose leaves are just beginning to turn yellow, I rest my chin on my knees and gaze across the valley to where Prem moves about in the garden. Looking back over the seven years he has been with me, I recall some of the nicest things about him. They come to me in no particular order—just pieces of cinema—coloured slides slipping across the screen of memory…

Prem rocking his infant son to sleep—crooning to him, passing his large hand gently over the child's curly head—Prem following me down to the police station when I was arrested (on a warrant from Bombay, charging me with writing an allegedly obscene short story!) and waiting outside until I reappeared; his smile, when I found him in Delhi, his large, irrepressible laughter, most in evidence when he was seeing an old Laurel and Hardy movie.

Of course, there were times when he could be infuriating, stubborn, deliberately pig-headed, sending me little notes of resignation—but I never found it difficult to overlook these little acts of self-indulgence. He had brought much love and laughter into my life, and what more could a lonely man ask for?

It was his stubborn streak that limited the length of his stay in the Headmaster's household. Mr Good was tolerant enough. But Mrs Good was one of those women who, when they are pleased with you, go out of their way to help, pamper and flatter; and who, when they are displeased, become vindictive, going out of their way to harm or destroy. Mrs Good sought power—over her husband, her dog, her favourite pupils, her servant… She had absolute power over the husband and the dog, partial power over her slightly bewildered pupils, and none at all over Prem, who missed the subtleties of her designs upon his soul. He did not respond to her mothering, or to the way in which she tweaked him on the cheeks, brushed against him in the kitchen and made admiring remarks about his looks and physique. Memsahibs, he knew, were not for him. So he kept a stony face and went diligently about his duties. And she felt slighted, put in her place. Her liking turned to dislike. Instead of admiring remarks, she began making disparaging remarks about his looks, his clothes, his manners. She found fault with his cooking. No longer was it 'lovely'. She even accused him of taking away the dog's meat and giving it to a poor family living on the hillside—no more heinous crime could be imagined! Mr Good threatened him with dismissal. So Prem became stubborn. The following day he withheld the dog's food altogether; threw it down the *khud* where it was seized upon by innumerable strays, and went off to the pictures.

It was the end of his job. 'I'll have to go home now,' he told me. 'I won't get another job in this area. The *mem* will see to that.'

'Stay a few days,' I said.

'I have only enough money with which to get home.'

'Keep it for going home. You can stay with me for a few days, while you look around. Your uncle won't mind sharing his food with you.'

His uncle did mind. He did not like the idea of working for his nephew as well; it seemed to him no part of his duties. And he was apprehensive that Prem might get his job.

So Prem stayed no longer than a week.

Here on the knoll the grass is just beginning to turn October yellow. The first clouds approaching winter cover the sky. The trees are very still. The birds are silent. Only a cricket keeps singing on the oak tree. Perhaps there will be a storm before evening. A storm like that in which Prem arrived at the cottage with his wife and child—but that's jumping too far ahead…

After he had returned to his village, it was several months before I saw him again. His uncle told me he had taken a job in Delhi. There was an address. It did not seem complete, but I resolved that when I was next in Delhi I would try to see him.

The opportunity came in May, as the hot winds of summer blew across the plains. It was the time of year when people who can afford it try to get away to the hills. I dislike New Delhi at the best of times, and I hate it in summer. People compete with each other in being bad-tempered and mean. But I had to go down—I don't remember why, but it must have seemed very necessary at the time—and I took the opportunity to try and see Prem.

Nothing went right for me. Of course the address was all wrong, and I wandered about in a remote, dusty, treeless colony called Vasant Vihar (Spring Garden) for over two hours, asking all the domestic servants I came across if they could put me in touch with Prem Singh of Village Koli, Pauri Garhwal. There were innumerable Prem Singhs, but apparently none who belonged to Village Koli. I returned to my hotel and took two days to recover from heatstroke before returning to Mussoorie, thanking God for mountains!

And then the uncle gave me notice. He'd found a better paid job in Dehra Dun and was anxious to be off. I didn't try to stop him.

For the next six months I lived in the cottage without any help. I did not find this difficult. I was used to living alone. It wasn't service that I needed but companionship. In the cottage it was very quiet. The ghosts of long-dead residents were sympathetic but unobtrusive. The song of the whistling thrush was beautiful, but I knew he was not singing for me. Up the valley came the sound of a flute, but I never saw the flute player. My affinity was with the little red fox who roamed the hillside below the cottage. I met him one night and wrote these lines:

> *As I walked home last night*
> *I saw a lone fox dancing*
> *In the cold moonlight.*
> *I stood and watched—then*
> *Took the low road, knowing*
> *The night was his by right.*
> *Sometimes, when words ring true,*
> *I'm like a lone fox dancing*
> *In the morning dew.*

During the rains, watching the dripping trees and the mist climbing the valley, I wrote a great deal of poetry. Loneliness is of value to poets. But poetry didn't bring me much money, and funds were low. And then, just as I was wondering if I would have to give up my freedom and take a job again, a publisher bought the paperback rights of one of my children's stories, and I was free to live and write as I pleased—for another three months!

That was in November. To celebrate, I took a long walk through the Landour Bazaar and up the Tehri road. It was a good day for walking, and it was dark by the time I returned to the outskirts of the town. Someone stood waiting for me on the road above the cottage. I hurried past him.

If I am not for myself,
Who will be for me?
And if I am not for others,
What am I?
And if not now, when?

I startled myself with the memory of these words of Hillel, the ancient Hebrew sage. I walked back to the shadows where the youth stood, and saw that it was Prem.

'Prem!' I said. 'Why are you sitting out here, in the cold? Why did you not go to the house?'

'I went, sir, but there was a lock on the door. I thought you had gone away.'

'And you were going to remain here, on the road?'

'Only for tonight. I would have gone down to Dehra in the morning.'

'Come, let's go home. I have been waiting for you. I looked for you in Delhi, but could not find the place where you were working.'

'I have left them now.'

'And your uncle has left me. So will you work for me now?'

'For as long as you wish.'

'For as long as the gods wish.'

We did not go straight home, but returned to the bazaar and took our meal in the Sindhi Sweet Shop; hot puris and strong sweet tea.

We walked home together in the bright moonlight. I felt sorry for the little fox dancing alone.

That was twenty years ago, and Prem and his wife and three children are still with me. But we live in a different house now, on another hill.

Once upon a Mountain Time

My solitude is not my own, for I see now how much it belongs to them—and that I have a responsibility for it in their regard, not just in my own. It is because I am one with them that I owe it to them to be alone, and when I am alone they are not 'they' but my own self. There are no strangers!

—Thomas Merton
From *Conjectures of a Guilty Bystander*

The trees stand watch over my day-to-day life. They are the guardians of my conscience. I have no one else to answer to, so I live and work under the generous but highly principled supervision of the trees—especially the deodars, who stand on guard, unbending, on the slope above the cottage. The oak and maples are a little more tolerant; they have had to put up with a great deal, their branches continually lopped for fuel and fodder. 'What would they think?' I ask myself on many an occasion. 'What would they like me to do?' And I do what I think they would approve of most!

Well, it's nice to have someone to turn to…

The leaves are a fresh pale green in the spring rain. I can look at the trees from my window—look down on them almost, because the window is on the first floor of the cottage, and the hillside runs away at a sharp angle into the ravine. The trees and I know each other quite intimately, and we have much to say to each other from time to time.

I do nearly all my writing at this window seat. The trees watch over me as I write. Whenever I look up, they remind me that they are there. They are my best critics. As long as I am aware of their presence, I can try to avoid the trivial and the banal.

Ramesh, the son of the municipal cleaner, looms darkly in the doorway. He is a stunted boy with a large head, but has wide, gentle eyes. His orange-coloured trousers brighten up the surrounding gloom.

'What do you want, Ramesh?'

'Newspapers.'

'To sell to the kabari?'

'No. For wrapping my schoolbooks.'

'Well, take a few.' I give him half a dozen old newspapers; the headlines already look meaningless. 'Sit down and wait for it to stop raining.'

He sits awkwardly on a *mora*.

'And what is your cousin Vinod doing these days?' (Vinod is a good-looking ne'er-do-well who seldom does anything apart from hanging around cinema halls.)

'Nothing.'

'Doesn't he go to school?'

'He has stopped going to school. He got a job at fifty rupees a month, but he left after a week. He says he will join the army in September.'

The rain stops and Ramesh departs. The clouds begin to break up, the sun strikes the steep hill on my left. A woman is chopping up sticks. I hear the tinkle of cowbells. Water drips from a leaking drainpipe. And suddenly, clear and pure, the song of the whistling thrush emerges like a dark, sweet secret from the depths of the ravine.

Bijju is back from school and is taking his parents' cattle out to graze. He sees me at the window and waves, then grabs his favourite cow Neelu by the tail and tells her to hurry up.

Bijju is twelve, a fair, good-looking Garhwali boy. His younger sister and brother are very pretty children. The father, an electrician, is a rather self-effacing man. The mother is a strong, hard woman. I have watched her on the hillside cutting grass. She has the muscular calves of a man, solid feet and heavy hands; but she is a handsome woman. They live in a rented outhouse further up the hill.

Bijju doesn't visit me very often. He is rather shy. But one day I looked out of the window and there he was in the branches of the oak tree, smiling at me rather hesitantly. We spoke to each other across the three or four yards that separate house from oak tree.

'If I jump, I can land in your tree,' I said.

'And if I jump, I will be in your house,' said Bijju.

'Come on then, jump!'

But he shook his head. He was afraid of me. The tree was safe. He put his arms round the thickest branch and held himself close to it. He looked very right in the tree, as though he belonged there, a boy of the woods, a tree spirit peeping out from a house of glossy new leaves.

'Come on, jump!'

'*You* jump,' he said.

In the evening, his sister brings the cows home. I meet her on the path above the house. She is only a year younger than Bijju, a very bonny girl who is going to be ravishingly beautiful when she grows up, if they don't marry her off too soon. She too has the same timid smile. But if these children are timid of humans, they are not afraid in the forest, and often wander far afield with Neelu the blue cow and others. (And S, who is eighteen and educated at an English-medium private school, wouldn't go alone into the forest if you paid him!) But the trees know their own. They will cherish the wild spirits and frighten the daylights out of the tame.

The whistling thrush is here, bathing in the rainwater puddle beneath the window. He loves this spot. So now, when there is no rain, I fill the puddle with water, just so that my favourite bird keeps coming.

His bath finished, he perches on a branch of the walnut tree. His glossy blue-black wings glitter in the sunshine. At any moment, he will start singing.

Here he goes! He tries out the tune, whistling to himself, and then, confident of the notes, sends his thrilling full-throated voice far over the forest. The song dies down, trembling, lingering in the air; starts again, joyfully, and then suddenly stops, as though the singer had forgotten the words or the tune.

Vinod, the ne'er-do-well, turns up with a friend, asking me to give them some work. They want to go to the pictures but have no money.

'You can dig up this slope below the house,' I tell them. 'The soil is good for growing vegetables.'

This sounds too much like hard work for Vinod, who says, 'We'll come and do it tomorrow.'

'No, we'll do it now,' says his more enterprising friend, and to my surprise they set to work.

Now and then, I look out of the window. They are digging away with fair enthusiasm.

After about half an hour, Vinod keeps sitting down for short rests, to the increasing irritation of his partner. They are soon snapping at each other. Vinod looks very funny when he sulks, because he has a snub nose, and somehow a snub nose and a ferocious expression only reminds me of Richmal Crompton's William. But the work gets done by evening, and they are quite pleased with their earnings.

Bijju is right at the top of a big oak. The branches sway to his movements. He grins down at me and waves. The higher he is in the tree, the more confident he becomes. It is only when he is down on the ground that he becomes shy and speechless.

He has allowed the cows to wander, and presently his mother's deep voice can be heard calling, 'Neelu, Neelu!' (The other cows don't have names.) And then: 'Where is that wretched boy?'

Sir Edmund Gibson has come up. He spends the summer in the big house just down the road. He is wheezing a lot and says he has water in his lungs—and who wouldn't, at the age of eighty-six.

'Ruskin, my advice to you,' he says, 'is never to live beyond the age of eighty.'

'Well, once ought to be enough, sir.'

He is a big man, but not as red in the face as he used to be. His Gurkha manservant, Tirlok, has to push him up the steep slope to my gate.

Sir Edmund was once the British Resident in the Kathiawar states. He knew my parents in Jamnagar, when I was just five or six. He is a bachelor and is looked after by his servants.

His farm at Ramgarh doesn't make any money, and he will probably give it to his retainers.

When Sir Edmund was Resident, he was once shot at from close range by a terrorist. The man took four shots and missed every time. He must have been a terrible shot, or perhaps the pistol was faulty, because Sir E presents a very large target.

He also treasures two letters from Mahatma Gandhi, which were written from prison.

'I liked Gandhi,' says Sir E. 'He had a sense of humour. No politician today has a sense of humour. They all take themselves far too seriously. But not Gandhi. He took his work seriously, but not himself. When I went to see him in prison, I asked him if he was comfortable, and he smiled and said, "Even if I was, I wouldn't admit it!"'

Sir E's servant brings tea, but there isn't any milk. I think I have exhausted Bijju's supply.

Now it's dusk and the trees are very still, very quiet. Far away, I can hear the *chuk-chuk-chuk* of a nightjar. The lights on Landour hill come on, one by one. Prem is singing in the kitchen. There is a whirr of wings as the king crows fly into the trees to roost for the night. A rustling in the dry leaves below the window. A snake? Field rats? Porcupines? It is now too dark to find out. The day has ended, and the trees move closer together in the dark.

We are treated to one of those spectacular electric storms that are fairly frequent at this time of the year, late spring or early summer. The clouds grow very dark, then send bolts of lightning sizzling across the sky, lighting up the entire range of mountains.

When the storm is directly overhead, there is hardly a pause in the frequency of the lightning; it is like a bright light being switched on and off with barely a second's interruption.

John Lang, writing in Dickens's magazine *Household Words* in 1853, almost exactly 120 years ago, had this to say about one of our storms:

> I have seen a storm on the heights of Jura—such a storm as Lord Byron describes. I have seen lightning, and heard thunder in Australia; I have, off Tierra del Fuego, the Cape of Good Hope, and the coast of Java, kept watch in thunderstorms which have drowned in their roaring the human voice, and made everyone deaf and stupefied; but these storms are not to be compared with a thunderstorm at Mussoorie or Landour.

Forgotten today, Lang was a popular writer in the mid-nineteenth century. He was also a successful barrister, who represented the Rani of Jhansi in her litigation with the East India Company. He spent his last years in Mussoorie and was buried in the Camel's Back cemetery. His grave proved to be almost as elusive as his books, and I found it with some difficulty, overgrown with moss and periwinkle. Prem and I cleaned it up until the inscription stood out quite clearly.

Prem won't come home on a stormy night like this. He is afraid of the dark, but more than that, he is afraid of thunderstorms. It is as though the gods are ganging up against him. So he will spend the night in the school quarters, where he is visiting his mother who is staying there with relatives.

In the morning, he turns up with a sheepish grin, saying it got very late and he didn't want to wake me in the middle of the night. I try to feign anger, but it is a gloriously fresh and spirited morning; impossible to feel angry. A strong breeze is driving the clouds away, and the sun keeps breaking through. The birds are particularly active. The king crows (who weren't here last year) seem to have taken up residence in the oaks. I don't know why they are called crows. They are slim, elegant black birds, with long forked tails, and their call, far from being a caw, is quite musical, though slightly metallic. The mynahs are very busy, very noisy, looking for a nesting site in the roof. The babblers are raking over fallen leaves, snapping up absent-minded grasshoppers. Now and then, the whistling thrush bursts into song, and then all other bird sounds pale into insignificance. Bijju has taken his cows to pasture and now scrambles up the hill, heading for home; he is late for school, and that is why he is in a hurry. He waves to me.

Both he and Prem have the high cheekbones and the deep-set eyes of the hill people. Prem, of course, is tall and dark. Bijju is small and fair; but he will grow into a sturdy young fellow.

The rain has driven the scorpions out of their rocks and crevices. I found one sitting on a loaf of bread. Up came his sting when we disturbed him. Prem tipped him out on the verandah steps and he scurried off into the bushes. I do not kill insects and other small creatures if I can help it, but there is a limit to my hospitality. I spared a centipede yesterday even though, last year, I was bitten by one which had occupied the seat of my pyjamas. Our hill scorpions and centipedes are not as dangerous as those found in the plains, and probably the same can be said for the people.

Prem tells me that his uncle is immune to scorpion stings, and allows himself to be stung in order to demonstrate his immunity. Apparently his mother was stung by a scorpion shortly before his birth!

Azure butterflies flit about the garden like flakes of sky.

Learnt two new words: bosky = wooded, bushy (bosky shadows); girding = jesting, jeering (girding schoolboys, girding monkeys).

Poor old Sir E is in a bad way. He has diarrhoea, and little or no control over the muscles that play a part in controlling the bowels. The Gurkha servant called me, and I went over with some tablets. Sir E looked quite exhausted and was panting from the exertion of walking from his bed to the toilet. The Gurkha is very good—gives Sir E his bath, dresses him, helps him on with his pyjamas.

Grateful for my alacrity in coming over with some medicine, Sir E offers me a whisky-and-soda (the first time he has ever done this), and pours himself a stiff brandy. He dozes off now and then, but the laboured breathing won't stop. He is a tough old tree, but I think he is beginning to find his massive frame something of a burden.

I make an attempt at conversation. 'Were you at Oxford or Cambridge?'

'Oxford. I joined Oxford in 1905 and left in 1909. Came out to India in 1910.'

He has an excellent memory, unlike Mr Biggs (a retired headmaster) who is ten years younger but will repeat the same story thrice in ten minutes.

'And when were you knighted?' I ask.

'1939 or 1940.'

He is too tired to do much talking. I let him doze off, and give my attention to the whisky. The log fire burns well, the flames cast their glow on Sir E's white hair and hanging jowls. The stertorous breathing grows in volume. He wakes up suddenly, complains that the fire is too hot; Tirlok opens the window. I finish the whisky; he doesn't offer another. It is his supper time, anyway, and I suggest soup and toast. 'Call me in the night if you have any trouble,' I say. He looks very grateful. The loneliness must press upon him a great deal.

I go out into the night. The trees are bending to a strong wind. From the foliage comes a deep sigh, the voice of leagues of trees sleeping and half disturbed in their sleep. The sky is clear, tremendous with stars.

For the first time this year I hear the barbet, a sure sign the summer is upon us. Its importunate cry carries far across the hills. It can keep this up for hours, like a beggar. Indeed, its plaint— *un-neow, un-neow!*—has been likened in the hills to that of the spirit of the village moneylender who has died before he can collect his dues. ('Un-neow!' is a cry for justice!)

It is difficult to spot the barbet. It is a fat green bird (no bigger than a mynah, but fatter), and it usually perches at the very top of a deodar or cypress.

The whistling thrush comes to bathe in the rainwater puddle. Sir E is much better and is sitting outside in the shade of an old oak. They are probably about the same age. What a rugged constitution this man must have; first, to survive, as a young man, all those diseases such as cholera, typhoid, dysentery, malaria, even the plague, which carried off so many Europeans in India (including my father); and now, an old man, to live and battle with congested lungs, a bad heart, weak eyes, bad teeth, recalcitrant bowels and god knows what else, and still be able to derive some pleasure from living. His old Hillman car is equally indestructible. But, like Sir E, it can't get up the hill any more; he uses it only in Dehradun.

I think his longevity is due simply to the fact that he refuses to go to bed when he is unwell. No amount of diarrhoea, or water in his lungs, will prevent him from getting up, dressing, writing letters or getting on with the latest Wodehouse (a contemporary of his) or *Blackwood's Magazine*, to which he has been subscribing for the last fifty years! He was pleased to find that some of my own essays were appearing in *Blackwood's*. Nothing will keep him from his four o'clock tea or his evening whisky-and-soda. He is determined, I am sure, to die in his chair, with all his clothes on. The thought of being taken unawares while still in his pyjamas must be something of a nightmare to him. (His favourite film, he once told me, was *They Died With Their Boots On*.)

The cicadas are tuning up for their first summer concert. Even Mrs Biggs, who is hard of hearing, can hear them. Yesterday, I met her on the road above the cottage and exchanged pleasantries. Up at Wynberg the girls' choir was hard at practice.

'The girls are in good voice today,' I remarked.

'Oh yes, Mr Bond,' she said, presuming I meant the cicadas. 'They do it with their legs, don't they?'

A week in Delhi. It is still only early summer, but the heat almost knocks one over. Slept on a roof, along with thousands of mosquitoes. It cools off in the early hours, but only briefly, before the sun comes shouting over the rooftops. The dust lies thick on floors, leaves, books, people. May's golden dust!

Now, back in the hills, I am struck first of all by the silence. The house, too, makes itself felt. It has been here too long not to have acquired a personality of its own. It is not a cheerful-looking place, nor is it exactly gloomy. My bedroom is rather dark (because it faces the abrupt slope of the hillside), but there is a wild cherry growing just outside the window—a cherry tree which I nurtured ever since it was a tiny seedling, five or six years ago, and which has now grown so tall that the branches tap against the roof whenever there is a breeze. It is a funny sort of cherry because it flowers in November instead of in the spring like other fruit trees. Small birds and small boys willingly eat the berries, which are too acid for adult palates.

The sitting room, with its two big windows looking out on the forest, is a bright room. Most of the wall space is taken up by my books. The rugs are worn and tattered—they have been with the house right from the beginning, I think—and I can't afford new ones.

On books and friends I spend my money;
For stones and bricks I haven't any.

Sir E, quite recovered from his recent illness, has gone down to Dehra again to attend to his farm and the demands of his farm workers. He should be back at the end of the month.

The brilliant blue-black of the whistling thrush shows up best when the sun is glinting off its back, but this seldom happens, because the bird likes to keep to the shade where it is almost black. Hopping about, it reminds me of Fred Astaire dancing in top hat and tails.

Now that it's getting hot, my small pool attracts a number of afternoon visitors—the mynahs, babblers, a bulbul, a magpie. After their dip they perch in the cherry tree to dry themselves, and I can watch them without getting up from my bed, where I take an afternoon siesta. I reserve the afternoons for doing nothing. 'Silence and non-action are the root of all things,' says Tao. Especially on a drowsy afternoon.

But I haven't seen the whistling thrush for several days. Perhaps he is offended at having to share the pool which he was the first to discover. I haven't heard his song either, which probably means that he has moved down to the stream where it is cooler and shadier.

Prem's mother and younger sister come for a few days. His mother is a very quiet woman and doesn't say much even to her son. She is quite handsome, although she looks rather worn and tired, due probably to her recent illness.

His little sister, about four, is a friendly little gazelle; not in the least pretty, but lively and intelligent. She will have to stay here for at least six months to be properly treated for her incipient tuberculosis. There is no treatment to be had in their village.

While I am resting, still exhausted from an attack of hill dysentery (who called this a health resort?), Sir E blows in, red-faced, as distressed as a stranded whale. His Gurkha servant has walked out, after quarrelling with his wife and mother-in-law, and has taken with him his twin sons (aged one and a half). I calm Sir E, tell him Tirlok will be back in a day or two—he is probably trying to show how indispensable he is!

Sir E takes out a cigarette and strikes a match, and the entire matchbox flares up, burning a finger. Definitely not his day. I apply Burnol.

'It's all that damned girl's fault,' he says. 'She has a vile temper, just like her mother. We were very wise not to marry, Ruskin.'

Wise or not, I seem to have acquired a family all the same.

∿

Hundreds of white butterflies are flitting through the forest.

When Prem told his mother that I kept a human skull in my sitting room (given to me by Anil, a medical student, and *not* pinched from the cemetery as some suppose), she told him not to spend too much time near it. If he did, he would be possessed by the spirit of the woman who had originally inhabited the skull.

But Prem, at the present time, is immune to spirits, having succumbed to the charms of his young wife who stays downstairs with his mother. They have only been married a few months. He leans over the balcony, chatting with her; advises her on how to keep the courtyard clean; then makes her a small broom from the twigs of a wild honeysuckle bush. She enjoys all the attention she is getting.

The sky is overcast this morning. Dust from the plains has formed a thick haze which hides the valley and the mountains. We are badly in need of rain. Down in the plains, over 200 people have died of heatstroke.

I haven't seen Bijju for some days, but this morning his sister, Binya, was out with the cows. What a sturdy little girl she is; and pretty, too. I will write a story about her.[*]

⌒

'We'll take you to the pictures one day, Sir Edmund.'

'Yes, I must see one more picture before I die.'

So there comes a time when we start thinking in terms of the last picture, the last book, the last visit, the last party. But Sir E's remark is matter of fact. He is given to boredom but not to melancholy.

And he has a timeless quality. I have noticed this in other old people; they look more permanent than the young.

He sums it all up by saying, 'I don't mind being dead, but I shall miss being alive.'

A number of small birds are here to bathe and drink in the little pool beneath the cherry tree: hunting parties of tits—grey tits,

---

[*]This story was called 'The Blue Umbrella'.

red-headed tits and green-backed tits—and two delicate little willow warblers. They take turns in the pool. While the green-backs are taking a plunge, the red-heads wait patiently on the moss-covered rocks, coming down later to sip daintily at the edge of the pool; they don't like getting their feet wet! Finally, when they have all gone away, the whistling thrush arrives and indulges in an orgy of bathing, as he now has the entire pool to himself.

The babblers are adept at snapping up the little garden skinks that scuttle about in the leaves and grass. The skinks are quite brittle and are easily broken to pieces with a few hard raps of the beak. Then down they go! Babblers are also good at sifting through dead leaves and seizing upon various insects.

The honeybees push their way through the pursed lips of the antirrhinum and disappear completely. A few minutes later they stagger out again, bottoms first.

1 June

The dry spell continues. It is only before sunrise that there is any freshness in the air.

At dawn I said, 'Day, you will not begin without me.' I was up with the whistling thrush at five. The cicadas were tuning up, the crickets were already in full cry, and the whistling thrush was calling most sweetly. As none of these songsters could be seen, it was as though the forest itself was singing.

Feeling the dawn wind stir, I was happy that I had met the day at its very beginning.

When the sun came up, the day became sultry and oppressive. I had to walk two miles to Ban Suman and back. There was no shade anywhere along the road. But we are equipped with legs for the purpose of walking. As more and more people grow dependent on their cars, a new species of humans will evolve. Around the turn of the twenty-second century, I can see legless humans being born. By then, of course, there will be flying wheelchairs.

A pall of dust hangs over the mountain.

Someone asked Sir E if he could shoot a bird on his land at Ramgarh. The man wanted the bird for dissection in a biology lab. Sir E refused.

'It's in the interests of science,' protested the man. 'Do you think a bird is better than a human?'

'Infinitely,' said Sir E. 'Infinitely better.'

He goes down today to pay his farmhands. He will return in a few days unless it gets cooler in Dehra. He complains of being very bored up here, for he can't get about, and in Dehra he has his Hillman. 'I'm *rotting* with boredom,' he says.

Vinod, I hear, is laid low with a fever—the result of a day's hard work. He is now in retirement for the rest of the season.

Walked five miles down the Tehri road to Suakholi, where I rested in a small tea shop, a loose stone structure with a tin roof held down by stones. It serves the bus passengers, mule drivers, milkmen and others who use this road.

I find a couple of mules tethered to a pine tree. The mule drivers, handsome men in tattered clothes, sit on a bench in the shade of the tree, drinking tea from brass tumblers. The shopkeeper, a man of indeterminate age—the cold dry winds from the mountain passes having crinkled his face like a walnut— greets me enthusiastically, as he always does. He even produces a chair, which looks like a survivor from the Savoy's 1890 ballroom. Fortunately, the Mussoorie antique dealers haven't seen it, or it would have been carried away long ago. In any case, the stuffing has come out of the seat. The shopkeeper apologizes for its condition: 'The rats were nesting in it.' And then, to reassure me: 'But they have gone now.'

Unlike the shopkeeper, the mule drivers have somewhere to go and something to deliver: sacks of potatoes. From Jaunpur to Jaunsar, the potato is probably the crop best suited to these stony, terraced fields. Oddly enough, it was introduced to the Himalayas by two Irishmen, Captain Young of Dehra and Mussoorie and

Captain Kennedy of Shimla, in the 1820s. The slopes of Young's house, Mullingar, were known as his Potato Farm. Looking up old books, I was surprised to learn that the potato wasn't known in India before the nineteenth century, and now it's an essential part of our diet in most parts of the country.

As the mule drivers lead their pack animals away, along the dusty road to Landour bazaar, I follow at a distance, singing 'Mule Train' in my best Nelson Eddy manner.[*]

A thunderstorm, followed by strong winds, brought down the temperature. That was yesterday. And today, June, it is cloudy, cool, drizzling a little, almost monsoon weather; but it is still too early for the real monsoon.

The birds are enjoying the cool weather. The green-backed tits cool their bottoms in the rainwater pool. A king crow flashes past, winging through the air like an arrow. On the wing, it snaps up a hovering dragonfly. The mynahs fetch crow feathers to line their nest in the eaves of the house. I am lying so still on the window seat that a tit alights on the sill within a few inches of my head. It snaps up a small dead moth before flying away.

Sir E is back. He found it too hot in the valley. Even up here he has given up wearing a necktie. I'll have him wearing a kurta and pyjamas before long; the only sensible dress in summer.

At dusk, I sit at the window and watch the trees and listen to the wind as it makes light conversation in the leafy tops of the maples. A large bat flits in and out of the trees. The sky is just light enough to enable me to see the bat and the outlines of the taller trees. Up on Landour hill, the lights are just beginning to come on. It is deliciously cool, eight o'clock, a perfect summer's evening. Prem is singing to himself in the kitchen. His wife and sister are chattering beneath the walnut tree. Down the hill, a *kakar* is barking, alarmed perhaps by the presence of a leopard. All the birds have gone to sleep for the night. Even the cicadas

---

*Not Nelson's song originally, but he sang it better than anyone else.

are strangely silent. The wind grows stronger and the tall maples bow before it: the maple moves its slender branches slowly from side to side, the oak moves its branches up and down. It is darker now; more lights on Landour. The cry of the barking deer has grown fainter, more distant, and now I hear a cricket singing in the bushes. The stars are out, the wind grows chilly, it is time to close the window.

Bijju is very much an outdoor boy, even when he isn't grazing cows. He isn't very strong in the chest, but his legs are sturdy; he was having no difficulty in scaling the high retaining wall. He grinned down at me. He is rather like the whistling thrush—absent for days, then unexpectedly reappearing in the forest or on the hillside. Bijju sings too, although his voice is more vigorous than melodic.

And that reminds me of the story of the whistling thrush. The bird was once a village boy who tried very hard to play the flute in the same style as the god Krishna. When the god heard his favourite melody being plagiarized, he was furious and turned the unfortunate boy into a bird. The whistling thrush still tries to copy the divine melody, but somehow it always breaks off right in the middle of a stanza. There ought to be a moral here, especially in a land full of plagiarists. Or to be fair, I should say film-land…

The Whistler. This is my name for the youth who labours part-time in the school. He is something of a character—scatterbrained, carefree, easy-going. He is always whistling—loudly and quite tunefully (this time a bird turned into a boy?)—so that you know when he's coming round a bend or through the trees, and even when it's dark you know who it is. He's usually out quite late, because he spends all his money at the pictures. He has three sisters, and they and the mother are all working as maids or ayahs, and as they are quite indulgent to him (the only brother) he doesn't have to work too hard. His shoes are always torn, even though his clothes look new.

He has a reputation for being a waster, but he returned the few rupees he borrowed from me last month. I suppose a youth who is always singing and whistling on the roads gives everyone the impression that he has nothing to do from morn till night, unlike that jolly miller of Dee who worked *and* sang the whole day through. (I know one man who forbids his children from singing in the home.)

But back to the Whistler, he is really quite enterprising. The other day he asked me for one of my books, and as I knew he hadn't squandered too many years in school, I gave him an easy Hindi translation of one of my children's books. But it was the paper he valued, not the words. He flogged it to the bania's small son, who took it apart and converted the large pages into envelopes, which were then used for selling gram and peanuts. In India, it doesn't take long for anything to be recycled. On the way home, I saw a couple of customers throwing their empty packets away, and these were promptly consumed by a stray cow. There went my beautiful story!

Is there a lesson to be learnt from this? Yes. Don't give away complimentaries.

It rained all night, and the morning is cool and fresh. Parrots are on the wing. I feel like tap-dancing like Gene Kelly, but you can't tap dance on a hillside, you'd break an ankle. Only the roads (and not all of them) are suitable for a song-and-dance act, and no doubt the Whistler will oblige before long. At forty, I must refrain from being too frisky and boyish. But I'll do a reel in the garden when no one is looking.

24 June

The first day of monsoon mist. And it's strange how all the birds fall silent as the mist comes climbing up the hill. Perhaps that's what makes the mist so melancholy; not only does it conceal the hills, it blankets them in silence too. Only an hour ago the trees were ringing with birdsong. And now the forest is deathly still, as though it were midnight.

Through the mist Bijju is calling to his sister. I can hear him running about on the hillside but I cannot see him.

Feeling sorry for Sir E (or maybe for myself), I walked over to see him. The door was closed, so I looked in at the French window (nothing could be more English than a French window, and no Agatha Christie mystery would be complete without one), I saw him sleeping in his chair with his chin on his chest. There was no dagger sticking out of his back, only a bit of stuffing from his old coat. My footsteps on the gravel woke him, and he got up and opened the door for me. He said he felt a bit tipsy; had taken his usual peg, but thought the quality of whisky varied from bottle to bottle, and wished he could lay his hands on a bottle of Scotch or even Irish. He could only offer me an Uttar Pradesh brand. I said I'd given up drinking, and this pleased him because in truth he hates anyone drinking his whisky; said he might give it up himself, it 'cost too damn much'! I told him it would be unwise to give up drinking at this stage of his life. As he had reached the age of eighty-six on two pegs a day, he was obviously thriving on it. Giving it up now would only play havoc with the orderly working of his system. I'd given it up in order to help an alcoholic friend abstain, and also because I wanted to give up *something*, and strong drink seemed the easiest thing to do without.

A cicada starts up in the tree nearest my window seat. What has he been doing all these weeks, and why does he choose this particular moment and this particular evening to play the fiddle so loudly? The cicadas are late this year, the monsoon has been late. But soon the forest will be ringing with the sound of the cicadas—an orchestra constantly tuning up but never quite getting into tune— and the sound of the birds will be pushed into the background.

Outside the front door, I found an elegant young praying mantis reclining on a leaf of the honeysuckle creeper. I say young because he hadn't grown to his full size, and was that very tender pale green which is the colour of a young mantis. They are light brown to begin with, like dry twigs, but as they grow older and the monsoon foliage becomes greener, they too change, and by mid-August they are dark green.

∿

As though to make up for lost time, the monsoon rains are now here with a vengeance. It has been pouring all day, and already the roof is leaking. But nothing dampens Prem's spirits. He is still singing love songs in the kitchen.

Kailash, whom I have known for a couple of weeks, asks me for twenty-five rupees.

'What do you need it for?' I ask.

'It's for my Sanskrit teacher,' he says. 'I have failed in Sanskrit but if I give the teacher twenty-five rupees he'll alter my marks. You see, I've passed in all the other subjects, but if I fail in Sanskrit I'll fail the entire exam and remain a pre-Inter student for another year.'

I took a little time to digest this information and ponder on the pitfalls of the examination system.

'He must be failing a lot of boys,' I said. 'Twenty-five rupees each! Are there many others?'

'Some. But he dare not fail the good ones. They can ask for a recheck. It's the borderline cases like me who give him a chance to make money.'

This placed me in a quandary. Should I yield to the evils of the examination system and provide the money for pass-marks? Or should I adopt a high moral stance and allow the boy to fail?

Whatever the evils of the exam system, they are not the fault of the student. And either way he isn't going to turn into a great Sanskrit scholar. So why be a hypocrite? I gave him the money.

Kailash slogs in his uncle's orchard all morning, gets a midday meal (no breakfast), and hasn't any shoes. And yet his uncle, a member of one of Garhwal's well-known upper-caste families, is a wealthy man.

Kailash tells me he will return to his village once he knows his result. According to him his uncle is such a miser that at mealtimes he pauses before each mouthful, wondering: 'Ought I to eat it? Or should I keep it for tomorrow?'

I am visited by another kind of student, a small girl from one of the private schools. Her mother has brought her to me for my autograph.

'She studies your book in Class six,' I was informed.

'And what book is that?' I asked the little girl.

'Tom Sawyer,' she replied promptly. So I signed for Mark Twain.

When a small storeroom collapsed during the last heavy rains, I was forced to rescue a couple of old packing cases that had been left there for three or four years—since my arrival here, in fact. The contents were well soaked and most of it had to be thrown away—old manuscripts that had been obliterated, negatives that had got stuck together, gramophone records that had taken on strange shapes (dear 'Ink Spots', how will I ever listen to you again?*)... Unlike most writers, I have no compunction about throwing away work that hasn't quite come off, and I am sure there are a few critics who would prefer that I throw away the lot! Sentimental rubbish, no doubt. Well, we can't please everyone; and we can't preserve everything either. Time and the elements will take their toll.

But a couple of old diaries, kept in exercise books almost twenty years ago, had managed to survive the rain, and I put them out in the sun to dry, and then, almost unwillingly, started browsing through them. It was instructive, and sometimes a little disconcerting, to discover the sort of person I had been in my twenties. In some ways, no different from what I am today. In other ways, radically different. A diary is a useful tool for self-examination, particularly if both diary and diarist are still around after some years.

One particular entry caught my eye, and I reproduce it here without any alteration, because it represented my credo as a young

---

*This was before the advent of audiotapes.

writer, and it set me wondering if I had lived up to my own expectations. (Nobody else had any expectations of me!)

The entry was made on 19 January 1958, when I was living on my own in Dehradun:

The things I do best are those things I do on my own, alone, of my own accord, without the advice or approval of others. Once I start doing what other people tell me to do, both my character and creativity take a dip. It is when I strike out on my own that I succeed best.

There was a time when I was much younger and poorer than I am now. I had been over a year in Jersey, in the Channel Islands; I was unhappy, and the atmosphere in which I was writing was one of discouragement and disapproval. And that was why I wrote so well—because I was defiant! That was why I finished the only book I have finished so far. I had to prove to myself that I could do it.

One night I was walking alone along the beach. There was a strong wind blowing, dashing the salt spray in my face, and the sea was crashing against the St Helier rocks. I told myself: I will go to London; I will take up a job; I will finish my book; I will find a publisher; I will save money and I will return to India, because I can be happier there than here.

And that was just what I did.

I had guts then.

What's more, I had an end in view.

The writing itself is not enough for me. Success and money are not enough. I had a little of both recently,[*] but they did not help me to do anything wonderful. I must have something to write for, just as I must have something to live for. And that's something I have yet to find.

There was more in that vein, but I give this excerpt as an example of a young man's determination to be a writer in what were then adverse circumstances. Thirty-five years later, I'm still trying.

----

[*]When *The Room on the Roof* was published (1956).

27 June

The rains have heralded the arrival of some seasonal visitors—a leopard; and several thousand leeches.

Yesterday afternoon the leopard lifted a dog from near the servants' quarters below the school. In the evening, it attacked one of Bijju's cows but fled at the approach of Bijju's mother, who came screaming imprecations.

As for the leeches, I shall soon get used to a little bloodletting every day. Bijju's mother sat down in the shrubbery to relieve herself, and later discovered two fat black leeches feeding on her fair round bottom. I told her she could use one of the spare bathrooms downstairs. But she prefers the wide open spaces.

Other new arrivals are the scarlet minivets (the females are yellow), flitting silently among the leaves like brilliant jewels. No matter how leafy the trees, these brightly coloured birds cannot conceal themselves, although, by remaining absolutely silent, they sometimes contrive to go unnoticed. Along come a pair of drongos, unnecessarily aggressive, chasing the minivets away.

A tree creeper moves rapidly up the trunk of the oak tree, snapping up insects all the way. Now that the rains are here, there is no dearth of food for the insectivorous birds.

In spite of there being water in several places, the whistling thrush still comes to my pool. He, at least, is a permanent resident.

Kailash has a round, cheerful face, only slightly marred by a swivel eye. His hair comes down over his forehead, hiding a deep scar. He is short, but quite compact and energetic. He chatters a good deal but in a general sort of way, and a response isn't obligatory.

It's quite possible that he will go away as soon as he gets his exam results. He's fed up with being the Cinderella of his uncle's house. He tells of how his miserly uncle went to see a rather permissive film, and was very shocked and wanted to walk out, but couldn't bear the thought of losing his ticket money; so he sat through the film with his eyes closed.

Sir E departed for Dehra with his large retinue of servants and their dependants, all of whom would have done justice to an eighteenth-century nabob. 'I am at the mercy of my servants,' he told me the other day.

But he had placed himself at their mercy long ago, by setting himself up as a country squire surrounded by 'faithful retainers'—all of whom received generous salaries but did little or no work. If he sold his white elephant of a farm, he'd be quite comfortable with one servant.

'I'll probably come up in September, after the rains,' he said. 'If I live that long... I'm just living from day to day.'

'So am I,' I told him. 'It's the best way to live.'

A couple of days passed before Kailash came to see me. I was beginning to wonder if he'd come again. Apparently the teacher had at first proved elusive; but the deed was done, and Kailash passed with the marks he needed. Ironically, his uncle was so impressed that he is now urging the boy to remain with him and complete the Intermediate exam.

'I must write a story about your uncle,' I remark.

'Don't give him a story,' says Kailash. 'A short note will do.'

Now that Prem is preoccupied with his wife, and the house is at the mercy of uninvited visitors, I stay out most of the time, and these days Kailash is my only companion. Yesterday we took Camel's Back Road, past the cemetery. He chatters away, and I can listen if I want to, or think of other things if I don't want to listen; apparently it makes no difference to him. He is a cheerful soul, with an infectious laugh. He walks with a slight swagger, or roll. He says he doesn't mind staying here now that he has me for a friend; that he can put up with two sour uncles as long as he knows I'm around. I suspect he's quite capable of pulling a fast one on his uncle; but all the same, I find myself liking him.

Moody. And when I'm moody I'm bad.

Prem says: 'It is easier to please God than it is to please you.'

'But God is easily pleased,' I respond. 'God makes absolutely no demands on us. We just imagine them.'

The eyes.

Prem's eyes have great gentleness in them.

His wife's eyes are round and mischievous and suggestive…

Suggestive enough to invite the attention of a mischievous or malignant spirit.

At about two in the morning, I am awakened by Prem's shouts, muffled by rain. Shouting back that I am on my way, for it is obviously an emergency, I leap out of bed, grab an umbrella, dash outside and then down the stairs to his room. His wife is sobbing in bed. Whatever had possessed her has now gone away, and the crying is due more to Prem's ministrations—he exorcizes the ghost by thumping her on the head—than to the 'possession' itself. But there is no doubt that she is subject to hallucinatory or subconscious actions. It is not simply a hysterical fit. She walks in her sleep, moves restlessly from door to window, holds conversations with an invisible presence, and resists all efforts to bring her back to reality. When she comes out of the trance, she is quite normal.

This sort of thing is apparently quite common in the hills, where people believe it to be a ghost taking temporary possession of a human mind. It's happened to Prem's wife before, and it also happens to her brother, so it seems to run in families. It never happens to Prem, who deeply resents the interruption to his sleep.

I calm the girl and then make them bring their bedding upstairs. I give her a sleeping tablet and she is soon fast asleep.

During a lull in the rain, I hear a most hideous sound coming from the forest—a maniacal shrieking, followed by a mournful hooting. But Prem and his wife sleep through it all. The rain starts again, and the shrieking stops. Perhaps it's a hyena. Perhaps something else.

A morning of bright sunshine, and the whistling thrush welcomes it with a burst of song. Where do the birds shelter when it rains? How does that frail butterfly survive the battering of strong winds and heavy raindrops? How do the snakes manage in their flooded holes?

I saw a bright green snake sunning itself on some rocks; no doubt waiting for its hole to dry out.

In my vagrant days, ten to fifteen years ago (long before the hippies made vagrancy a commonplace), I was a great frequenter of tea shops, those dingy little shacks with a table and three chairs, a grimy tea kettle, and a cracked gramophone. Tea shops haven't changed much, and once again I find myself lingering in them, sometimes in company with Kailash, who, although he doesn't eat much, drinks a lot of tea.

One can sit all day in a tea shop and watch the world go by. Amazing the number of people who actually do this! And not all of them unemployed. The tea shop near the clock tower is ideal for this purpose. It is a busy part of the bazaar but the tea shop, though small, is gloomy within, and one can loll about unseen, observing everyone who passes by a few feet away in the sunlit (or rain-spattered) street. The tea itself is indifferent, the buns are stale, the boiled eggs have been peppered too liberally. Kailash is unusually quiet; there is no one else in the shop. People who would stop me in the road pass by without glancing into the murky interior. This is the ideal place; not as noble as my window opening into the trees, but familiar, reminiscent of days gone by in Dehra, when cares sat lightly upon me simply because I did not care at all. And now perhaps I have begun to care too much.

I gave Bijju a cake. He licked all the icing off it, only then did he eat the rest.

It was a dark windy corner in Landour bazaar, but I always found the old man there, hunched up over the charcoal fire on which he roasted his peanuts. He'd been there for as long as I could remember, and he could be seen at almost any hour of the day or night. Summer or winter, he stayed close to his fire.

He was probably quite tall, but we never saw him standing up. One judged his height from his long, loose limbs. He was very thin, and the high cheekbones added to the tautness of his tightly stretched skin.

His peanuts were always fresh, crisp and hot. They were popular with the small boys who had a few paise to spend on their way to and from school, and with the patrons of the cinemas, many of whom made straight for the windy corner during intervals or when the show was over. On cold winter evenings, or misty monsoon days, there was always a demand for the old man's peanuts.

No one knew his name. No one had ever thought of asking him for it. One just took him for granted. He was as fixed a landmark as the clock tower or the old cherry tree that grew crookedly from the hillside. The tree was always being lopped; the clock often stopped. The peanut vendor seemed less perishable than the tree, more dependable than the clock.

He had no family, but in a way all the world was his family, because he was in continuous contact with people. And yet he was a remote sort of being; always polite, even to children, but never familiar. There is a distinction to be made between aloneness and loneliness. The peanut vendor was seldom alone; but he must have been lonely.

Summer nights he rolled himself up in a thin blanket and slept on the ground, beside the dying embers of his fire. During the winter, he waited until the last show was over, before retiring to the rickshaw-coolies' shed where there was some protection from the biting wind.

Did he enjoy being alive? I wonder now. He was not a joyful person; but then, neither was he miserable. I should think he was a genuine stoic, one of those who do not attach overmuch importance to themselves, who are emotionally uninvolved, content with their limitations, their dark corners. I wanted to get to know the old man better, to sound him out on the immense questions involved in roasting peanuts all his life; but it's too late now. The last time I visited the bazaar, the dark corner was deserted; the old man had vanished; the coolies had carried him down to the cremation ground.

'He died in his sleep,' said the tea-shop owner. 'He was very old.'

Very old. Sufficient reason to die.

But that corner is very empty, very dark, and whenever I pass it I am haunted by visions of the old peanut vendor, troubled by the questions I failed to ask; and I wonder if he was really as indifferent to life as he appeared to be.

✓

Prem brought his wife some of her favourite mangoes. This afternoon he took her into my room so that she could listen to the radio. They both fell asleep at opposite ends of the bed; are still asleep as I write this in the next room, at my window. If I curled up a little, I could fall asleep here on the window seat. Nothing would induce me to disturb those innocents; they look far too blissful in their slumbers.

✓

Kailash and I are caught in a storm and it's by far the worst storm of the year. To make matters worse, there is absolutely no shelter for a mile along the main road from the town. It was fierce, lashing rain, quite cold, whipping along on the wind from all angles. The road was soon a torrent of muddy water, as earth and stones came rushing down the hillsides. Our one umbrella was useless and was very nearly blown away. The cardboard carton in which we were carrying vegetables was soon reduced to pulp. We broke into a run, although we could hardly see our way. There were blinding flashes of lightning—is an umbrella a good or a bad conductor of electricity? Kailash sees humour in these situations and was in peals of laughter all the way home, even when we slid into a ditch.

He takes my hand and holds it between his hands. He is happy. He has got his self-confidence back, and can now deal with his uncles and Sanskrit teachers.

In the morning, I work on a story. There is a dove cooing in the garden. Now it is very quiet, the only sound is the distant tapping of a woodpecker. The trees are muffled in ferns and creepers. It is mid-monsoon.

Kailash, his hair falling in an untidy mop across his forehead, drags me out of the house and over the wet green grass on the hillside. I protest that I do not like leeches, so we make for the high rocks. He laughs, talks, chuckles, and when he grins his large front teeth make him look like a 1940s' Mickey Rooney. When he looks sullen (this happens when he talks about his uncle), he looks Brando-ish. He has the gift of being able to convey his effervescence to me. Am I, at thirty-eight, too old to be gambolling about on the hill slopes like a young colt? (Am I, sobering thought, going to be a character of enforced youthfulness like the man on the boat in *Death in Venice?* Well, better that than the Gissing hero of *New Grub Street* who's old at forty.) If I am fit enough to gambol, then I must gambol. If I can still climb a tree, then I must climb trees, instead of just watching them from my window. I was in such high spirits yesterday that I kept playing the clown, and I haven't done this in years. To walk in the rain was fun, and to get wet was fun, and to fall down was fun, and to get hurt was fun.

'Will it last?' asks Kailash.

'This feeling of love between us?'

'*This* won't last. Not in this way. But if something *like* it lasts, we should be happy.'

∽

Prem is happy, laughing, giggling all the time. Sometimes it is a little annoying for me, because he is obviously unaware of what is happening around him—such as the fact that part of the roof blew away in the storm—but I am a good Taoist, I say nothing,

I wait for the right moment! Besides, it's a crime to interfere with anyone's happiness.

Prem notices the roof is missing and scolds his wife for seeing too many pictures. 'She's seen ten pictures in two months. More than she'd seen in her whole life, before coming here.' She pulls a face. Says Prem: 'My grandfather will be here any day to take her home.'

'Then she can see pictures with your grandfather,' I venture. 'While we repair the roof.'

'I wouldn't go anywhere with that old man,' she says.

'Don't speak like that of my grandfather. Do you want a beating? Look at Binya'—we all look at Binya, who is perched very prettily on the wall—'she hasn't seen more than two pictures in her life!'

'I'll take her to the pictures,' I offer.

Binya gives me a radiant smile. She'd love to go to the pictures, but her mother won't allow it.

Prem relents and takes his wife to the pictures.

Binya's mother has a bad attack of hiccups. Serves her right, for stealing my walnuts and not letting me take Binya to the pictures.

In the evening, I find Prem teaching his wife the alphabet, using the kitchen door as a blackboard. It is covered with chalk marks. Love is teaching your wife to read and write!

ᔕ

These entries were made in 1973, twenty years ago.

The following year I did not keep a journal, but these are some of the things that happened:

Sir E had a stroke and, like a stranded whale, finally heaved his last breath. According to his wishes, he was cremated on his farm near Dehra.

To Prem and Chandra was born a son, Rakesh, who immediately stole my heart—and gave me many a sleepless night, for as a baby he cried lustily.

Kailash went into the army and disappeared from my life, as well as from his uncle's.

Bijju and Binya were to remain a part of the hillside for several years.

Walking the Streets of Delhi

I made my home in Mussoorie in 1963, but of course I was to revisit Delhi many times, even spending a couple of winters there.

On one of these visits, in 1971, I reached my friend Kamal's house in Rajouri Garden, and mentioned that I had walked from Connaught Place, a distance of some eight miles. His family greeted me with a pained and bewildered silence.

Finally my friend's mother, a practical Punjabi lady, asked: 'How did you lose your money?' She kept hers knotted in the end of her sari, and firmly believed that people who kept their money in easily snatched handbags and wallets were asking for trouble.

'I haven't lost anything,' I said.

'Aren't the buses running?'

'Oh, the buses are running. One nearly ran over me.'

'Then why did you walk?'

'I thought I'd see more that way.'

The rest of the story is told in my journal.

The consensus of opinion in my friend's house is that I am a little mad. They have never heard of anyone in Delhi walking from choice. They prefer to wait long periods for overcrowded buses and hang on by their eyebrows, even if the distance to be covered is only a furlong. As in big cities the world over, the people of Delhi are rapidly losing the use of their legs.

I suppose Delhi is one of the least attractive cities in which to walk about. Crossing roads can be hazardous. Single and double-decker buses (many emitting smokescreens of diesel fumes), wildly driven taxis, unpredictable scooter-rickshaws, slow-moving cars and tongas, and thousands of wavering, wayward cyclists, make for chaos on the streets. On the main roads the traffic is fast and furious, and cyclists are frequently knocked over and killed. But Delhi has an acute transport problem, and the cycle is the poor man's only guarantee of getting to work in time. He cannot afford a scooter, and he cannot wait for a bus. And yet, in this city bursting with the Punjabi nouveau riche there are thousands who do have their own scooters and cars, and the number and variety of vehicles on the road increase at an alarming rate.

Setting out on another long walk, I realized that the pavement is meant for almost every purpose except walking. I am on the Najafgarh Road, heading in the general direction of central Delhi. It is a straight road, but this is no straight walk. To find a thirty-yard stretch of unoccupied pavement is most unlikely. In a territory where every square foot of land has a high price, why should so much good pavement go to waste?

The first two wayside stalls belong to sellers of lottery tickets. Theirs is a thriving business. All over Delhi, at almost every street corner, there is someone selling lottery tickets. The prizes are attractive enough. The owner of the winning ticket collects ₹250,000—sometimes more—and there are a number of other prizes. And the income accruing to the state is also tremendous—so much so that almost every state in the country, including Delhi, has climbed on the lottery bandwagon. After all, it is easier than collecting taxes. No one, not even the street sweeper, grudges giving a rupee to the government if there is a chance in a million of his winning a fortune.

While the poor man is quite willing to part with his rupee, it is the rich man, the thriving businessman, who often goes in for lottery tickets in a big way, sometimes buying up forty or fifty tickets at a time. He believes that while it is great to be rich, there is nothing like getting richer.

How times have changed. Ten years ago, if I asked a Sikh boy what he would like to be on growing up, he would unhesitatingly have said, 'I'll join the Army'—or the Navy, or the Air Force. He was proud of his martial traditions. Yesterday, while talking to an intelligent twelve-year-old Sikh, I asked the same question and received this reply: 'I'll open a cinema or deal in spare parts.'

No spirit of adventure, no vision of faraway places—unless it be of a cloth shop in Bangkok! The boy confessed that what he really wanted in life was a television set bigger and better than his neighbour's.

But Delhi is not entirely Punjabi. Here, on the Najafgarh Road I find a community of Lohiawalas, a gypsy tribe of blacksmiths who have wandered into Delhi, camped on the pavement, and gone about their ancient and traditional way of living, supremely indifferent to the fast pace, the noise of traffic, the neon signs and Western clothes that surround them on all sides. Their bullock-carts (in which they travel and sleep and live and die and have their babies) stand just off the pavement; these are lined with old iron, stamped with decorative patterns and studded with coloured stones.

A charcoal fire has been made in a hole in the ground, and this is kept alive by a bellows worked by a wheel turned by an attractive woman wearing a black blouse and black skirt. This sombre attire is set off by heavy silver anklets and a pair of very lively eyes. Another pair of bellows has been fashioned out of goat's skin. A man is beating out a strip of red-hot tin on his anvil. A boy is filling a bent bicycle-pump with sand (to keep it firm) before straightening it out with his hammer. The entire family, including bearded old men, wizened old women ready to take off on broomsticks, and naked grandchildren, is at work. Handsome people these; and although they live in dirt and squalor, they seem quiet and dignified.

A little farther along the road are some people making what appear to be straw mats. These turn out to be roofs for the small shacks belonging to the Rajasthani labourers who live on the other side of an open drain. The walls of these shacks are about four feet high, the rooms about six feet square. There is no sanitation. People use the drain. They bathe at a public tap. During the rains, water moves sluggishly along this drain, but now it is dry except for pools of stagnant, slimy water, a grey liquid tinged with green. It must hold treasures for anyone searching for biological specimens. (And indeed, the enterprising Delhiwala has not ignored this possibility, for farther along, on Link Road, frogs are on sale to biology students.)

At this side of the road lies a dead pony, knocked down at night by a speeding truck. A portion has been eaten away by dogs and jackals. It is now being pecked at by crows; when these birds tire of the stinking carcass they move on to a nearby fruit stall. No one seems to notice this, least of all the fruit vendors. Well-dressed people pass by without a glance at the dead horse or the open drain. Is it apathy, or is it that Delhi people—city people—are unobservant by nature? Does city life dull the perceptions? Are the giant cinema hoardings so overpowering, so dazzling, that everything else pales into insignificance beside them?

Some of the shack-dwellers have tried to make their homes attractive. They have whitewashed their walls, adorned them with crude but colourful drawings of birds and animals. But what a contrast there is between these humble homes and the elegant villas and bungalows of Kirti Nagar, Patel Nagar and Pusa Road, three prosperous areas of Delhi which lie on my route. A tenant has to pay anything from three to five hundred rupees a month for a small flat in one of these fine houses.

I went flat-hunting once, but I was turned away by the house-owners—not because of race, colour or religion, but because I was a bachelor. In India, staying single is something of a crime against society. Bachelors have a rough time; they seldom get invited into homes where there are girls of marriageable age.

'Are Delhi bachelors such monsters?' I asked a house agent in Rajinder Nagar.

'Most of them are very well-behaved,' he said. 'But you see, parents no longer have much confidence in their daughters. A girl sees too many films, and then she wants to have a tragic affair with the first good-looking male who comes along.'

It has taken me two hours of foot-slogging to reach Connaught Place, which is still the premier shopping centre of New Delhi, I remember it well from my childhood, in the war years, when my father was stationed at Air Headquarters in New Delhi. The capital was a small, sparsely populated town in those days. We lived in temporary RAF hutments on Wellesley Road. A multi-storeyed hotel now occupies the site. The jungle where I hunted rabbits has long since been cleared to make way for the expensive residential area of Sunder Nagar. But the central vista, leading from India Gate up to Lutyens's complex of Parliament House and the President's Estate, is still a lovely stretch of green grass, still water and shady jamun trees.

Connaught Place has not changed much. The milk bar I frequented as a boy is still there, although they do not sell milk any more; now it is espresso coffee and hamburgers. The Regal cinema has switched over to Hindi films. In its cellar is a discotheque. Shopfronts are more flashy, but service-lanes have not altered. And of course the faces and clothes are different. The British uniforms of the war years have given way to the uniforms of the hippies, who slouch about in beads and togas, unaccepted and even scorned by the local citizens. Indians are not impressed by people who do not dress well. Their concept of the true Englishman is of the sahib who dresses for dinner even when there is no dinner; they *like* that kind of Englishman. No one is as clothes-conscious as a Punjabi. He likes his shoes polished, his shirt pressed, his suit spotless—a difficult business in Delhi, where the dust, even in winter, is as thick as in the time of Emperor Shah Jahan who, proud of his new capital, asked the Persian Ambassador how it compared with his Isphahan, and received the double-edged reply: 'By God! Isphahan cannot be compared with the dust of your Delhi!'

But Shah Jahan's Delhi, the old walled city near the Yamuna, is not on my route today. I am tired and hungry, and I lunch at a dhaba, a cheap eating-house, one of many lining the outer pavements round Connaught Place. If one does not mind the filthy surroundings, there is good meat to be had in these little restaurants, most of them run by Punjabis who learned their cooking in Lahore. Certainly the food here is better and cheaper than the watered-down dishes served in some of the smart restaurants in the inner circle. The dish-washers and servers are barefooted hill boys, working in the city because their small fields in the hills do not provide a sufficient living for their families. They work quite cheerfully (for they are cheerful by nature), in spite of hard words, cuffs and meagre wages.

Outside, on the road, a small crowd has gathered round a turbaned Pathan. For a moment I fear violence for this exotic stranger; then I realize that the crowd is merely curious, even in good humour. The Pathan is extolling the virtues of an aphrodisiac mixture which he is trying to sell. 'Be happy!' he cries. 'And make your bulbul happy!'

In spite of the family planning hoarding directly behind him, he appears to be doing good business. It is, after all, the wedding season.

I am forcibly reminded of this on my way home in the evening. The roads in and out of every residential area are blocked by shamianas put up for wedding receptions. This is illegal, but the fine is a small one, and when a father is spending thousands on his daughter's wedding, he dosen't mind paying a fine of forty rupees. He accepts the summons with good humour, and carries on with the reception. This is the month most propitious for marriages. After 15 January, four months must pass before a Hindu will marry off his daughter. Astrology plays as great a part in the lives of the people here today as it did three hundred years ago when the traveller Francois Bernier observed that no one in Delhi, Hindu or Muslim, undertook any project without first consulting his astrologer. Today, matchmakers must still study the stars in their courses before pairing a boy with a girl.

Most fathers love to give their daughters a good send-off, and Delhi marriages are splendid, glittering affairs. The bridegroom traditionally arrives on a white horse, but Delhiwalas, who like being up-to-date, often use cars, jeeps or even tractors (because of the high perch they provide).

I find myself involved in a procession on Pusa Road. It is impossible to get past the throng of people, so I must remain with them for some distance. If I choose to attend the reception, no one will turn me away. The bride's people will be under the impression that I am one of the bridegroom's guests, and the bridegroom's group will feel sure that I belong to the bride's party. As most of the guests are seeing each other for the first time, it is possible for any well-dressed person to join the festivities. This frequently happens.

There has, of course, to be a band, and bands are chosen mainly on the strength of the volume of noise they are able to produce and sustain. A trumpet, sounding a foot away from my ear, sends me reeling to the rear of the procession. Drums, bugles, clarinets and saxophones burst into a great profanity of sound. It is not Indian music they play, but a combination of military marches and popular Hindi film tunes. There is nothing like it anywhere else on earth.

The bandsmen wear red coats and white spats, but shoes are optional. On their heads they wear what appear to be Salvation Army caps. They will play on their instruments (often independently of each other) for as long as they are paid to play, and must deliver a final burst at daybreak when the bride leaves her father's house.

It is a colourful procession, headed by small urchin boys carrying gas lamps. After them comes the band; then the bridegroom's beautifully clothed friends and relatives; and finally the bridegroom, enthroned on top of a gaily caparisoned jeep.

I take a side road and leave the procession, but find my way blocked by another marriage party. This time a heavily-built Sikh, slightly tipsy, embraces me as a long-lost brother. He seems to know me. Quite possibly I knew him when he was a smooth-cheeked lad of fifteen; but now, disguised by a magnificent beard, he reminds me of no one I have ever known. But he wants me to join his party, and so, to humour him, I accompany him for about a hundred yards, when he suddenly forgets me and rushes off to some other old acquaintance.

I have to reconnoitre another three processions, and four more shamianas, before I reach Rajouri Garden. I keep going by eating boiled eggs. These are sold on the roadside, and the egg-seller will even peel the egg for you, and serve it sliced, with pepper and salt, on a piece of newspaper. Unfortunately all the egg-sellers disappear when summer comes, because people believe that eggs are 'heating' and should only be eaten during the winter months. I suppose the same reasoning applies to the Pathan's tonic mixture. I am almost home. It does not look as though anyone in Delhi sleeps at night, but I am ready for bed, and all the brass bands in the city (and there must be over a hundred of them) will not keep me from sleeping.

But there is something I must do first.

The seller of lottery tickets has been staring hopefully at me, and I hate to disappoint him last thing at night. So I produce a rupee and buy a ticket; and, in doing so, I feel that I have finally identified myself with the good people of Delhi.

Simply Living

These thoughts and observations were noted in my diaries through the 1980s, and may give readers some idea of the ups and downs, highs and lows, during a period when I was still trying to get established as an author.

March 1981

After a gap of twenty years, during which it was, to all practical purposes, forgotten, *The Room on the Roof* (my first novel) gets reprinted in an edition for schools.

(This was significant, because it marked the beginning of my entry into the educational field. Gradually, over the years, more of my work became familiar to school children throughout the country.)

Stormy weather over Holi. Room flooded. Everyone taking turns with septic throats and fever. While in bed, read Stendhal's *The Red and the Black*. I seem to do my serious reading only when I'm sick.

Felt well enough to take a leisurely walk down the Tehri Road. Trees in new leaf. The fresh light green of the maples is very soothing.

I may not have contributed anything towards the progress of civilization, but neither have I robbed the world of anything. Not one tree or bush or bird. Even the spider on my wall is welcome to his (her) space. Provided he (she) stays on the wall and does not descend on my pillow.

April

Swifts are busy nesting in the roof and performing acrobatics outside my window. They do everything on the wing, it seems—including feeding and making love. Mating in midair must be quite a feat.

Someone complimented me because I was 'always smiling'. I thought better of him for the observation and invited him over. Flattery will get you anywhere!

(This is followed by a three-month gap in my diary, explained by my next entry.)

Shortage of cash. Muddle, muddle, toil and trouble. I don't see myself smiling.

Learn to zigzag. Try something different.

August

Kept up an article a day for over a month. Grub Street again!
DARE
WILL
KEEP SILENCE
These words helped Napoleon, but will they help me?
Try cursing!
I curse the block to money.
I curse the thing that takes all my effort away.
I curse all that would make me a slave.
I curse those who would harm my loved ones.
And now stop cursing and give thanks for all the good things you have enjoyed in life.

'We should not spoil what we have by desiring what we have not, but remember that what we have was the gift of fortune.'

(Epicurus)

'We ought to have more sense, of course, than to try to touch a dream, or to reach that place which exists but in the glamour of a name.'

(H.M. Tomlinson, *Tide Marks*)

October

A good year for the cosmos flower. Banks of them everywhere. They like the day-long sun. Clean and fresh—my favourite flower *en-masse*.

But by itself, the wild commelina, sky-blue against dark green, always catches the heart.

∿

A latent childhood remains tucked away in our subconscious. This I have tried to explore...

A...stretches out on the bench like a cat, and the setting sun is trapped in his eyes, golden brown, glowing like tiger's eyes. (Oddly enough, this beautiful youth grew up to become a very sombre-looking padre.)

December

A kiss in the dark—warm and soft and all-encompassing—the moment stayed with me for a long time.

Wrote a poem, 'Who kissed me in the dark?' but it could not do justice to the kiss. Tore it up!

On the night of the 7th, light snowfall. The earliest that I can remember it snowing in Landour. Early morning, the hillside looked very pretty, with a light mantle of snow covering trees, rusty roofs, vehicles at the bus stop—and concealing our garbage dump for a couple of hours, until it melted.

January 1982

Three days of wind, rain, sleet and snow. Flooded out of my bedroom. We convert dining room into dormitory. Everything is bearable except the wind, which cuts through these old houses like a knife—under the roof, through flimsy verandah enclosures and ill-fitting windows, bringing the icy rain with it.

Fed up with being stuck indoors. Walked up to Lal Tibba, in flurries of snow. Came back and wrote the story 'The Wind on Haunted Hill'.

I invoke Lakshmi, who shines like the full moon.

Her fame is all-pervading.

Her benevolent hands are like lotuses.

I take refuge in her lotus feet.

Let her destroy my poverty forever.

Goddess, I take shelter at your lotus feet.

February

My boyhood was difficult, but I had my dreams to sustain me. What does one dream about now?

But sometimes, when all else fails, a sense of humour comes to the rescue.

And the children (Raki, Muki, Dolly) bring me joy. All children do. Sometimes I think small children are the only sacred things left on this earth. Children and flowers.

Further blasts of wind and snow. In spite of the gloom, wrote a new essay.

March

Blizzard in the night. Over a foot of snow in the morning. And so it goes on...unprecedented for March. The Jupiter Effect? At least the snow prevents the roof from blowing away, as happened last year. Facing east (from where the wind blows) doesn't help. And it's such a rickety old house.

ᔕ

Mid-March and the first warm breath of approaching summer. Risk a haircut. Ramkumar does his best to make me look like a 1930s film star. I suppose I ought to try another barber, but he's too nice. 'I look rather strange,' I said afterwards (like Wallace Beery in *Billy the Kid*). 'Don't worry,' he said. 'You'll get used to it.'

'Why don't you give me an Amitabh Bachchan haircut?'

'You'll need more hair for that,' he says.

Bus goes down the mud, killing several passengers. Death moves about at random, without discriminating between the innocent and the evil, the poor and the rich. The only difference is that the poor usually handle it better.

Late March

The blackest clouds I've ever seen squatted over Mussoorie, and then it hailed marbles for half an hour. Nothing like a hailstorm to clear the sky. Even as I write, I see a rainbow forming.

And Goddess Lakshmi smiles on me. An unprecedented flow of cheques, mainly accrued royalties on 'Angry River' and 'The Blue Umbrella'. A welcome change from last year's shortages and difficulties.

Perfection

The smallest insect in the world is a sort of fairyfly and its body is only a fifth of a millimetre long. One can only just see it with the naked eye. Almost like a speck of dust, yet it has perfect little wings and little combs on its legs for preening itself.

Late April

Abominable cloud and chilly rain. But Usha brings bunches of wild roses and irises. And her own gentle smile.

Mid-May

Raki (after reading my biodata): 'Dada, you were born in 1934! And you are still here!' After a pause: 'You are very lucky.'

I guess I am, at that.

June

Did my sixth essay for *The Monitor* this year.

(Have written off and on, for *The Christian Science Monitor* of Boston from 1965 to 2002).

Wrote an article for a new magazine, *Keynote*, published in Bombay, and edited by Leela Naidu, Dom Moraes and David Davidar. It was to appear in the August issue. Now I'm told that the magazine has folded. (But David Davidar went on to bigger things with Penguin India!)

If at first you don't succeed, so much for skydiving.

July

Monsoon downpour. Bedroom wall crumbling. Landslide cuts off my walk down the Tehri road.

Usha: a complexion like apricot blossom seen through a mist.

September

Two dreams:

A constantly recurring dream or, rather, nightmare—I am forced to stay longer than I had intended in a very expensive hotel and know that my funds are insufficient to meet the bill. Fortunately, I have always woken up before the bill is presented!

Possible interpretation: fear of insecurity. My own variation of the dream, common to many, of falling from a height but waking up before hitting the ground.

Another occasional dream: living in a house perched over a crumbling hillside. This one is not far removed from reality!

Glorious day. Walked up and around the hill, and got some of the cobwebs out of my head.

That man is strongest who stands alone!

Some epigrams (for future use).

A well-balanced person: someone with a chip on both shoulders.

Experience: the knowledge that enables you to recognize a mistake when you make it the second time.

Sympathy: what one woman offers another in exchange for details.

Worry: the interest paid on trouble before it becomes due.

October

Some disappointment, as usual in connection with films (the screenplay I wrote for someone who wanted to remake *Kim*), but if I were to let disappointments get me down, I'd have given up writing twenty-five years ago.

A walk in the twilight. Soothing. Watched the winter line from the top of the hill.

Raki first in school races.

Savitri (Dolly) completes two years. Bless her fat little toes.

Advice to myself: conserve energy. Talk less!

'Better to have people wondering why you don't speak than to have them wondering why you speak.'

(Disraeli)

Wrote 'The Funeral'. One of my better stories, and thus, more difficult to place.

If death was a thing that money could buy,

The rich, they would live, and the poor, they would die.

In California, you can have your body frozen after death in the hope that a hundred years from now some scientist will come along and bring you to life again. You pay in advance, of course.

December

I never have much luck with films or filmmakers. Mr K.S. Varma, finally (after five years), completed his film of my story 'The Last Tiger', but could not find a distributor for it. I don't regret the small sum I received for the story. He ran out of money—and tigers!—and apparently went to heroic lengths to complete the film in the forests of Bihar and Orissa. He used a circus tiger for the more intimate scenes, but this tiger disappeared one day, along with one of the actors. Tom Alter played a *shikari* and went on to play other, equally hazardous roles: he's still around, the tiger having spared him, but the film was never seen (and hasn't been seen to this day).

∽

A last postcard from an old friend: 'Ruskin, dear friend—but you won't be, unless you keep your word about lunching with us on Xmas Day. PLEASE DO COME, both Kanshi and I need your presence. It will be a small party this time as most of our friends are either *hors-de-combat* or dead! Bring Rakesh and Mukesh. Please let me know. I have been in bed for two days with a chill. Please don't disappoint.

Love,
Winnie

(We did go to the Christmas party, but sadly, the chill became pneumonia and there were no more parties with Winnie and Kanshi, who were such good company. I still miss them.)

January 1984

To Maniram's home near Lal Tibba. He was brought up by his grandmother—his mother died when he was one. Keeps two calves, two cows (one brindled), and a pup of indeterminate breed. Made me swallow a glass of milk. Haven't touched milk for years, can't stand the stuff, but drank it so as not to hurt his feelings. (Mani and his Granny turned up in my children's story *Getting Granny's Glasses*.)

On the 6th, it was bitterly cold and the snow came in through my bedroom roof. Not enough money to go away, but at least there's enough for wood and coal. I hate the cold—but the children seem to enjoy it. Raki, Muki and Dolly in constant high spirits.

February

Two days and nights of blizzard—howling winds, hail, sleet, snow. Prem bravely goes out for coal and kerosene oil. Worst weather we've ever had up here. Sick of it.

March

Peach, plum and apricot trees in blossom. Gentle weather at last. Schools reopen.

Sold German and Dutch translation rights in a couple of my children's books. I wish I could write something of lasting worth. I've done a few good stories but they are so easily lost in the mass of wordage that pours forth from the world's presses.

Here are some statistics that I got from the UK a couple of years ago:

There are over nine million books in the British Museum and they fill 86 miles of shelving.

There are over 50,000 living British authors. They don't get rich. The latest Society of Authors survey shows that only 55 per cent of those whose main occupation is writing earn over £700 a year.

Britain has 8,500 booksellers, as well as many other shops where books are sold.

The first book to be printed in Britain was *The Dictes and Sayings of the Philosophers*, which was translated and printed by William Caxton in 1477.

As many books were published in Britain between 1940 and 1980 as in the five centuries from Caxton's first book.

Who says the reading habit is dying?

∿

April

The 'adventure wind' of my boyhood—I felt it again today. Walked five miles to Suakholi, to look at an infinity of mountains.

The feeling of space—limitless space—can only be experienced by living in the mountains.

It is the emotional, the spiritual surge, that draws us back to the mountains again and again. It was not altogether a matter of mysticism or religion that prompted the ancients to believe that their gods dwelt in the high places of this earth. Those gods, by whatever name we know them, still dwell there. From time to time we would like to be near them, that we may know them and ourselves more intimately.

May

Completed my half-century and launched into my 51st year.

Fifty is a dangerous age for most men. Last year there was nothing to celebrate, and at the end of it my diary went into the dustbin. There was an abortive and unhappy love affair (dear reader, don't fall in love at fifty!), a crisis in the home (with Prem missing for weeks), conflicts with publishers, friends, myself. So skip being fifty. Become fifty-one as soon as possible; you will find yourself in calmer waters. If you fall in love at the age of fifty, inner turmoil and disappointment is almost guaranteed. Don't listen to what the wise men say about love. P.G. Wodehouse said the whole thing more succinctly: 'You know, the way love can change a fellow is really frightful to contemplate.' Especially when a fifty-year-old starts behaving like a sixteen-year-old!

Most of my month's earnings went to the dentist. And I notice he's wearing a new suit.

June

A name—a lovely face—turn back the years: 45 years to be exact, when I was a small boy in Jamnagar, where my father taught English to some of the younger princes and princesses—among them M—whose picture I still have in my album (taken by my father). She wrote to me after reading something I'd written, wanting to know if I was the same little boy, i.e., Mr Bond's mischievous son. I responded, of course. A link with my father is so rare; and besides, I had a crush on her. My first love! So long ago—but it seems like yesterday...

ᴖ

Monsoon breaks.

Money-drought breaks.

And if there's a connection, may the rain gods be generous this year.

(The rest of the year's entries were fairly mundane, implying that life at Ivy Cottage, Landour, went on pretty smoothly. But the rain gods played a trick or two. Although they were fairly generous to begin with, the year ended with a drought, as my mid-December entry indicates: 'Dust covers everything, after nearly two and half months of dry weather. Clouds build up, but disperse.' Always receptive to Nature's unpredictability, I wrote my story *Dust on the Mountain*.)

1995

On the flyleaf of this year's diary are written two maxims: 'Pull your own strings' and 'Act impeccably'. I'm not sure that I did either with much success, but I did at least try. And trying is what it's all about...

January

My book of poems and prayers finally published by Thomson Press, *seven years* after acceptance. Received a copy. Hope it won't be the only one. Splendid illustrations by Suddha. (Shortly afterwards Thomson Press closed down their children's book division and my book vanished too!)

Can thought (consciousness) exist outside the body? Can it be trained to do so? Can its existence continue after the body has gone? Does it *need* a body? (but without a body it would have nothing to do.)

Of course, thoughts can travel. But do they travel of their own volition, or because of the bodily energy that sustains them?

We have the wonders of clairvoyance, of presentiments, and premonitions in dreams. How to account for these?

Our thinking is conditioned by past experience (including the past experience of the human race), and so, as Bergson said: 'We think with only a small part of the past, but it is with our entire past, including the original bent of the soul, that we desire, will, and act.'

'The original bent of the soul...' I accept that man has a soul, or he would be incapable of compassion.

February

We move from mind to matter:

Tried a pizza—seemed to take an hour to travel down my gullet.

Two days later: Swiss cheese pie with Mrs Goel, who's Swiss—and more adventures of the digestive tract.

Next day: supper with the Deutschmanns from Australia. Australian pie.

Following day: rest and recovery. Then reverted to good old dal bhaat.

Accompanied N—to Dehradun and ended up paying for our lunch. The trouble with rich people is that they never seem to have any money on them. That's how they stay rich, I suppose.

March

Sold *A Crow for All Seasons* to the Children's Film Society for a small sum. They think it will make a good animated film. And so it will. But I'm pretty sure they won't make it. They have forgotten about the story they bought from me five years ago! (Neither film was ever made.)

April

The wind in the pines and deodars hums and moans, but in the chestnut, it rustles and chatters and makes cheerful conversation. The horse-chestnut in full leaf is a magnificent sight.

∿

Children down with mumps. I go clown with a viral fever for two days. Recover and write three articles. Hope for the best. It is not in mortals to *command* success.

∿

Men get their sensual natures from their mothers, their intellectual make-up from their fathers; women, the other way round. (Or so I'm told!)

June

Not many years ago, you had to walk for weeks to reach the pilgrim destinations—Badrinath, Gangotri, Kedarnath, Tungnath... Last week, within a few days, I covered them all, as most of them are now accessible by motorable road. I liked some of the smaller places, such as Nandprayag, which are still unspoilt. Otherwise, I'm afraid the dhaba-culture of urban India has followed the cars and buses into the mountains and up to the shrines.

July

The deodar (unlike the pine) is a hospitable tree. It allows other things to grow beneath it, and it tolerates growth upon its trunk and branches—moss, ferns, small plants. The tiny young cones are like blossoms on the dark green foliage at this time of the year.

∿

Slipped and cracked my head against the grid of a truck. Blood gushed forth, so I dashed across to Dr Joshi's little clinic and had three stitches and an anti-tetanus shot. Now you know why I don't travel well.

∿

M.C. Beautiful, seductive. 'She walks in beauty like the night...'

August

Endless rain. No sun for a week. But M.C. playful, loving. In good spirits, I wrote a funny story about cricket. I'd find it hard to write a serious story about cricket. The farcical element appeals to me more than the 'nobler' aspects of the game. Uncle Ken made more runs with his pads than with his bat. And out of every ten catches that came his way, he took one!

October

Paid rent in advance for next year; paid school fees to end of this year. Broke, but don't owe a paisa to a soul. Ice cream in town with Raki. Came home to find a couple of cheques waiting for me!

M.C. Quick as a vixen, but makes the chase worthwhile.

We walk in the wind and the rain. Exhilarating.

Frantic kisses.

Time to say goodbye!

When love is swiftly stolen,

It hasn't time to die.

When in love, I'm inspired to write bad verse.

Teilhard de Chardin said it better:

'Some day, after we have mastered the winds, the waves, the tides and gravity, we shall harness for God the energies of love. Then for the second time in the history of the world, man will have discovered fire.'

February 1986

Destiny is really the strength of our desires.

⌣

Raki back from the village. I'm happy he has made himself popular there, adapted to both worlds, the comparative sophistication of Mussoorie and the simple earthiness of village Bachhanshu in the remoteness of Garhwal. Being able to get on with everyone, rich or poor, old or young, makes life so much easier. Or so I've found! My parents' broken marriage, father's early death, and the difficulties of adapting to my stepfather's home, resulted in my being something of a loner until I was thirty. Now I've become a family person without marrying. Selfish?

⁓

Returned to two great comic novels—H.G. Wells's *History of Mr Polly* and George and Weedon Grossmith's *The Diary of Nobody*. *Polly* has some marvellous set-pieces, while *Nobody* never fails to make me laugh.

⁓

M.C. returns with a spring in the Springtime. The same good nature and sense of humour.

Three things in love the foolish will desire:

Faith, constancy, and passion; but the wise
Only an hour's happiness require
And not to look into uncaring eyes.

(Kenneth Hopkins)

March

Getting Granny's Glasses received a nomination for the Carnegie Medal. *Cricket for the Crocodile* makes friends.

After a cold wet spell, Holi brings warmer days, ladybirds, new friends.

May

So now I'm 52. Time to pare life down to the basics of doing.

    a)   what I have to do
    b)   what I want to do

Much prefer the latter.

June

Blood pressure up and down.

Writing for a living: it's a battlefield!

People do ask funny questions. Accosted on the road by a stranger, who proceeds to cross-examine me, starting with: 'Excuse me, are you a good writer?' For once, I'm stumped for an answer.

Muki's no better. Bangs my study door, sees me give a start, and says: 'This door makes a lot of noise, doesn't it?'

August

Thousands converge on the town from outlying villages, for a local festival. By late evening, scores of drunks staggering about on the road. A few fights, but largely good-natured.

The women dress very attractively and colourfully. But for most of the menfolk, the height of fashion appears to be a new pyjama-suit. But I'm a pyjama person myself. Pyjamas are comfortable, I write better wearing pyjamas!

September

Month began with a cheque that bounced. Refrained from checking my blood pressure.

Monsoon growth at its peak. The ladies' slipper orchids are tailing off, but I noticed all the following wild flowers: balsam (two kinds), commelina, agrimony, wild geranium (very pretty), sprays of white flowers emanating from the wild ginger, the scarlet fruit of the cobra lily just forming tiny mushrooms set like pearls in a retaining wall; ferns still green, which means more rain to come; escaped dahlias everywhere; wild begonias and much else. The best time of year for wild flowers.

February 1987

Home again, after five days in hospital with bleeding ulcers. Loving care from Prem. Support from Ganesh and others. Nurse Nirmala very caring. I prefer nurses to doctors.

Milk, hateful milk!

After a week, back in hospital. Must have been all that milk. Or maybe Nurse Nirmala!

March

To Delhi for a check-up. Public gardens ablaze with flowers. Felt much better.

'A merry heart does good like a medicine, but a broken spirit dries the bones.'

'He who tenderly brings up his servant from a child, shall have him become his son at the end.'

(Book of Proverbs)

May

Lines for future use:

Lunch (at my convent school) was boiled mutton and overcooked pumpkin, which made death lose some of its sting.

Pictures on the wall are not just something to look at. After a time, they become company.

Another bus accident, and a curious crowd gathered with disaster-inspired speed.

He (Upendra) has a bonfire of a laugh.

(Forgot to use these lines, so here they are!)

May

Ordered a birthday cake, but it failed to arrive. Sometimes I think inertia is the greatest force in the world.

Wrote a ghost story, something I enjoy doing from time to time, although I must admit that, try as I might, I have yet to encounter a supernatural being. Unless you can count dreams as being supernatural experiences.

August

After the drought, the deluge.

Landslide near the house. It rumbled away all night and I kept getting up to see how close it was getting to us. About twenty feet away. The house is none too stable, badly in need of repairs. In fact, it looks a bit like the Lucknow Residency after the rebels had finished shelling it.

(It did, however, survive the landslide, although the retaining wall above our flat collapsed, filling the sitting-room with rubble.)

November

To Delhi, to receive a generous award from Indian Council for Child Education. Presented to me by the Vice President of India. Got back to my host's home to discover that the envelope contained another awardee's cheque. He was due to leave for Ahmedabad by train. Rushed to railway station, to find him on the platform studying my cheque which he had just discovered in his pocket. Exchanged cheques. All's well that ends well.

A Delhi Visit

A long day's taxi journey to Delhi. It gets tiring towards the end, but I have always found the road journey interesting and at times quite enchanting—especially the rural scene from outside Dehradun, through Roorkee and various small wayside towns, up to Muzaffarnagar and the outskirts of Meerut: the sugar-cane being harvested and taken to the sugar factories (by cart or truck); the fruit on sale everywhere (right now, it's the season for bananas and 'chakotra' lemons); children bathing in small canals; the serenity of mango groves...

Of course, there's the other side to all this—the litter that accumulates wherever there are large centres of population; the blaring of horns; loudspeakers here and there. It's all part of the picture. But the picture as a whole is a fascinating one, and the colours can't be matched anywhere else.

Marigolds blaze in the sun. Yes, whole fields of them, for they are much in demand on all sorts of ceremonial occasions: marriages, temple pujas, and garlands for dignitaries—making the humble marigold a good cash crop.

And not so humble after all. For although the rose may still be the queen of flowers, and the jasmine the princess of fragrance, the marigold holds its own through sheer sturdiness, colour and cheerfulness. It is a cheerful flower, no doubt about that—brightening up winter days, often when there is little else in bloom. It doesn't really have a fragrance—simply an acid odour, not to everyone's liking—but it has a wonderful range of colour, from lower yellow to deep orange to golden bronze, especially among the giant varieties in the hills.

Otherwise this is not a great month for flowers, although at the India International Centre (IIC) in Delhi, where I am staying, there is a pretty tree with fragile pink flowers—the Chorisia speciosa, each bloom having five large pink petals, with long pistula.

My Trees in the Himalayas

Living in a cottage at 7,000 ft in the Garhwal Himalayas, I am fortunate to have a big window that opens out on the forest so that the trees are almost within my reach. If I jumped, I could land quite neatly in the arms of an oak or horse chestnut. I have never made that leap, but the big langurs—silver-grey monkeys with long, swishing tails—often spring from the trees onto my corrugated tin roof, making enough noise to frighten all the birds away.

Standing on its own outside my window is a walnut tree, and truly this is a tree for all seasons. In winter, the branches were bare; but they were smooth, straight and round like the arms of an apsara. In spring each limb produces a bright green spear of new growth, and by midsummer the entire tree is in leaf. Toward the end of the monsoon, the walnuts, encased in their green jackets, have reached maturity. When the jackets begin to split, you can see the hard brown shells of the nuts, and inside each shell is the delicious meat itself. Look closely at the nut, and you will notice that it is shaped rather like the human brain. No wonder the ancients prescribed walnuts for headaches.

Every year this tree gives me a basket of walnuts. But last year, the nuts were disappearing one by one, and I was at a loss as to who had been taking them. Could it have been Bijju, the milkman's small son? He was an inveterate tree climber, but he was usually to be found on the oak trees, gathering fodder for his herd. He admitted that his cows had enjoyed my dahlias, which they had eaten the previous week, but he stoutly denied having fed them walnuts, saying they did not care for them.

Later, I found a fat langur sitting in the walnut tree. I watched him for some time to see if he was going to help himself to the nuts, but he was only sunning himself. When he thought I wasn't looking, he came down and ate the geraniums; but he did not take any walnuts.

It wasn't the woodpecker either. He was out there every day, knocking furiously against the bark of the tree, trying to pry an insect out of a narrow crack. He was strictly non-vegetarian and none the worse for it.

The nuts seemed to disappear early in the morning while I was still in bed, so one day I surprised everyone, including myself, by getting up before sunrise. I was just in time to catch the culprit climbing out of the walnut tree. She was an old woman who sometimes came to cut grass on the hillside. Her face was as wrinkled as the walnuts she had been pinching. But in spite of her age, her arms and legs were sturdy. When she saw me, she was as swift as a civet cat in getting out of the tree.

'And how many walnuts did you gather today, Grandmother?' I asked.

'Just two,' she said with a giggle, offering them to me on her open palm. I accepted one, and thus encouraged, she climbed higher into the tree and helped herself to the remaining nuts. It was impossible for me to object. I was taken with admiration for her agility. She must have been twice my age, but I knew I could never get up that tree. To the victor, the spoils!

Last winter the PWD decided to take a new road past my doorstep, and the first casualty was the walnut tree. Along with a large number of different trees growing below the cottage, it fell to the contractors' axes.

Recently when I met the old woman on the road, I asked her, 'Where do you get your walnuts now, Grandmother?'

'Nowhere,' she answered stoically. 'That was the last walnut tree on the hillside.'

Unlike the prized walnuts, the horse chestnuts are inedible. Even the rhesus monkeys throw them away in disgust. But the tree itself is a friendly one, especially in summer when it is in full leaf. The lightest breeze makes the leaves break into conversation, and their rustle is a cheerful sound. The spring flowers of the horse chestnut look like candelabra, and when the blossoms fall, they carpet the hillside with their pale pink petals. It stands erect and dignified and does not bend with the wind. In spring, the new leaves, or needles, are a tender green, while during the monsoon, the tiny young cones spread like blossoms in the dark green folds of the branches.

The deodar enjoys the company of its own kind: where one deodar grows, there will be others. A walk in a deodar forest is awe-inspiring—surrounded on all sides by these great sentinels of the mountains, you feel as though the trees themselves are on the march.

I walk among the trees outside my window often, acknowledging their presence with a touch of my hand against their trunks. The oak has been there the longest, and the wind has bent its upper branches and twisted a few so that it looks shaggy and undistinguished. But it is a good tree for the privacy of birds. Sometimes it seems completely uninhabited until there is a whining sound, as of a helicopter approaching, and a party of long-tailed blue magpies flies across the forest glade.

Most of the pines near my home are on the next hillside. But there is a small Himalayan blue a little way below the cottage, and sometimes I sit beneath it to listen to the wind playing softly in its branches.

When I open the window at night, there is almost always something to listen to—the mellow whistle of a pygmy owlet, or the sharp cry of a barking deer. Sometimes, if I am lucky, I will see the moon coming up over the next mountain, and two distant deodars in perfect silhouette.

Some night sounds outside my window remain strange and mysterious. Perhaps they are the sounds of the trees themselves, stretching their limbs in the dark, shifting a little, flexing their fingers, whispering to one another. These great trees of the mountains, I feel they know me well, as I watch them and listen to their secrets, happy to rest my head beneath their outstretched arms.

And Now We Are Twelve

People often ask me why I've chosen to live in Mussoorie for so long—almost forty years without any significant breaks.

'I forgot to go away,' I tell them, but of course, that isn't the real reason.

The people here are friendly, but then people are friendly in a great many other places. The hills, the valleys are beautiful; but they are just as beautiful in Kulu or Kumaon.

'This is where the family has grown up and where we all live,' I say, and those who don't know me are puzzled because the general impression of the writer is of a reclusive old bachelor.

Unmarried I may be, but single I am not. Not since Prem came to live and work with me in 1970. A year later, he was married. Then his children came along and stole my heart; and when they grew up, their children came along and stole my wits. So now I'm an enchanted bachelor, head of a family of twelve. Sometimes I go out to bat, sometimes to bowl, but generally I prefer to be twelfth man, carrying out the drinks!

In the old days, when I was a solitary writer living on baked beans, the prospect of my suffering from obesity was very remote. Now there is a little more of author than there used to be, and the other day five-year-old Gautam patted me on my tummy (or balcony, as I prefer to call it) and remarked: 'Dada, you should join the WWF.'

'I'm already a member,' I said. 'I joined the World Wildlife Fund years ago.'

'Not that,' he said. 'I mean the World Wrestling Federation.'

If I have a tummy today, it's thanks to Gautam's grandfather and now his mother who, over the years, has made sure that I am well-fed and well-proportioned.

Forty years ago, when I was a lean young man, people would look at me and say, 'Poor chap, he's definitely undernourished. What on earth made him take up writing as a profession?' Now they look at me and say, 'You wouldn't think he was a writer, would you? Too well nourished!'

It was a cold, wet and windy March evening when Prem came back from the village with his wife and first-born child, then just four months old. In those days, they had to walk to the house from the bus stand; it was a half-hour walk in the cold rain, and the baby was all wrapped up when they entered the front room. Finally, I got a glimpse of him, and he of me, and it was friendship at first sight. Little Rakesh (as he was to be called) grabbed me by the nose and held on. He did not have much of a nose to grab, but he had a dimpled chin and I played with it until he smiled.

The little chap spent a good deal of his time with me during those first two years of his in Maplewood—learning to crawl, to toddle and then to walk unsteadily about the little sitting room. I would carry him into the garden, and later, up the steep gravel path to the main road. Rakesh enjoyed these little excursions, and so did I, because in pointing out trees, flowers, birds, butterflies, beetles, grasshoppers, et al., I was giving myself a chance to observe them better instead of just taking them for granted.

In particular, there was a pair of squirrels that lived in the big oak tree outside the cottage. Squirrels are rare in Mussoorie though common enough down in the valley. This couple must have come up for the summer. They became quite friendly, and although they never got around to taking food from our hands, they were soon entering the house quite freely. The sitting room window opened directly on to the oak tree whose various denizens—ranging from stag beetles to small birds and even an acrobatic bat—took to darting in and out of the cottage at various times of the day or night.

Life at Maplewood was quite idyllic, and when Rakesh's baby

brother, Suresh, came into the world, it seemed we were all set for a long period of domestic bliss; but at such times tragedy is often lurking just around the corner. Suresh was just over a year old when he contracted tetanus. Doctors and hospitals were of no avail. He suffered—as any child would from this terrible affliction—and left this world before he had a chance of getting to know it. His parents were broken-hearted. And I feared for Rakesh, for he wasn't a very healthy boy, and two of his cousins in the village had already succumbed to tuberculosis.

It was to be a difficult year for me. A criminal charge was brought against me for a slightly risque story I'd written for a Bombay magazine. I had to face trial in Bombay and this involved three journeys there over a period of a year and a half, before an irate but perceptive judge found the charges baseless and gave me an honourable acquittal.

It's the only time I've been involved with the law and I sincerely hope it is the last. Most cases drag on interminably, and the main beneficiaries are the lawyers. My trial would have been much longer had not the prosecutor died of a heart attack in the middle of the proceedings. His successor did not pursue it with the same vigour. His heart was not in it. The whole issue had started with a complaint by a local politician, and when he lost interest so did the prosecution. Nevertheless the trial, once begun, had to be seen through. The defence (organized by the concerned magazine) marshalled its witnesses (which included Nissim Ezekiel and the Marathi playwright Vijay Tendulkar). I made a short speech which couldn't have been very memorable as I have forgotten it! And everyone, including the judge, was bored with the whole business. After that, I steered clear of controversy publications. I have never set out to shock the world. Telling a meaningful story was all that really mattered. And that is still the case.

I was looking forward to continuing our idyllic existence in Maplewood, but it was not to be. The powers-that-be, in the shape of the Public Works Department (PWD), had decided to build a 'strategic' road just below the cottage and without any warning to us, all the trees in the vicinity were felled (including the friendly old oak) and the hillside was rocked by explosives and bludgeoned by bulldozers. I decided it was time to move. Prem and Chandra (Rakesh's mother) wanted to move too; not because of the road, but because they associated the house with the death of little Suresh, whose presence seemed to haunt every room, every corner of the cottage. His little cries of pain and suffering still echoed through the still hours of the night.

I rented rooms at the top of Landour, a good thousand feet higher up the mountain. Rakesh was now old enough to go to school, and every morning I would walk with him down to the little convent school near the clock tower. Prem would go to fetch him in the afternoon. The walk took us about half an hour, and on the way Rakesh would ask for a story and I would have to rack my brains in order to invent one. I am not the most inventive of writers, and fantastical plots are beyond me. My forte is observation, recollection and reflection. Small boys prefer action. So I invented a leopard who suffered from acute indigestion because he'd eaten one human too many and a belt buckle was causing an obstruction.

This went down quite well until Rakesh asked me how the leopard got around the problem of the victim's clothes.

'The secret,' I said, 'is to pounce on them when their trousers are off!'

Not the stuff of which great picture books are made, but then, I've never attempted to write stories for beginners. Red Riding Hood's granny-eating wolf always scared me as a small boy, and yet parents have always found it acceptable for toddlers. Possibly they feel grannies are expendable.

Mukesh was born around this time and Savitri (Dolly) a couple of years later. When Dolly grew older, she was annoyed at having been named Savitri (my choice), which is now considered very old fashioned; so we settled for Dolly. I can understand a child's dissatisfaction with given names.

My first name was Owen, which in Welsh means 'brave'. As I am not in the least brave, I have preferred not to use it. One given name and one surname should be enough.

When my granny said, 'But you should try to be brave, otherwise how will you survive in this cruel world?' I replied: 'Don't worry, I can run very fast.'

Not that I've ever had to do much running, except when I was pursued by a lissome Australian lady who thought I'd make a good obedient husband. It wasn't so much the lady I was running from, but the prospect of spending the rest of my life in some remote cattle station in the Australian outback. Anyone who has tried to drag me away from India has always met with stout resistance.

Up on the heights of Landour lived a motley crowd. My immediate neighbours included a Frenchwoman who played the sitar (very badly) all through the night; a Spanish lady with two husbands, one of whom practised acupuncture—rather ineffectively as far as he was concerned, for he seemed to be dying of some mysterious debilitating disease. The other came and went rather mysteriously, and finally ended up in Tihar Jail, having been apprehended at Delhi airport carrying a large amount of contraband hashish.

Apart from these and a few other colourful characters, the area was inhabited by some very respectable people, retired brigadiers, air marshals and rear admirals, almost all of whom were busy writing their memoirs. I had to read or listen to extracts from their literary efforts. This was slow torture. A few years before, I had done a stint of editing for a magazine called *Imprint*. It had involved going through hundreds of badly written manuscripts, and in some cases (friends of the owner!) rewriting some of them for publication. One of life's joys had been to throw up that particular job, and now here I was, besieged by all the top brass of the Army, Navy and Air Force, each one determined that I should read, inwardly digest, improve, and if possible find a publisher for their outpourings. Thank goodness they were all retired. I could not be shot or court-martialled. But at least two of them set their wives upon me, and these intrepid ladies would turn up around noon with my 'homework'—typescripts to read and edit! There was no escape. My own writing was of no consequence to them. I told them that I was taking sitar lessons, but they disapproved, saying I was more suited to the tabla.

When Prem discovered a set of vacant rooms further down the Landour slope, close to the school and bazaar, I rented them without hesitation. This was Ivy Cottage. Come up and see me sometimes, but leave your manuscripts behind.

When we came to Ivy Cottage in 1980, we were six, Dolly having just been born. Now, twenty-four years later, we are twelve. I think that's a reasonable expansion. The increase has been brought about by Rakesh's marriage twelve years ago, and Mukesh's marriage two years ago. Both precipitated themselves into marriage when they were barely twenty, and both were lucky. Beena and Binita, who happen to be real sisters, have brightened and enlivened our lives with their happy, positive natures and the wonderful children they have brought into the world. More about them later.

Ivy Cottage has, on the whole, been kind to us, and particularly kind to me. Some houses like their occupants, others don't. Maplewood, set in the shadow of the hill, lacked a natural cheerfulness; there was a settled gloom about the place. The house at the top of Landour was too exposed to the elements to have any sort of character. The wind moaning in the deodars may have inspired the sitar player but it did nothing for my writing. I produced very little up there.

On the other hand, Ivy Cottage—especially my little room facing the sunrise—has been conducive to creative work. Novellas, poems, essays, children's stories, anthologies, have all come tumbling on to whatever sheets of paper happen to be nearest me. As I write by hand, I have only to grab for the nearest pad, loose sheet, page-proof or envelope whenever the muse takes hold of me; which is surprisingly often.

I came here when I was nearing fifty. Now I'm seventy, and

instead of drying up, as some writers do in their later years, I find myself writing with as much ease and assurance as when I was twenty. And I enjoy writing. It's not a burdensome task. I may not have anything of earth-shattering significance to convey to the world, but in conveying my sentiments to you, dear readers, and in telling you something about my relationship with people and the natural world, I hope to bring a little pleasure and sunshine into your life.

Life isn't a bed of roses, not for any of us, and I have never had the comforts or luxuries that wealth can provide. But here I am, doing my own thing, in my own time and my own way. What more can I ask of life? Give me a big cash prize and I'd still be here. I happen to like the view from my window. And I like to have Gautam coming up to me, patting me on the tummy, and telling me that I'll make a good goalkeeper one day.

It's a Sunday morning, as I come to the conclusion of this chapter. There's bedlam in the house. Siddharth's football keeps smashing against the front door. Shrishti is practising her dance routine in the back verandah. Gautam has cut his finger and is trying his best to bandage it with Sellotape. He is, of course, the youngest of Rakesh's three musketeers, and probably the most independent-minded. Siddharth, now ten, is restless, never quite able to expend all his energy. 'Does not pay enough attention,' says his teacher. It must be hard for anyone to pay attention in a class of sixty! How does the poor teacher pay attention?

If you, dear reader, have any ambitions to be a writer, you must first rid yourself of any notion that perfect peace and quiet is the first requirement. There is no such thing as perfect peace and quiet except perhaps in a monastery or a cave in the mountains. And what would you write about, living in a cave? One should be able to write in a train, a bus, a bullock cart, in good weather or bad, on a park bench or in the middle of a noisy classroom.

Of course, the best place is the sun-drenched desk right next to my bed. It isn't always sunny here, but on a good day like this, it's ideal. The children are getting ready for school, dogs are barking in the street, and down near the water tap there's an altercation between two women with empty buckets, the tap having dried up. But these are all background noises and will subside in due course. They are not directed at me.

Hello! Here's Atish, Mukesh's little ten-month old infant, crawling over the rug, curious to know why I'm sitting on the edge of my bed scribbling away, when I should be playing with him. So I shall play with him for five minutes and then come back to this page. Giving him my time is important. After all, I won't be around when he grows up.

Half an hour later. Atish soon tired of playing with me, but meanwhile Gautam had absconded with my pen. When I asked him to return it, he asked, 'Why don't you get a computer? Then we can play games on it.'

'My pen is faster than any computer,' I tell him, 'I wrote three pages this morning without getting out of bed. And yesterday I wrote two pages sitting under Billoo's chestnut tree.'

'Until a chestnut fell on your head,' says Gautam, 'Did it hurt?'

'Only a little,' I said, putting on a brave front.

He had saved the chestnut and now he showed it to me. The smooth brown horse-chestnut shone in the sunlight.

'Let's stick it in the ground,' I said. 'Then in the spring a chestnut tree will come up.'

So we went outside and planted the chestnut on a plot of wasteland. Hopefully a small tree will burst through the earth at about the time this little book is published.

The Garden of Memories

Sitting in the sun on a winter's afternoon, feeling my age just a little (I'm over seventy), I began reminiscing about my boyhood in the Dehra of long ago, and found myself missing the old times—friends of my youth, my grandmother, our neighbours, interesting characters in our small town, and, of course, my eccentric relative—the dashing young Uncle Ken!

Yes, Dehra was a small town then—uncluttered, uncrowded, with quiet lanes and pretty gardens and shady orchards.

The only time in my life that I was fortunate enough to live in a house with a real garden—as opposed to a backyard or balcony or windswept verandah—during those three years when I spent my winter holidays (December to March) in Granny's bungalow on Old Survey Road.

The best months were February and March, when the garden was heavy with the scent of sweet peas, the flower beds were a many-coloured quilt of phlox, antirrhinum, larkspur, petunia and Californian poppy. I loved the bright yellows of the Californian poppies, the soft pinks of our own Indian poppies, the subtle perfume of petunias and snapdragons and, above all, the delicious, overpowering scent of the massed sweet peas, which grew taller than me.

Flowers made a sensualist of me. They taught me the delight of smell, colour and touch—yes, touch too, for to press a rose to one's lips is much like a gentle, hesitant, exploratory kiss...

Granny decided on what flowers should be sown, and where. Dhuki, the gardener, did the digging and weeding, sowing and transplanting. He was a skinny, taciturn old man, who had begun to resemble the weeds he flung away. He did not mind answering my questions, but never did he allow our brief conversations to interfere with his work. Most of the time he was to be found on his haunches, hoeing and weeding with a little spade called a *khurpi.* He would throw out the smaller marigolds because he said Granny did not care for them. I felt sorry for these colourful little discards, collected them and transplanted them to a little garden patch of my own at the back of the house, near the garden wall.

Another so-called weed that I liked was a little purple flower that grew in clusters all over Dehra, on any bit of wasteland, in ditches, on canal banks. It flowered from late winter into early summer, and it will be growing in the valley and beyond long after gardens have become obsolete, as indeed they must, considering the rapid spread of urban clutter. It brightens up fields and roads where you least expect a little colour. I have since learnt that it is called ageratum, and that it is actually prized as a garden (lower in Europe, -where it is described as Blue Mink in the seed catalogues. Here it isn't blue but purple, and it grows all the way from Rajpur (just above Dehra) to the outskirts of Meerut; then it disappears.

Other garden outcasts include the lantana bush—an attractive wayside shrub—the thorn apple, various thistles, daisies and dandelions. But both Granny and Dhuki had declared a war on weeds, and many of these commoners had to exist outside the confines of the garden. Like slum children, they survived rather well in ditches and on the roadside, while their more pampered fellow citizens were prone to leaf diseases and parasitic infections of various kinds.

The verandah was a place where Granny herself could potter about, attending to various ferns, potted palms and colourful geraniums. She averred that geraniums kept snakes away, although she never said why. As far as I know, snakes don't have a great sense of smell.

One day, I saw a snake curled up at the bottom of the verandah steps. When it saw me, or became aware of my footsteps, it uncoiled itself and slithered away. I told Granny about it, and observed that it did not seem to be bothered by the geraniums.

'Ah,' said Granny. 'But for those geraniums, the snake would have entered the house!' There was no arguing with Granny. Or with Uncle Ken, when he was at his most pontifical.

One day, while walking near the canal bank, we came upon a green grass snake holding a frog in its mouth. The frog was half in, half out, and with the help of my hockey stick, I made the snake disgorge the unfortunate creature. It hopped away, none the worse for its adventure.

I felt quite pleased with myself. 'Is this what it feels like to be God?' I mused aloud.

'No,' said Uncle Ken. 'God would have let the snake finish its lunch.'

Uncle Ken was one of those people who went through life without having to do much, although a great deal seemed to happen around him. He acted as a sort of catalyst for events that involved the family, friends, neighbours, the town itself. He believed in the fruits of hard work: other people's hard work,

Ken was good-looking as a boy, and his sisters (including my mother, the youngest) doted on him. He took full advantage of their devotion, and, as the girls grew up and married, Ken took it for granted that they and their husbands would continue to look after his welfare. You could say he was the originator of the welfare state: his own.

I'll say this for Uncle Ken, he had a large fund of curiosity in his nature, and he loved to explore the town we lived in, and any other town or city where he might happen to find himself. With one sister settled in Lucknow, another in Ranchi, a third in Bhopal and a fourth in Shimla, Uncle Ken managed to see a cross section of India by dividing his time between all his sisters and their long-suffering husbands.

Uncle Ken liked to walk. Occasionally he borrowed my bicycle, but he had a tendency to veer off the main road and into ditches and other obstacles. After a collision with a bullock cart, in which he tore his trousers and damaged the handlebar of my bicycle, he concluded that walking was the best way of getting around Dehra.

Uncle Ken dressed quite smartly for a man of no particular occupation. He had a blue striped blazer and a red striped blazer; he usually wore white or off-white trousers, immaculately pressed (by Granny). He was the delight of shoeshine boys, for he would always have his shoes polished. Summers he wore a straw hat, telling everyone he had worn it for the Varsity Boat Race while rowing for Oxford (he hadn't attended college there, let alone rowed for the college team); winters he wore one of Grandfather's old felt hats. He seldom went bareheaded. At thirty he was almost completely bald, prompting Aunt Mabel to remark, 'Well, Ken, you must be grateful for small mercies. At least you'll never have bats getting entangled in your hair.'

Thanks to all his walking, Uncle Ken had a good digestion, which kept pace with a hearty appetite. Our walks would be punctuated by short stops at chaat shops, sweet shops, fruit stalls, confectioners, small bakeries and other eateries.

'Have you brought any pocket money along?' he would ask, for he was usually broke.

'Granny gave me five rupees.'

'We'll try some rasgullas, then.'

And the rasgullas would be followed by gulab jamuns, until my five rupees were finished. Uncle Ken received a small allowance from Granny, but he ferreted it away to spend on clothes, preferring to spend my pocket money on perishables such as ice creams, kulfis and Indian sweets.

On one occasion, when neither of us had any money, Uncle Ken decided to venture into a sugarcane field on the outskirts of the town. He had broken off a stick of cane, and was busy chewing on it, when the owner of the field spotted us and let out a volley of imprecations. We fled from the field, with the irate farmer giving chase. I could run faster than Uncle Ken, and did so. The farmer would have caught up with Uncle Ken if the latter's hat hadn't blown off, causing a diversion. The farmer picked up the hat, examined it, seemed to fancy it, and put it on. Several small boys clapped and cheered. The farmer marched off, wearing the hat, and Uncle Ken wisely decided against making any attempt to retrieve it.

'I'll get another one,' he said philosophically.

He wore a pith helmet, or sola topi, for the next few days, as he thought it would protect him from sticks and stones. For a while he harboured a paranoia that all the sugarcane farmers in the valley were looking for him, to avenge his foray into their fields. But after some time he discarded the topi because, according to him, it interfered with his good looks.

Granny grew the best sweet peas in Dehra. But she never entered them at the Annual Flower Show held every year in the second week of March. She did not grow flowers to win prizes, she said; she grew them to please the spirit of Grandfather, who still hovered about the house and grounds he'd built thirty years earlier.

Miss Kellner, Granny's crippled but valued tenant, said the flowers were grown to attract beautiful butterflies, and she was right. In early summer, swarms of butterflies flitted about the garden.

Uncle Ken had no compunction about winning prizes, even though he did nothing to deserve them. Without telling anyone, he submitted a large display of Granny's sweet peas for the flower show, and when the prizes were announced, lo and behold, Kenneth Clerke had been awarded first prize for his magnificent display of sweet peas.

Granny refused to speak to him for several days.

Uncle Ken had been hoping for a cash prize, but they gave him a flower vase. He told me it was a Ming vase. But it looked more like Meerut to me. He offered it to Granny, hoping to propitiate her; but, still displeased with him, she gave it to Mr Khastgir, the artist next door, who kept his paintbrushes in it.

Although I was sometimes a stubborn and unruly boy (my hero was Richmal Crompton's William), I got on well with old ladies, especially those who, like Miss Kellner, were fond of offering me chocolates, marzipans, soft nankhatai biscuits (made at Yusuf's bakery in the Dilaram Bazaar), and pieces of crystallized ginger. Miss Kellner couldn't walk—had never walked—and so she could only admire the garden from a distance, but it was from her that I learnt the names of many flowers, trees, birds and even butterflies.

Uncle Ken wasn't any good with names, but he wanted to catch a rare butterfly. He said he could make a fortune if he caught a leaf butterfly called the Purple Emperor. He equipped himself with a butterfly net, a bottle of ether, and a cabinet for mounting his trophies; he then prowled all over the grounds, making frequent forays at anything that flew.

He caught several common species—Red Admirals, a Tortoiseshell, a Painted Lad, even the occasional dragonfly—but the high-flying Purple Emperor and other exotics eluded him, as did the fortune he was always aspiring to make.

Eventually he caught an angry wasp, which stung him through the netting. Chased by its fellow wasps, he took refuge in the lily pond and emerged sometime later, draped in lilies and waterweeds.

After this, Uncle Ken retired from the butterfly business, insisting that tiger hunting was safer.

The Dehra I Know

Formally, it's now known as Dehra Dun, but in the 1940s and '50s, when we were young, everyone called it Dehra.

That's where I spent much of my childhood, boyhood, and early manhood, and it was the Dehra I wrote about in many of my books and stories.

It was very different from the Dehra Dun of today—much smaller, much greener, considerably less crowded; sleepier too, and somewhat laid-back, easy-going; fond of gossip, but tolerant of human foibles. A place of bicycles and pony-drawn tongas. Only a few cars; no three-wheelers. And you could walk almost anywhere, at any time of the year, night or day.

The Dehra I knew really fell into three periods. The Dehra of my childhood, staying in my grandmother's house on the Old Survey Road (not much left of that bungalow now). The Dehra of my schooldays, when I would come home for the holidays to stay with my mother and stepfather—a different house on almost every visit, right up until the time I left for England. And then the Dehra of my return to India, when I lived on my own in a small flat above Astley Hall and wrote many of my best stories.

While I was in England, I wrote my first novel *The Room on the Roof*, which was all about the Dehra I had left and the people and young friends I had known and loved. It was a little immature, but it came straight from the heart—the heart and mind of a seventeen-year-old—and if it's still fresh today, fifty years after its first publication, it's probably because it was so spontaneous and unsophisticated.

Back in Dehra, I wrote a sequel of sorts, *Vagrants in the Valley*.

It wasn't as good, probably because I had exhausted my adolescence as a subject for fiction; but it did capture aspects of life in Dehra and the Doon valley in the early '50s.

I had returned to India and Dehra when I was twenty-one, and set up my writing shop, so to speak, in that flat above Bibiji's provision store.

Bibiji was my stepfather's first wife. He and my mother had moved to Delhi, leaving Bibiji with the provision store. I got on very well with her and helped her with her accounts, and she gave me the use of her rooms above the shop. I think it's only in India that you could find such a situation—a young offspring of the Raj, somewhat at odds with his mother and Indian stepfather, choosing to live with the latter's abandoned first wife!

Bibiji made excellent parathas, shalgam (turnip) pickle, and kanji, a spicy carrot juice. And so, romantic though I may have been, I was far from being the young poet starving in a garret, nor was Bibiji to be pitied. She was Dehra's first woman shopkeeper, and she managed very well.

Bibiji was of course much older than me; heavily built, strong. She could toss sacks of flour about the shop. Her son, rather mischievous, kept out of her reach; a cuff about the ears would send him sprawling. She suffered from a hernia, and was immensely grateful to me for bringing her a hernia-belt from England; it provided her with considerable relief.

I was quite happy cooking up stories, most of them written after dark by the light of a kerosene lantern. Bibiji hadn't been able to pay the flat's accumulated electricity bills, and as a result the connection had been cut. But this did not bother me. I was quite content to live by candlelight or lamplight. It lent a romantic glow to my writing life.

And a lot of romance went into those early stories. There was the girl on the train in 'The Eyes Are Not Here', and the girl selling baskets on the platform at Deoli, and Aunt Mariam's amours behind the Dilaram Bazaar, and romantic episodes in places as unlikely as

Shamli and Bijnor (Pipalnagar). However, as my intention is to give the reader a picture of Dehra as I knew it, the stories in this collection are all set in Dehra Dun and its immediate environs. I was writing for anyone who would read me. It was only much later that I began writing for children.

Some favourite places for my fictional milieu were the parade-ground or maidaan, the Paltan Bazaar and its offshoots, the litchi gardens of Dalanwala, the tea-gardens, the quiet upper reaches of the Rajpur Road (non-transformed into shopping malls), the sal forests near Rajpur, the approach to Dehra by road or rail, and of course the railway station which is much the same as it used to be.

When I was a boy, many of the bungalows (such as the one built by my grandfather) had fairly large grounds or compounds—flower gardens in front, orchards at the back. Apart from litchis, the common fruit trees were papaya, guava, mango, lemon, and the pomalo, a sort of grapefruit. Most of those large compounds have now been converted into housing-estates. Dehra's population has gone from fifty thousand in 1950 to over seven lakh at present. Not much room left for fruit trees!

Some of the stories, such as 'A Handful of Nuts' and 'Living Without Money', were written long after I'd left Dehra, but I think the atmosphere of the place comes through quite strongly in them. When a writer looks back at a particular place or period in his life, he tries to capture the essence of the place and the experience.

During the two years I freelanced from Bibiji's flat (1956–58), I produced over thirty short stories, a couple of novellas, and numerous articles of an ephemeral nature. I managed to sell some of the stories to the BBC's Home service programme—*The Thief, Night Train at Deoli, The Woman on Platform 8, The Kitemaker*—others to the *Elizabethan, Illustrated Weekly of India, Sunday Statesman* (over the years, a few have been lost.) In India, ₹50 was the most you got for a short story or article back then, but you could live quite comfortably on three or four hundred rupees a month—provided your mode of transport was limited to the bicycle. Only successful businessmen and doctors owned cars.

My stepfather was an exception. He was an unsuccessful businessman who used a different car every month. That was because, before leaving Dehra, he ran a motor workshop, and if a car was left with him for repairs or overhauling ('oiling and greasing' he called it) he would use it for a month or two on the pretext of trying it out, before returning it to its owner. This he would do only when the owner's patience had reached its limit; sometimes the car had to be taken away by force. Occasionally, my stepfather would relent and return the car of his own accord—along with a bill for having looked after it for so long!

His talents went unappreciated in Dehra. When he moved to Delhi he became a successful salesperson.

Some of the characters in my Dehra stories were fictional, some were based on real people; Granny was real, of course. And so were the boys in 'The Room' and 'Vagrants'. But did Rusty really make love to Meena Kapoor? It's a question I have often been asked and must leave unanswered. It might have happened. But then again, it might not. I prefer to leave it as a sweet mystery that will never be solved.

One thing is certain. Dehra played an integral part in my development as a writer. More than Shimla, where I did my schooling. More than London, where I lived for nearly four years. More than Delhi, where I spent a number of years. As much as Mussoorie, where I have passed half my life. It must have been the ambience of the place, something about it, that suited my temperament.

But it's a different place now, and no longer do I feel like 'singin' in the rain' as I walk down the Rajpur Road. I am in danger of being knocked down by a speeding vehicle if I try out my old song-and-dance routine. So I keep well to the side of the pavement and look out for known landmarks—an old peepal tree, a familiar corner, a surviving bungalow, a bookshop, the sabzi-mandi, a bit of wasteland where once we played cricket.

There was a wild flower, a weed, that grew all over Dehra and still does. We called it Blue Mint. It grows in ditches, in neglected gardens, anywhere there's a bit of open land. It's there nearly all the year round. I've always associated it with Dehra. The burgeoning human population has been unable to suppress it. This is one plant that will never go extinct. It refuses to go away. I have known it since I was a boy, and as long as it's there I shall know that a part of me still lives in Dehra.

Joyfully I Write

I am a fortunate person. For over fifty years I have been able to make a living by doing what I enjoy most—writing.

Sometimes I wonder if I have written too much. One gets into the habit of serving up the same ideas over and over again, with a different sauce perhaps, but still the same ideas, themes, memories, characters. Writers are often chided for repeating themselves. Artists and musicians are given more latitude. No one criticized Turner for painting so many sunsets at sea, or Gauguin for giving us all those lovely Tahitian women, or Husain for treating us to so many horses, or Jamini Roy for giving us so many identical stylized figures.

In the world of music, one Puccini opera is very like another, a Chopin nocturne will return to familiar themes, and in the realm of lighter, modern music the same melodies recur with only slight variations. But authors are often taken to task for repeating themselves. They cannot help this, for in their writing they are expressing their personalities. Hemingway's world is very different from Jane Austen's. They are both unique worlds, but they do not change or mutate in the minds of their author-creators. Jane Austen spent all her life in one small place, and portrayed the people she knew. Hemingway roamed the world, but his characters remained much the same, usually extensions of himself.

In the course of a long writing career, it is inevitable that a writer will occasionally repeat himself, or return to themes that have remained with him even as new ideas and formulations enter his mind. The important thing is to keep writing, observing, listening and paying attention to the beauty of words and their arrangement.

And, like artists and musicians, the more we work on our art, the better it will be.

Writing, for me, is the simplest and greatest pleasure in the world. Putting a mood or an idea into words is an occupation I truly love. I plan my day so that there is time in it for writing a poem, or a paragraph, or an essay, or part of a story or longer work; not just because writing is my profession, but from a feeling of delight.

The world around me—be it the mountains or the busy street below my window—is teeming with subjects, sights, thoughts, that I wish to put into words in order to catch the fleeting moment, the passing image, the laughter, the joy, and sometimes, the sorrow. Life would be intolerable if I did not have this freedom to write every day. Not that everything I put down is worth preserving. A great many pages of manuscripts have found their way into my waste-paper basket or into the stove that warms the family room on cold winter evenings. I do not always please myself. I cannot always please others because, unlike the hard professionals, the Forsyths and the Sheldons, I am not writing to please everyone, I am really writing to please myself!

My theory of writing is that the conception should be as clear as possible, and that words should flow like a stream of clear water, preferably a mountain stream! You will, of course, encounter boulders, but you will learn to go over them or around them, so that your flow is unimpeded. If your stream gets too sluggish or muddy, it is better to put aside that particular piece of writing. Go to the source, go to the spring, where the water is purest, your thoughts as clear as the mountain air.

I do not write for more than an hour or two in the course of the day. Too long at the desk, and words lose their freshness.

Together with clarity and a good vocabulary, there must come a certain elevation of mood. Sterne must have been bubbling over with high spirits when he wrote *Tristram Shandy*. The sombre intensity of *Wuthering Heights* reflects Emily Brontë's passion for life, fully knowing that it was to be brief. Tagore's melancholy comes through in his poetry. Dickens is always passionate; there are no half measures in his work. Conrad's prose takes on the moods of the sea he knew and loved.

A real physical emotion accompanies the process of writing, and great writers are those who can channel this emotion into the creation of their best work.

'Are you a serious writer?' a schoolboy once asked.

'Well, I try to be *serious*,' I said, 'but cheerfulness keeps breaking in!'

Can a cheerful writer be taken seriously? I don't know. But I was certainly serious about making writing the main occupation of my life.

In order to do this, one has to give up many things—a job, security, comfort, domesticity—or rather, the pursuit of these things. Had I married when I was twenty-five, I would not have been able to throw up a good job as easily as I did at the time; I might now be living on a pension! God forbid. I am grateful for continued independence and the necessity to keep writing for my living, and for those who share their lives with me and whose joys and sorrows are mine too. An artist must not lose his hold on life. We do that when we settle for the safety of a comfortable old age.

Normally writers do not talk much, because they are saving their conversation for the readers of their books—those invisible listeners with whom we wish to strike a sympathetic chord. Of course, we talk freely with our friends, but we are reserved with people we do not know very well. If I talk too freely about a story I am going to write, chances are it will never be written. I have talked it to death.

Being alone is vital for any creative writer. I do not mean that you must live the life of a recluse. People who do not know me are frequently under the impression that I live in lonely splendour on a mountain top, whereas in reality, I share a small flat with a family of twelve—and I'm the twelfth man, occasionally bringing out refreshments for the players!

I love my extended family, every single individual in it, but as a writer, I must sometimes get a little time to be alone with my own thoughts, reflect a little, talk to myself, laugh about all the blunders I have committed in the past, and ponder over the future. This is contemplation, not meditation. I am not very good at meditation, as it involves remaining in a passive state for some time. I would rather be out walking, observing the natural world, or sitting under a tree contemplating my novel or navel! I suppose the latter is a form of meditation.

When I casually told a journalist that I planned to write a book consisting of my meditations, he reported that I was writing a book on meditation per se, which gave it a different connotation. I shall go along with the simple dictionary meaning of the verb *meditate*—to plan mentally, to exercise the mind in contemplation.

So I was doing it all along!

I am not, by nature, a gregarious person. Although I love people, and have often made friends with complete strangers, I am also a lover of solitude. Naturally, one thinks better when one is alone. But I prefer walking alone to walking with others. That ladybird on the wild rose would escape my attention if I was engaged in a lively conversation with a companion. Not that the ladybird is going to change my life. But by acknowledging its presence, stopping to admire its beauty, I have paid obeisance to the natural scheme of things of which I am only a small part.

It is upon a person's power of holding fast to such undimmed beauty that his or her inner hopefulness depends. As we journey through the world, we must inevitably encounter meanness and selfishness. As we fight for our survival, the higher visions and ideals often fade. It is then that we need ladybirds! Contemplating that tiny creature, or the flower on which it rests, gives one the hope—better, the certainty—that there is more to life than interest rates, dividends, market forces and infinite technology.

As a writer, I have known hope and despair, success and failure; some recognition, but also long periods of neglect and critical dismissal. But I have had no regrets. I have enjoyed the writer's life to the full, and one reason for this is that living in India has given me certain freedoms that I would not have enjoyed elsewhere. Friendship when needed. Solitude when desired. Even, at times, love and passion. It has tolerated me for what I am—a bit of a dropout, unconventional, idiosyncratic. I have been left alone to do my own thing. In India, people do not censure you unless you start making a nuisance of yourself. Society has its norms and its orthodoxies, and provided you do not flaunt all the rules, society will allow you to go your own way. I am free to become a naked ascetic and roam the streets with a begging bowl; I am also free to live in a palatial farmhouse if I have the wherewithal. For twenty-five years, I have lived in this small, sunny second-floor room looking out on the mountains, and no one has bothered me, unless you count the neighbour's dog who prevents the postman and courier boys from coming up the steps.

I may write for myself, but as I also write to get published, it must follow that I write for others too. Only a handful of readers might enjoy my writing, but they are my soulmates, my alter egos, and they keep me going through those lean times and discouraging moments.

Even though I depend upon my writing for a livelihood, it is still, for me, the most delightful thing in the world.

I did not set out to make a fortune from writing; I knew I was not that kind of writer. But it was the thing I did best, and I persevered with the exercise of my gift, cultivating the more discriminating editors, publishers and readers, never really expecting huge rewards but accepting whatever came my way. Happiness is a matter of temperament rather than circumstance, and I have always considered myself fortunate in having escaped the tedium of a nine-to-five job or some other form of drudgery.

Of course, there comes a time when almost every author asks himself what his effort and output really amounts to. We expect our work to influence people, to affect a great many readers, when, in fact, its impact is infinitesimal. Those who work on a large scale must feel discouraged by the world's indifference. That is why I am happy to give a little innocent pleasure to a handful of readers. This is a reward worth having.

As a writer, I have difficulty in doing justice to momentous events, the wars of nations, the politics of power; I am more at ease with the dew of the morning, the sensuous delights of the day, the silent blessings of the night, the joys and sorrows of children, the strivings of ordinary folk and, of course, the ridiculous situations in which we sometimes find ourselves.

We cannot prevent sorrow and pain and tragedy. And yet when we look around us, we find that the majority of people are actually enjoying life! There are so many lovely things to see, there is so much to do, so much fun to be had, and so many charming and interesting people to meet... How can my pen ever run dry?

Picnic at Fox Burn

In spite of the frenetic building activity in most hill-stations, there are still a few ruins to be found on the outskirts—neglected old bungalows that have fallen or been pulled down, and which now provide shelter for bats, owls, stray goats, itinerant sadhus and sometimes the restless spirits of those who once dwelt in them.

One such ruin is Fox-Burn, but I won't tell you exactly where it can be found, because I visit the place for purposes of meditation (or just plain contemplation) and I would hate to arrive there one morning to find about fifty people picnicking on the grass.

And yet it did witness a picnic of sorts the other day, when the children accompanied me to the ruin. They had heard it was haunted, and they wanted to see the ghost.

Rakesh is twelve, Mukesh is six, and Dolly is four, and they are not afraid of ghosts.

I should mention here, that before Fox-Burn became a ruin, back in the 1940s, it was owned by an elderly English woman, Mrs Williams, who ran it as a boarding-house for several years. In the end, poor health forced her to give up this work, and during her last years, she lived alone in the huge house, with just a chowkidar to help. Her children, who had grown up on the property, had long since settled in faraway lands.

When Mrs Williams died, the chowkidar stayed on for some time until the property was disposed of; but he left as soon as he could. Late at night there would be a loud rapping on his door, and he would hear the old lady calling out: 'Shamsher Singh, open the door! Open the door, I say, and let me in!'

Needless to say, Shamsher Singh kept the door firmly closed.

He returned to his village at the first opportunity. The hill-station was going through a slump at the time, and the new owners pulled the house down and sold the roof and beams as scrap.

'What does Fox-Burn mean?' asked Rakesh, as we climbed the neglected, overgrown path to the ruin.

'Well, Burn is a Scottish word meaning stream or spring. Perhaps there was a spring here, once. If so, it dried up long ago.'

'And did a fox live here?'

'Maybe a fox came to drink at the spring. There are still foxes living on the mountain. Sometimes you can see them dancing in the moonlight.'

Passing through a gap in a wall, we came upon the ruins of the house. In the bright light of a summer morning it did not look in the least spooky or depressing. A line of Doric pillars were all that remained of what must have been an elegant porch and verandah. Beyond them, through the deodars, we could see the distant snows. It must have been a lovely spot in which to spend the better part of one's life. No wonder Mrs Williams wanted to come back.

The children were soon scampering about on the grass, whilst I sought shelter beneath a huge chestnut tree.

There is no tree so friendly as the chestnut, especially in summer when it is in full leaf.

Mukesh discovered an empty water-tank and Rakesh suggested that it had once fed the burn that no longer existed. Dolly busied herself making nosegays with the daisies that grew wild in the grass.

Rakesh looked up suddenly. He pointed to a path on the other side of the ruin, and exclaimed: 'Look, what's that? Is it Mrs Williams?'

'A ghost!' said Mukesh excitedly.

But it turned out to be the local washerwoman, a large white bundle on her head, taking a short-cut across the property.

A more peaceful place could hardly be imagined, until a large black dog, a spaniel of sorts, arrived on the scene. He wanted someone to play with—indeed, he insisted on playing—and ran circles round us until we threw sticks for him to fetch and gave him half our sandwiches.

'Whose dog is it?' asked Rakesh.

'I've no idea.'

'Did Mrs Williams keep a black dog?'

'Is it a ghost dog?' asked Mukesh.

'It looks real to me,' I said.

'And it's eaten all my biscuits,' said Dolly.

'Don't ghosts have to eat?' asked Mukesh.

'I don't know. We'll have to ask one.'

'It can't be any fun being a ghost if you can't eat,' declared Mukesh.

The black dog left us as suddenly as he had appeared, and as there was no sign of an owner, I began to wonder if he had not, after all, been an apparition.

A cloud came over the sun, the air grew chilly.

'Let's go home,' said Mukesh.

'I'm hungry,' said Rakesh.

'Come along, Dolly,' I called.

But Dolly couldn't be seen.

We called out to her, and looked behind trees and pillars, certain that she was hiding from us. Almost five minutes passed in searching for her, and a sick feeling of apprehension was coming over me, when Dolly emerged from the ruins and ran towards us.

'Where have you been?' we demanded, almost with one voice.

'I was playing—in there—in the old house. Hide and seek.'

'On your own?'

'No, there were two children. A boy and a girl. They were playing too.'

'I haven't seen any children,' I said.

'They've gone now.'

'Well, it's time we went too.'

We set off down the winding path, with Rakesh leading the way, and then we had to wait because Dolly had stopped and was waving to someone.

'Who are you waving to, Dolly?'

'To the children.'

'Where are they?'

'Under the chestnut tree.'

'I can't see them. Can you see them, Rakesh? Can you, Mukesh?'

Rakesh and Mukesh said they couldn't see any children. But Dolly was still waving.

'Goodbye,' she called. 'Goodbye!'

Were there voices on the wind? Faint voices calling goodbye? Could Dolly see something we couldn't see?

'We can't see anyone,' I said.

'No,' said Dolly. 'But they can see me!'

Then she left off her game and joined us, and we ran home laughing. Mrs Williams may not have revisited her old house that day but perhaps her children had been there, playing under the chestnut tree they had known so long ago.